D1083087

The Secret Deaths of Arthur Lowe

U.L. Harper

ISBN: 9781520965277

To Brianna

Also from U.L. Harper

In Blackness

In Blackness: The Reinvention of Man

ACKNOWLEDGMENTS

I must thank the beta-readers of this novel. A very patient bunch. Many thanks to Eric Greenwell who has been there since the beginning. Rhonda Gilmore was huge in her contributions. Ashley Farrand has somehow been with me for years, and did a great job seeing my vision through. A big thank you to my splendid wife for putting up with me while I finished this thing. I'm yelling to another coast to give a huge what up to Clobber Monotype, a friend who has been reading my work since about 9th grade. There are too many to thank and not enough space. But everyone who knows my journey, I see you.

Beginning of the Modern World

Shaking and in tears, it's a struggle to lift his wife's lifeless body off the bloody carpet and onto the bed.

With her finally on their bed, Arthur relaxes his hand on her shoulder, lets the life-shaping energy he controls move through him and into her. In the past, he brought people who weren't too physically injured by their cause of death back to life. It never took long, but Sandra had a gunshot wound to her head. It might take longer.

It's been decades since having a reason to animate an object, even longer to bring someone back to the living, which to him were the same thing. His wife dying would be every reason to use his ability.

He slips off her sweats and t-shirt but leaves on her panties. He stops redressing her in one of his shirts, because it settles on him that she killed herself in front of him out of spite. Her last words to him were "fuck you, Arthur." And then she ended it.

Arthur maneuvers her onto her side, tucks her into the fetal position. To remedy looking at the gun wound to her face, he places a blanket over her—a temporary measure, merely until she comes back to him. With the blanket over her, it's more like she's asleep than dead.

In the passing weeks, he tells acquaintances Sandra is sick and they can see her health has improved. In the meantime, a slight aroma gathers around her. Not as bad as it could be for a normal death. There's a smell, nonetheless, like old wet food of some sort. Beans and yogurt, and some kind of old meat.

He checks on her regularly to see if she's changed position, to see if there are signs she's come back to the living. The process never takes this long, but he's patient because of her injuries.

If anybody suspects something is wrong they'll ask too many questions. So, to keep up appearances, he accepted a dinner invitation from next door neighbors and friends Glenda and Raheem.

Knowing the best lies are half true, he knocks on their door.

Raheem yells from the other side, tells Arthur to let himself in, which he does.

Glenda and Raheem sit at the dining room table with their kids— Shelly, a stunningly cute little girl nine years of age, with thick, kinky dark hair like her mother, and Tracy, an energetic, yet obedient, young boy, ten years of age.

The adults have small talk about the needed rain in arid Southern

California, about the stupid patrons at Raheem's work, and, yes, that awkward pungent stench overcoming the public. It gets worse every day.

Glenda and Raheem cut the conversation short in order to bring in the food—chicken, vegetables, mashed potatoes, and water. Raheem leads grace. The kids bow their heads. Glenda squints. Raheem bows his head. Arthur does not participate.

As they eat, the family their heads as they politely chew. They clank plates with their utensils. Something is wrong, or at the very least, being hidden by their bowed heads.

"It's hard to believe how sick she is." Glenda cuts into her boneless chicken breast. Her tight pigtails with pink barrettes clipped on the ends.

"As suddenly as she got sick, you'd think it was contagious." Although holding a spoon, Raheem speaks with his hands. "You're not contagious, are you?"

"Arthur," Glenda's voice is rhythmic. "How is she?"

Glenda's hair has silver streaks. Her complexion much darker than Raheem's, who is more yellow than brown. She's dark like Arthur. Arthur has less hair and his belly won't stop growing. Raheem is in great shape but weighs more than ever. He doesn't go to the gym as often because he lacks the give-a-shit.

Arthur bites into his chicken. "She'll be okay, contrary to popular opinion. Believe it or not, she's been more sick than this."

Raheem scoops peas on his spoon. "I've heard people have died from this particular flu bug."

"She hasn't left the room for over a week, has she?" Glenda asks.

Raheem begins, "Hey, man, if you need help with anything—"

"Truth is, I'm good," Arthur says. "We don't need help."

Glenda places both of her hands on the table. "Nobody is trying to, I guess, seem like they know everything. I hear you. We're thinking she's probably more sick than you think she is. What are the chances of her needing a doctor?"

Raheem leans forward. "Dog, I'm going to chime in on someone I deeply care about and say, why don't you get her checked out? She's hella not good. She's not just your wife. She's a friend of ours too. I know sometimes you get a certain way...so you can't hear what people are saying, but hear this. Arthur, go get Sandra some damned help."

Damn it, an intervention. "We're fine. We saw a doctor."

"Kids." Raheem jabs a finger towards the living room.

Their food mostly eaten, Tracy and Shelly excuse themselves.

Raheem leans back. "You're being disrespectful as shit by lying to me in my house."

"'Heem…" Arthur starts.

"*Ra* heem."

"I'm sorry if I come off rude. It's hard to see her like that. It's harder with you calling me a liar."

"Would she be better off in the hospital?" Glenda says.

Arthur drops his knife and fork on his plate, lets them clang together. "This isn't going to work. Again, thanks for dinner."

Raheem folds his arms. "You sure you talked to somebody about her?"

"I inquired," Arthur lies. "I really don't want to talk about it."

Glenda stops mid-chew. "I think she's sick because of the air. It might not be the Flu. Just take her to the doctor. They're probably dealing with it a whole lot down there."

"Thank you for the meal. Thank you for being honest and *exactly* who you guys are." For a second, he admires Tracy and Shelly watching television. "Beautiful family. You're giving them the childhood I *wish* I had, you know that?"

"Okay, thank you." Raheem says, pushing himself away from the table. "You're going to deflect the whole thing?"

Arthur leaves, certain lying makes the situation worse. The only person worth talking to about Sandra would be Sandra.

***

In his home office, Arthur fires up his computer, opens a new word processing file and names it "Sandra". To help in thinking about her, he writes to her.

***

My dear Sandra,

When I think back to that moment when you shot yourself, I get stuck. Thinking about it, I spend my days watching the sun from the office window. Before I know how much time has gone, the sun has faded into nothing. I don't know why I feel guilty, but I *do* feel guilty. Nearly twenty-five years of marriage and I never abused you, never cheated on you, and never intentionally lied to you, but I can see you were mad at me. I feel guilty.

I should have known whatever I did—and I don't know what I

did—was wrong. Because of my ignorance, I cleaned your blood from off the bedroom mirror, wiped bits of skull from the dresser, picked up pieces of forehead from the carpet. The puddles are gone, but the blood stains will always be there.

I've thought about leaping off a building, wishing a stray bullet from somewhere would strike me in the gut and end my life. Plenty of people are like you and me and have pondered putting a gun to their head and pulling the trigger. We're not the minority. People want to die. But they want people to have cared for them too. Me and you—people in general—have mental lists of who we think will give a damn about us dying. If I kill myself, with you gone, I wonder who will mourn me.

I keep racking my brain about how it happened. Where in the world did you gather the courage to kill yourself?

Not Her Boy

My Beautiful Wife,

I'm thinking, in this writing, I can tell you things I've never told you or I might not have admitted already. I'm a closed person, even to you. But you knew that.

I believe you'll come back to me, read this, and through this writing we'll become closer. There are things I've learned that changed who I am.

Here's something I learned years ago, something you may not have known about me. My adoptive mother thought of me as *a* boy rather than *her* boy. I was never going to be her boy. I know that now.

Maybe back then I had an idea about my real parents. They're probably dead by now.

I wound up with Dana and Bixby. Dana wanted to love me. Sometimes people unconsciously adopt characteristics of who or what they want. Nobody is as strong or as weak as they seem. She wanted to be a mother or see herself as one.

At something like six years old and in one of my first nights in my new home, I wandered into my room after dinner and pretended to go to sleep, not knowing what to say to my new parents. Throughout dinner they spoke to me basically in baby talk, which for some reason discouraged me.

The house was larger than the group home I had experienced. You remember my house don't you, several blocks from yours? The bathrooms and bedrooms seemed bigger when I was smaller. The ceiling higher. Everything seemed so large through those kid eyes.

Dana and Bixby thought they had saved me. To be honest, a kid in my situation probably had no future. I had no parents, and if not for Dana and Bixby, I would have joined a system that would take care of me but not actually *give a damn* about me. It's the system you join unconditionally when your real parents don't want you. From my understanding my parents were exactly the type of people to drop a kid off somewhere and hand him over to the state, because that's what happened.

Dana and Bixby rarely talked about the girl they originally decorated the room for. They wanted to adopt a girl. The right one didn't pop up.

They wound up with me. To their credit, they didn't go for a kid who looked like them. At the time, I had a big, curly fro, like three inches high. Me being Black with all dark features and them being white with all white features. Dana with her straight, sandy blond hair, and Bixby with his brown, thinning hair, and freckles.

"What are you doing?" Bixby said to my new mom from the doorway of my new room. He was trying to speak quietly to keep me from waking. He failed.

"You'll wake him," she whispered.

"Not before you do. Let him sleep. When he's up, he's up."

Bixby made sense when sense had to be made. Nice and tall. Even then I could tell that at one point he had been in really good shape, like a former runner.

Although he pulled her to the other room, I could still hear them talking. I'll always remember what they said about me that time when they thought I was asleep and couldn't hear them. He wanted a son of his own, not an adopted one. She wanted a child but was basically scared of giving birth due to complications that ran in her family. The consequences to their situation was that I grew on them more like a pet than an actual person. They loved me like a stray animal.

Considering the circumstances, at first, we did well with each other. Dana figured out rather quickly how much I liked the park. I liked the sand and the trees and the grass and the pinecones and the gopher holes. I loved the baseball fields and how people played soccer and Frisbee on them. Whenever at the park, I sweat. For me, at all of six years old, sweating meant doing something important. I took playing seriously. I came down the slide with a scowl. I swung on the swings with everything I had. When I threw dirt, I threw it hard. Mom watched me with pride. She coached me along, gave me positive reinforcement, said things like "good job" and "keep it up". She once told me that if I worked as hard in the classroom as I did on the playground, my life would be perfectly fine.

One day Dana watched me play in the sandbox from the bench near it. I might have had a birthday by then, so I would have been seven, I think. The playground was more dangerous back then. Nowadays they make playgrounds to placate kids. Back then they made playgrounds to grow you, regardless of the physical or mental cost. You learned lessons of life on the playground. They had the two-story tall spaceship slides made with metal, sometimes three-stories high depending on the park. On hot days you got burned going down—simply part of it. Whoever built it knew it burned, shrugged off the idea like most parents did.

My mom watched me from the bench as I worked on executing my plan to make a deer out of sand. Somewhere, earlier in the week, I had seen something about deer on the news, on TV somewhere. I wanted to make my deer gallop like it did on whatever show I saw the actual deer in. I can remember the confidence I had that I could do it.

First, I managed to make the hooves: small sand patties made from both dried sand and some of the sand wet by the sprinklers.

"Arthur!" Dana called to me. "Arthur! Why don't you come here? I want you to meet someone."

She had been conversing with a guy I would get to know rather well. We've talked about this day before, although I don't think you know all of these details. She had been conversing with your dad. He had all those tattoos, and he wore that baseball cap. I remember the cap because from my distance it kept me from seeing his face. You sat right next to him. I was too busy with my sand deer to move. I paid Dana some mind, stopping my sand bath to stare at her. Creativity called me louder than she called me, so I went back to working with the sand deer. If I made it move, Dana would ultimately be impressed, so I pushed on.

As she called me over again, I ignored her, made the legs to the deer. Then the rest of the body. Lastly, I smashed together the head, poked my index and middle fingers in the ball of dirt, called the two holes eyes. I touched its belly and felt the deer start to wiggle out of my hand. It galloped off, kicking dirt behind it, first into the grass, and then into the bushes. Mom, who had turned her head in time to see what I did, leapt to her feet and hurried past me after the deer, wide-eyed. "What the hell is that?"

At the time, I thought I hadn't done anything to scare her. On the contrary, I did something so fantastic that the only way she knew to react was with fear.

She followed the trail of sand from the deer to a nearby bush where it had collapsed.

Your dad came over to me, holding your hand. You had on a white dress with blue trim. He sat on the concrete walkway that made up the edge of the sandbox. Me and my mom didn't know that you guys had seen my sand deer, but you had. Years later, you told me yourself.

Your dad said, "Hey, little guy."

"Hey!" Dana shouted from her short distance. "Hey!"

"What's going on?" your dad said, his eyes never leaving Dana. "What...happened?"

"I don't want anybody..." Mom said it in a huff jogging from behind me. She gripped my hand. "Nothing... I'm sorry, I'm sorry.

Good to meet you. Arthur, let's go."

"Is it because that thing?" I asked.

"Yes. Because of the thing. Let's go."

"The thing is fine," your dad said. "It's okay."

"What thing?" my mom said.

Your dad didn't press it with her. "Oh." He stood back and shut up about it.

She didn't grab my hand like she would if we were crossing a street. She had my wrist, squeezed it tightly, as if we had escaped. Instead of speaking up, I cried. She paid me no attention. My mom stomped towards our yellow station wagon. I tripped over my untied shoelaces. She lifted me so we wouldn't lose pace.

Once through the park and into the parking lot, she raised me up, held me under her arm like a surfer holds a surfboard. She threw me in the car, strapped me in like I was luggage, and we were off. Halfway home she muttered my name while shaking her head. She managed to transfer her stress over to me, causing my chest to tighten. I had scared the shit out of her. Despite how much I cried, she ignored me. Not once did she ask me to be quiet.

Finally, at home, she opened my door, unstrapped me, and with a straight face told me to go inside. I scampered towards the house, realizing I could lose my home and parents over this.

I busted through the living room, stomping my feet, I remember, swinging my arms.

Bixby sat on the couch with no shoes and socks or shirt on, watching television.

"Arthur!" he shouted in my direction.

I shut my bedroom door behind me, waited for the worst to happen. Soon they'd enter my room, explain they'd give me back, that they weren't going to keep me. I stared at my bedroom door, wiped so many tears from my face that my cheeks became raw.

***

Love of My Life,

They had set up my room for a young girl.

Stuffed bears and tigers and mice and bunnies were propped up like dominoes along the edges of the beige walls. I didn't mind.

Puzzles waited for me on a small table in the corner near the wood rocking chair, next to a bunch of toy cars. None of this distracted me from their arguing. In the beginning, Dana and Bixby always had disagreements, but they never argued like they did this time. I heard stomping across the hardwood floor in the living room, as Dana tried to explain what I had done with the sand at the park. Bixby didn't believe her about me making the sand come to life. He said he didn't want to call her a liar but she had been lying, which, to him, meant she had been hiding something.

"Why would I even bring up another man if I was trying to hide him from you?" she said in a raised voice.

"I can't speak for motivations, only for what you did. Arthur didn't make dirt come to life. *Come on.*"

I picked up the old teddy bear. While holding it, it reached out and gently grabbed my wrist. The black piece of thick knitting bent in a U across its face gave it a permanent smile. That plush bear smile was what I really needed. Any smile was a smile.

I set the old bear down on his feet to see what he would do. He didn't do anything but shadow me. For a while, we curled on the bed next to each other. It seems like it'd be awkward, but it wasn't. I felt embraced, although it didn't touch me.

By evening I still hadn't been fed. Old Bear sat in the rocking chair. It looked at me as I sat on their going-to-be daughter's bed.

One of the puzzles on the table had a lot of color. The box said the puzzle had a thousand pieces. Bixby had placed the puzzles in my room so me and him would have something to do together. So, I grabbed a puzzle, opened the box and dumped all the pieces on the carpet, spread them around. The old bear jumped out of the chair, got on his plush knees, and helped me start assembling the picture. It picked out pieces. His paws were too fat to set the pieces in their proper place, so I did the actual assembling. With his help, I did a thousand-piece puzzle in less than an hour. The puzzle made an image of an orange sunset on a glassy lake.

After we finished the puzzle, I fell asleep right there on the rug. Bixby woke me.

The ceiling light brightened the room.

I began to cry, not looking forward to facing my situation. He asked me to sit up, to come over to the bed. I did.

The old bear was lifeless in the rocking chair.

Dad sat next to me. "I can see you're upset. You're not in trouble. Do you know what I mean by upset?"

I nodded again.

"It's okay to be upset. How it comes out is what's important. I want you to look at me and use your words. Wipe your face. Now, wipe your face. Okay, now use your words."

I jumped off the bed and grabbed the old bear from the chair. "Nothing."

"Nothing? What does that mean? Full sentences, guy. Tell me what you're upset about."

I was so nervous talking to him that I could barely breathe.

"I'll wait," Bixby said, folding his arms. "I'm not going anywhere." He stood, backpedaled to the door, and shut it with his heel.

"She's mad at me for nothing!"

"Calm down. What is she mad at you about?"

"She said…"

"I can't talk to you unless you use your words."

"She's not my mommy anymore. Are you my daddy?"

"Whoa whoa whoa, what? Of course, I'm your…" He fluttered his eyelids. "Why wouldn't you think I was your dad, Arthur? Arthur, look at me. Look at me, Arthur. I'm going to ask you a serious question and I need you to answer it right now and truthfully." Bixby knelt on one knee. "Arthur, who is the man your mom was with in the park?" He took a step back so he could see me better.

"I don't know," I said. I don't think Bixby was a jealous guy. Learning that Demetri, your dad, was in the park with us still set him off. Bixby might have had a few things in his closet and had been projecting. That's seeing everything from afar and with a lot of thought. Maybe he cheated on Dana. If he did cheat on her, he never actually got caught.

"You've seen him before?" he asked. "Did he have his hands on mommy in any way. His hand might have been on her lap? Or around her waist."

I shrugged, confused by the questioning.

"You've never met Demetri till today?"

"No," I said, shaking my head.

"What did you guys talk about?"

"Nothing."

"Nothing. Nothing. Okay, why don't you get in your pajamas? You're not in trouble. I still want you in bed, okay? I know you haven't eaten. We're working on that. You're not in trouble. I want you to lie there and not think about anything. We're going to talk about it, just not now. Go ahead. Hop to it." Bixby clapped his hands.

I dropped the old bear on the bed, grabbed my pajamas from the seat of the rocking chair, and began to undress. Before I finished, Bixby had left the room. With him gone, the old bear sat up on the bed, hung his feet off the end. In my pajamas, I rocked in the chair, stared at it. It had no choice but to smile back at me. It waved to me. I waved back. The old bear's presence gave me the patience to wait for Bixby to come back.

When Dad knocked at door, the old bear flopped to the floor, lifeless.

Dad opened the door. "Hey, Big A. You ready to eat?"

"Is Mom still mad at me?"

"She's fine." He looked at the puzzle me and the old bear were working on, then at the one we had completed. He gave the puzzles a sideways glance. "I know you don't like meatloaf. Doesn't stop dinner from being meatloaf."

"She's not mad at me?"

"Don't worry about it. Listen, let's get that grub."

If Mom was mad, I didn't want to be anywhere near her. "Can I have it in here?"

"Actually. Yes."

Me and Dad ate dinner together in my room. Very cool.

On his way out of my room he said, "Good job with the puzzle. Damn good job, actually." He clicked off the lights, leaving me on my bed to go to sleep.

Not too long after Bixby left me alone, I stared across the room at a silhouette of the bear tiptoeing towards me. It had a hard time climbing onto the bed. It curled up next to me, something that, like the sand deer, I knew I couldn't mention.

Begin the Stench

First, a pounding on the living room door, and then Glenda's voice yelling from the other side. "Arthur!"

Arthur stops typing, bolts to the living room.

He swings the door open. "What's going on?"

"Raheem won't wake up."

"What?"

"He passed out and won't wake up."

"What happened?"

"We were sitting there—"

"Did you call 911?"

"Yes, I called 911. I can't wake him."

"Are you sure? He's at the house?"

"Yes. *Yes*, he's at the house."

"I'll go back over with you." The smell outside is so bad, he covers his face while making his way to her place.

She does the same.

He leaps up her porch steps. "Is he sick from the smell, do you think?"

"I don't know."

"What happened last time?"

"His throat swelled up. He couldn't breathe, but this time there wasn't any of that."

"That you know of."

For years Arthur told himself if an emergency happened, he'd be ready. Then, today, the day an emergency, he's barefoot, with no shirt on.

Glenda follows close behind wearing an L.A. Rams jersey.

He stops in the living room. "Where are the kids?"

"School."

"He's in the room?"

"He won't wake up."

"Is he in the room or not?"

"Yes, *yes*," she says, "he's in the room."

Arthur enters Glenda and Raheem's bedroom. Raheem lies on the bed. Arthur grips his wrist with two fingers and a thumb. No pulse. Arthur places his left hand over his right, intertwines his fingers. With his arms straight and locked, Arthur firmly presses twenty times on

Raheem's chest cavity. Surely, how he's doing the CPR is all wrong. The stamina to pull this off abandoned him years ago. He tilts Raheem's head back, opens his mouth, gives a few breaths. Unfortunately, 'Heem had gone to sleep on the bed. Such a soft surface would make CPR more difficult.

Arthur pumps Raheem's chest, blows into his mouth, cups his nose. "Call 911 again!"

He's dead.

With Glenda in the doorway, Arthur briskly walks over and kicks the door shut, locks it with Glenda on the other side.

Glenda pounds on the door. "Arthur, what the *hell* are you doing?"

He drags Raheem off the bed. His dead weight shakes the hollow floor.

Glenda continues to pound and scream. "What are you doing? Unlock the door. Unlock the door! What. The. Hell. Are. You. Doing?" Each word comes with a powerful crack from her fist on their hollow, wooden door.

Her pounding commences into half-hearted, sporadic slaps, like a wrestler weakly tapping out of a lost match.

***

Raheem died on his back with his head turned to the side, palms up, and his legs crossed.

"Arthur." From the other side of the bedroom door, Glenda sounds like a small child faking an adult's voice. "Tell me... What's going on?"

The scream of sirens approach from the distance.

"I can still help," Arthur says.

"If they hurry—"

"—He'll be alright. You'll be better off if you just...calm down. I think he'll be alright."

The bedroom windows have a perfect view to watch the fire trucks pull up to the house, park parallel to cars along the curb. Firemen exit their vehicles. They never seem in a hurry.

Glenda's footsteps travel away from the door, probably to greet the firemen.

Arthur places his hand on Raheem's shoulder. Arthur's energy, like a breeze, filters through him, transfers to Raheem.

Looking through the window, neighbors from across the street, from down the street, and from next door gather on their front lawns expecting something horrible. Nothing like this ever happens on this block. The anticipation of seeing a tragedy blankets their faces. They want the spectacle, the gossip fodder.

Raheem sits up on the bed, in a daze. He scans the room. Raheem takes off his shirt, showing drooping pectoral muscles, once taut, until age, laziness and gravity got a hold of them. He looks over himself.

Arthur opens the bedroom door, moments before the firemen and Glenda arrive.

"How's it going, I guess?" Arthur says to the firemen.

"Hello, sir," one of them says in a slightly raised voice to Raheem, as if Raheem is mostly deaf.

Raheem slowly turns his head in the fireman's direction.

"We okay?" the fireman says in the raised tone. He's got a toolbox of equipment.

Glenda stands in the doorway, her hands on her forehead.

"I'm the one who helped him," Arthur says.

"I don't understand." Glenda looks like she's figuring out a riddle.

"That's okay," Arthur responds.

She runs to Raheem, grabs him by the back of his head and kisses his forehead. "Shit, I thought you were dead."

"I'm okay," Raheem says, standing, and then lying on the bed.

"I thought you were dead," she repeats, reaching over and tightly hugging him.

"We should take you in," a different fireman says.

"For what?" Glenda frowns at the fireman. "He's fine. Right, baby, you're fine."

"A lot of people are getting looked at," the fireman says.

"Because of that damned smell," she says. "For the life of me, what is it?"

"That's the question." The fireman nods. "That's the question. M'sure people are getting sick from it." He focuses on Raheem. "Your head doesn't hurt? You're not thirsty? Not nauseous, anything like that? Sore throat?"

Raheem searches the room. "No, sir."

The firemen swap glances.

One of them grins at Raheem. "Good luck to ya. Get a gas mask. Everyone should have one."

Raheem closes his eyes again, then immediately falls asleep. For a second, everyone stares at him, despite the rise and fall of his chest.

"You know our number," one of the firemen says.

The firemen file out of the bedroom, wander down the hall, depart the house, and finally find their way through the crowd of neighbors and other lookee-loos.

***

Glenda rises, takes a few steps towards the middle of the bedroom. She gives off the appearance of calm and collected. "Is he okay, do you think?"

"The professionals seem to think so."

"Still, do you think he's okay?"

"Don't *you*? I thought you didn't want him going with them."

She says, "What if he gets worse?"

"You know he stopped breathing for a while there."

She crosses her arms, embraces herself as if she's cold. "Did we tell the paramedics that? You think I should take him in?"

"He's going to be fine."

"When did *you* become so positive?"

"I'm not being positive; I'm telling you what I know. Do I think he's healthy? Probably not. Will he survive? Yeah."

"It'd be better if he wasn't lying there like that."

Raheem's chest rises and falls in a steady rhythm.

She leans over Raheem. "I know I should probably take him in. Do you think he's okay?"

"Listen… You want to let him rest?"

She lets out a hefty sigh. "Shit, you're right. I need to let him be. Okay."

Arthur strolls behind her as she heads to the living room.

He sits on the opposite end of her sofa. She twiddles her thumbs in her lap, her eyes glazing over. He locks up when she starts to cry. He cried for hours after Sandra killed herself. He didn't have a problem joining Glenda in shedding a few tears.

She grabs her nose, and then gets up and hurries off to the kitchen. She returns a moment later to her spot on the couch, offers him a damp rag to put over his face.

He reaches for it. "Helps with the smell, I take it."

"Doesn't make it any worse."

Arthur does as she suggests.

She gazes off in thought. "I'm trying to wrap my head around the fact that… How long did you say he stopped breathing?"

"I don't think he was breathing when I first got in the room."

"Are you sure?"

"First thing I noticed."

15

"Obviously, you did something to help him. I'm so lucky, thank God."

"One thing we have in common—our better halves are sick."

"Stating it doesn't help," she says.

"Death is a hell of a thing. I'm saying it's okay if you think about Raheem dying. For me, I know I'm not going to be able to let Sandra go. I was like five or six when I met her. I can't have somebody come pick her up, take her away, stick her in the dirt, and pile it on."

Glenda clasps her hands together, still holding the rag. "That smell is literally killing people. It's why they said we should have gas masks."

Dead air seeps between their conversation.

"I'm going to go home…and be by myself," he says, standing, turning his back on her.

"You're leaving me here?"

"I'm right there next door. You guys are good, right? You're fine?"

"Yeah, sure, we're perfectly fine."

Arthur departs, knowing her lucky ass can still have conversations with Raheem. He could still speak to Sandra, too, but it'll have to be through words on the computer. If that's the only way to speak to her for the time being then that's what he'll do.

Back in his office, he double-clicks the Sandra icon to open the document. He begins to write.

The Mother Incidents

My Queen,

Raheem died today.

I brought him back, just like I'm trying to do with you. You're so injured it's taking longer. That's what I tell myself.

With you gone I can see how you're much, much more than just a body and a brain. You're my history. History is energy a person can't access. My childhood disappeared with you. All those opportunities at Kennedy Elementary that Bixby tried to harness are gone.

Kennedy seemed normal except for the neighborhood which didn't have any apartments. I noticed all the grass. My house back then had grass, though, you know, our general neighborhood didn't. It surprised me that the houses near Kennedy weren't surrounded by fences like in our neighborhood near my home school, Lincoln.

Some things were normal at Kennedy but not normal at Lincoln. At Lincoln, you spoke with the Principal if you were in trouble. Even then he didn't speak to you as much as he spoke *at* you. At Kennedy, I met the Principal the first day and I wasn't in trouble. He wanted to greet me and my dad. It's something he did with all the new families.

Aside from Kennedy having a better history of nurturing intellect than my old school, my dad also liked it because of the sports. Seeing that Kennedy had sports in their after-school program as well as intellectual activities, it made perfect sense.

The Principal, Mr. Howard, wore a suit and had a glistening dome for a head. His black-rimmed glasses made him look professional. Mr. Howard and dad shook hands, and then me and my dad strolled down the hallway towards room 7, Ms. Kimbrel's class.

"This is going to be an important person, Arthur. As important as Ms. Beatty. New school, new teachers, and a new Principal. Pretty cool, huh. What do you think?"

"The hallway's big."

"I guess it's bigger than your last one. By the time you're done at this school these halls will seem small."

We entered my first-grade classroom and laid eyes on Ms. Kimbrel.

Everybody stopped to look at us. Ms. Kimbrel started for us from the front of the class with a great, meaningful smile. Nobody had ever been that happy to see me. She wore a pink dress that came down to her pink flats, and the dress swung as if a breeze had swept underneath. One person tried to grab it as she passed.

She beamed. "You must be Arthur."

"This is my son," Bixby said.

They shook hands. After a few worthless words she briefly cupped his elbow. I remember this so clearly because Bixby kind of gasped when she did it. She smelled like roses on a warm, quiet, summer day. She had a slim figure. Slimmer and taller than dad. Not by much, but taller. Way taller than mom.

She bent her knees, leaned down with her hands clasped. After a hesitation, she held her hand out for me, just like she did for Bixby. I had never shaken a woman's hand. My previous teacher, Ms. Beatty, I don't remember touching her. Ms. Beatty had old-lady glasses and short, graying, curly hair, and the type of pearl necklace that old people wear. She was as old as the school system itself, and although I liked her, she didn't inspire. She didn't produce feelings in a person. Ms. Kimbrel, on the other hand, had soft hands. Her grasp alone told you stuff. By squeezing my hand, she told me hello.

"Hi," I responded.

"Class," she said, "remember I said we'd have a new class member? Say hi to Arthur." The class did so, all in unison.

When she let go of my hand, a kind of energy disconnected. I understood why that boy had tried to grab her dress when she passed. I could see why my dad gasped when she grabbed his elbow.

Again, Sandra, I'm telling you, the environment was completely different than at Lincoln. I think you went to Carver before you moved into the neighborhood.

Kids at Kennedy were different, the teachers were different. The Principal was different. The halls bigger. There were more windows to see through. Lincoln had closed, tinted windows with shades over them. Safety was the excuse they gave.

As I sat, most of the class stared at me. The other part sat, aloof. Meanwhile, my dad and Ms. Kimbrel hit it off, saying nothing, although letting words fall out of their mouths. Every few seconds she touched his wrist or his shoulder. It looked as if Bixby liked the new school as much as I did.

Despite the pleasantness of Kennedy, it took a few weeks to feel comfortable, to let go. Once people stopped calling me the new kid, and started using my name, it got better.

At my previous school they picked on people for fun. I had friends, but we were all picked on at some point. It's something you got used to. In contrast, at Kennedy, that sort of thing would get you in trouble.

I felt bad leaving Clarence and Frank back there. I can't say I missed their friendship because I made friends at Kennedy rather quickly.

You remember Justin and Charles from high school and junior high. In elementary school, Justin always wore overalls, no matter the weather. A huge silver buckle in the middle. Every pair slightly flooded. His parents dressed him that way, too lazy to get him a t-shirt and pants to match. Every damned day he had on those overalls.

Kids used to ask if Charles was a boy or a girl because of his long, wavy hair. They didn't think he was a girl. They asked just to be mean.

Outside of my afro, you would have noticed the holes in my pants. I didn't think anything of them until I realized nobody else at school had holes in their pants.

That's who we were. Me, Justin, and Charles. Our interest in digging in dirt brought us together, especially at lunch. We liked to hang at the far corner of the playground, near a planted tree next to one of the two kickball backstops. The other backstop was where the games took place. Gigi, the playground supervisor, she organized some damned good games. We were too small to play with the third-grade kids. We didn't care for kickball or anything else going on.

For a few consecutive days, we had been digging in one of the planters at lunch. That tree had a stick supporting it, helping it grow upward. One day it would be as huge as the one on the edge of the grass area across the playground. Three stories high, a canopy of branches and leaves over the entire grass area.

"If you dig far enough down," Justin said, "you'll get to the Indian dirt."

"What's Indian dirt?" Charles said. The rims of his glasses were thick and durable, needing to be because of his habit of letting them drop off his face.

Justin replied, "It's named after the red marks left on some people's arms after you give them an Indian burn. You know how it's all red?"

Charles looked perplexed.

"How far down do we have to dig?" I asked.

"Way down," Justin said. "Like way down. All recess for a month."

I said, "I made dirt into an animal before."

"An animal out of Indian dirt?" Charles said.

"It ran and everything. Well, is sand dirt?"

"Nah ah," Justin said.

"For reals," I said, "if you pat it... If you pack it down..."

19

My new friends did not believe a word I said. They stuck their knees in the dirt. With their bare hands, they started digging for Indian dirt.

Charles's glasses fell off.

I imagined his glasses were kind of like the leaves on the giant tree across the playground; the glasses were part of him, even if they weren't connected. I saw that vision everywhere. Things were connected and separate at the same time.

Charles peeled a piece of bark from the tree and tried to use it as a shovel for digging. The bark wasn't stiff enough, but he tried digging anyway. I stood with my hands in my pockets, torn between the hope they'd find the Indian dirt and the idea of the tree really being alive. Wasn't the skin of the tree its bark? Didn't it bleed if you peeled it or cut it enough? The tree spoke with the help of the wind, by tapping its leaves together. This tree didn't have many leaves, but the huge one in the grass area had plenty to say; it had wisdom with its age.

I told them to stop digging because they could kill the tree. I was so much more in tune with the physical world around me when I was a kid.

"You can't kill dirt," Justin said. He smacked his palms together. Dust flew up in his face, not that he minded.

"The tree," I said. "The tree, you guys."

They stopped what they were doing, heeded my warning. Charles dusted himself off, placed his glasses back on his face and gazed up at the tree.

"Nah ah," Justin said.

I wasn't sure we'd kill the tree. I could find out though. All I had to do, oddly enough, was ask the big tree. With all those leaves, it knew if we could kill this smaller tree or not. The small tree didn't have enough leaves to have much to say. The big tree had plenty of leaves to clap together and speak through the wind with. I started over to the large tree. Before I got there the bell rang, so I bolted for the line to enter the classroom. I mean, who didn't want to be first in line?

After that, the leaves and trees talking seemed to leave me alone, so I forgot about them for a while. What happened to you is what brought them to the forefront again. You might remember you choked one day. But I don't think you have an actual memory of me bringing you back to life.

Before I talk about you choking, wasn't it perfect that Ms. Kimbrel headed the after-school program?

You didn't have her class during the day. I did, so I got to see her all day because she was my teacher. I loved that bungalow at the back of the school, for the program. I remember going to the program and taking the bus to the YMCA. It took forever for me to understand swimming was designed to be the first part of the program because of how hot it got in September. I don't think I could find that YMCA, now if my life depended on it.

A few weeks in, you joined. You already knew how to swim, so you swam on the deep side of the pool. You guys didn't do the same drills as us non-swimmers. You guys on the deep side were diving to the bottom and gathering items, testing your speed. Meanwhile, I didn't like putting my head under water. It felt like drowning every time the water touched my face. Figuring out how to swim felt more like something to overcome rather than something to learn.

The reason I didn't talk to you at school was because you could swim, and I couldn't. It sounds silly, but it's true. I didn't like talking to people who were a lot better than me at something. Basically, unless you liked to dig in the dirt, I didn't feel comfortable talking to you.

Dad sometimes picked me up from the program. He thought I didn't need to get on the bus home if he got off work at the dealership in enough time to pick me up. That's what he said, at least. Before leaving, he'd always talk with Ms. Kimbrel about my progress, sometimes in private. If you asked my mom, she might say otherwise, but I don't think Bixby ever cheated on her. Obviously, something existed between Ms. Kimbrel and him, but I don't think he flat-out cheated. Still, Mom thought Bixby saw Ms. Kimbrel too much. She didn't like him talking to Ms. Kimbrel outside of the classroom.

One day (this is after swimming in first grade had ended and the program had moved on to gymnastics) while I was practicing on the small balance beam, Mom shows up. She certainly saw me because I yelled to her and would have run to her, except she ignored me. Instead of coming over or smiling at me or acknowledging me, she scanned the room. Across the bungalow, Ms. Kimbrel sat at her desk, her hair in a ponytail, her glasses on her nose. A baby blue, collared, after-school program shirt hung off her athletic frame. My mom was usually at work, during this time. Not today. She leaned over and said something to Ms. Kimbrel. While saying it, my mom tapped Ms. Kimbrel's desk several times, hard, with her index finger. A scowl on her face.

Ms. Kimbrel stood, scooted her chair out of the way and took a step back. She came from around the desk and gestured towards the exit, before leading Mom outside.

At first, my instructor, Mr. Dale, wouldn't let me go to my mom because he hadn't met her, for one, and for two, she and Ms. Kimbrel had left the bungalow, so it might be inappropriate to speak with my mom at the moment. Three, he didn't believe she was my mom. She was light-skinned, and I had dark skin. So, he thought I was lying. Instead of waiting for his approval, I ditched the activity and ran into my mom's and Ms. Kimbrel's discussion.

Mom blurted to Ms. Kimbrel, "I don't want my husband near you. If nothing's happened, like you say, then I don't need all the other—" she looked at me and then back at Ms. Kimbrel, "—doo-doo going on."

"Uh huh. Is that a threat?" Ms. Kimbrel raised an eyebrow.

"I'm not making threats. I'm sure you can respect what I'm telling you."

"There is nothing like that going on."

At that moment, here comes your dad, all chipper, saying hello to Mom. She waved to him and turned away.

"You don't remember me?" he said to my mother.

"Oh, hey," Dana said. "Your daughter's here too?"

"Giving her whatever edge there is to give," he said.

Ms. Kimbrel gave him a weak grin, waved him inside. He paused for a second, in his sandals and tattoos and Angel's baseball cap. Once he was inside, a huge gust of wind pushed us all back. Across the playground, the leaves in the trees tapped against one another, saying something. At first, I couldn't tell what, as I tried to ignore it.

"Are you okay?" Ms. Kimbrel said to me. "You have that look on your face."

"What look?" Mom said. She examined me. "What's wrong, Arthur?" in that same tone she used that day in the car after I made the sand deer.

"I'm not by myself," I heard myself say.

"We're right here with you," Ms. Kimbrel said in the sweetest, most fake tone I'd ever heard from her.

"Arthur," Dana said, holding out a hand. "Come on. Let's go."

"You go," I yelled. I didn't want to leave when the wind talked to me, when the leaves spoke to me.

Mom scoffed at my assertiveness.

"I'm waiting for Dad."

"The hell you are. Now let's go." She extended her hand again.

I don't know how to word what happened next so that it makes any more sense. The wind entered me through my mouth and nose and eyes and pores and ears, it entered me. Gently, yet swiftly. The gust stopped because I had it in me. It made me lighter. If you've ever huffed glue, you kind of know what I felt like. If you haven't huffed glue, then you need to huff glue.

"What's going on with you?" Dana asked.

"I have the wind in me."

"The what?"

"The breeze, mommy, the breeze."

Your dad exited the bungalow with a large question mark on his face. "Is she in the bathroom?"

"She's not inside?" Ms. Kimbrel replied.

"Didn't see her. No. Your people couldn't find her either. It's not that big a room. She's just not in there. The bathroom is right there, right?" He pointed to the restrooms connected to the building a few hundred feet away. He started in that direction with worry on his face. His sandals rapidly smacked the bottom of his feet.

"She's not in there, mommy."

"Do you know where she is?" Mom asked me. "If you know, tell him."

"She's not over there, mister," I yelled to your dad.

Demetri quickly walked back in our direction. "You know where, young man?"

The wind had become a small, tireless, light ball that pinged around inside of me. First it settled in my legs. By the time Demetri made it back to us it was in my feet. Not kidding, the wind was in my feet.

"Where the hell is she?" he said, as he peered down at me.

Ms. Kimbrel suggested we call the houses of anyone Sandra knew, or any relatives

"There are no relatives in the area." Demetri took off his cap, ran his fingers through his thinning hair. "She doesn't have friends like that. She's seven, wandering the neighborhood like she's in *high school.*"

My feet began to guide me.

"Where are you going?" Mom said.

I didn't know. I started into a run, grinned the whole time, because of the wind that tickled me from the inside.

Your dad, my mom, and Ms. Kimbrel followed me all the way out to the front of the school, all the way down the block. They followed me, as I giddily followed my feet.

I found you, barely past the flagpole, lying on the yellowing grass. Demetri sprinted over to you. Ms. Kimbrel ran back to the bungalow to call for help. You know, this is long before 911, so she had to make it all the way back to the bungalow and probably be put on hold.

Mom held me back, with a firm grip. "No."

My feet wanted to get over to you; the wind inside of me wanted to be closer.

23

"No," Mom said again, this time softly. "I don't think she's breathing," she whispered. "Oh my God, she's not breathing."

Your dad had you in his arms, breathed into your mouth. He pushed on your chest. I had seen this in movies. How he did it, it didn't look like it did on television.

"Somebody go call for help!" Demetri yelled to the neighborhood.

Your skin had become pasty. Come to find out, you choked on something. You were trying to get to the school nurse's for help. You had died, probably not that long before we arrived.

Demetri lost his shit and started for my mom in a rage, as if she had done something wrong.

I wiggled from her grip, sprinted passed Demetri, right to your body. The wind that was inside of me, I breathed it into you. Right after I did it, you drew in a deep breath, coughed a bronchitis cough. You stood, only to have your dad rush over and lift you off the ground. You must remember all this, but you've never talked about it, at least not to me. You were the first person I brought back to life or animated. I didn't know what I was doing. I was happier back then. I want to say the older I got, the more bitter I got, and the more bitter people became when I brought them back. It's what it seems like.

"What kind of shit was that?" your dad said, and then he just stared at me.

"What'd you do, Arthur?" Mom yelled to me.

I knew I would be in trouble. Way worse than the time with the sand deer.

For most of the way home, Mom didn't say anything. And then...

"What happened with that little girl? Do you know?"

It's one of those moments when the truth wouldn't do me any good. "I don't know."

"Are you sure?"

"If I tell you, you'll get mad."

"Why would I get mad?"

"You got mad about the sand."

"You can't get in trouble for helping her. What's her name?"

"Sandra?"

"Why do you say it with a question? Is her name Sandra?"

"Yes."

"Okay. You can't get in trouble for helping Sandra. What did you do?"

"The trees and leaves and wind didn't think it was her time to die. The wind got in my feet and took me to her and then it came out of me and brought her back to life."

Dana pretended to not take what I said seriously. Realistically, she thought about how I did the sand deer thing, and how I did the thing with the wind to help you. She had to be thinking about how I wasn't really her kid to begin with.

***

My Dear Sandra,

Believe me that things were different between me and Mom from that day forward. Often, a lot of the times when Bixby mentioned me in conversation, she wouldn't listen. In return, he stared at her behind her back, while he tried to figure her out. Before I saved you, Bixby would stop by my room while I worked on a puzzle. He'd tell me how great I could be, curious about how my mind worked. After I saved you, he came into my room to call Dana nosy, to say she didn't give a shit.

Once, he said, "Son, you have to think before you get married. Do it for more than love. Be better than that. Sheesh, you have to be better than that."

"Okay."

"I'm being honest with you. Marry someone who gives a damn, no matter what. I didn't curse right now. Damn is a bad word for you. Not for me. Damn is a perfectly fine word for me," he laughed. "If I were to curse, I'd say your mother is an uncaring bitch. I'm not going to curse though. Don't tell her I said that. Finish your puzzle. Is that a thousand pieces? You've barely worked on it. Why don't you ever work on it when I'm with you? You want to do one? Let's do one."

I didn't want to do the puzzle as much as I wanted to hang out with my old bear.

"That's fine, not now?" he said.

Once Bixby left to work, the old bear leapt from the chair. He had that big smile on his face. Always happy to see me. I was happy to see him too. Together we finished the thousand-piece puzzle in a few hours. It must have been a weekend because I wasn't at school and Mom hadn't gone to work. On weekends, she worked at night.

After the puzzle I went out to the backyard and roller-skated up and down the walkway with the old bear under my arm.

I used to really love to skate.

I set the old bear down, to make sure nobody from the adjacent yards were looking. The old bear didn't lie there like normal stuffed bears would. He walked across the backyard lawn, looked around in the garage and all that. He rolled around in the grass, dusted himself off, did twirls till he got dizzy and collapsed. I laughed, watched him spin, fresh with life.

When I got done skating, I kicked off my skates, grabbed him, and we went inside.

Mom served me a late lunch. I watched reruns of *I Love Lucy* by myself. She refused to sit with me. She put me on one side of the house, herself on the other. What I did for you scared her more than I could imagine at the time.

I retreated into my bedroom again, closed the door behind me. Me and the stuffed animal went to work on another puzzle. I did this particular puzzle for Bixby, so I'd have something more to talk to him about when he got home. He'd get home and she'd go to work. They'd switch off.

Me and the old bear both worked on the puzzle and danced. One dance I made up all by myself. I named it the Oopdicti, a word that meant nothing.

As we danced, a silhouette of a person stood outside the window behind the closed shades. Mom, standing there, peeking inside, watching me and the doll having a good time. I froze, not knowing what to do, as the silhouette disappeared. The back door opened. The screen door slammed behind it. Her feet stepped closer and closer to my bedroom.

The old bear jumped into the chair, went limp while I waited for her.

The knob turned, and Dana pushed the door open. At first, she looked at me, then scanned the room. Her eyes settled on the bear before she cautiously entered.

Come to find out, my mom had been well aware of my old bear for a while. Seeing it dance, coupled with the sand deer, and me doing my thing with Sandra, made her somewhat hardened to the reality of the old bear, so she was less than amused by me and the antics of it.

She took several large steps before arriving at the chair the bear lay in. "If I rip its head off, will it scream?"

She lifted the old bear by his ear, held him as if he were used toilet paper.

It grabbed her hand.

Startled, she let go of it. It hit the floor, but pushed itself right up onto its cute, plush feet. On its hind legs, it smiled his ear-to-ear sewn on grin. She jumped back to create space between it and her, and then she kicked the old bear across the room. She had observed it enough before this moment to assume, like me, that it wouldn't be animated with her in the room.

In the corner, the bear shook his head while it walked towards us, as its face began to stretch. Its face stretched until we heard and saw the seams of the smile rip.

"Mommy, it's fine," my old bear said, as doll stuffing oozed from its torn open mouth.

Her eyes were closed while she frantically mumbled something incomprehensible into her cupped hands.

The bear moved its torn lips again. "Mommy, it's fine." The voice sounded exactly like mine. Freaked me out. The bear went from being a cute, interesting companion to diabolical in a heartbeat.

Me and Dana fled the room, nearly tripped over one another. She slammed the door behind us. We pushed on it to make sure the diabolical stuffed animal couldn't get out.

After a few minutes, we relaxed, certain it wouldn't open the door. "Mommy, it's fine," I said.

She quickly put a trembling finger to her lips. "Sssshhhh," she whispered. "Don't talk. Stay right here."

Shaking, she sauntered, slowly, first to the living room where she grabbed her car keys, and then out of the front door.

Hours later when Bixby got home from work, she hadn't come back yet. I was still pushing on my bedroom door.

***

Witnessing the old bear do what it did, and then hearing him sound like me, ruined her, and ruined me for her.

If I could go back and talk to Dana, I would tell her I needed the old bear to help me grow up. On some level, I probably still do.

Having her as basically my enemy, it felt like getting kicked in the chest, daily. I cried all the time, and nothing needed to set me off. I slept, woke up in tears. I wept at school when no one watched.

Bixby popped into my room less frequently. There were times when I thought I felt his presence in the doorway. By the time I turned to greet him, he would be walking away, sulking. When we were all together, which didn't happen too often, things felt better than when I was alone. My grades didn't suffer because I already knew what school wanted me to know. I could read and write at the proper level with no problem.

The back of the playground with Justin and Charles and the dirt,

saved me. The leaves waving to me and clapping and staying with me
kept me alive. Life will keep you going if you adhere to it.

Finally, Bixby came into my room, sat next to me on my unmade
bed, as I lay there, depressed.

"You okay, guy?" he said. "You're a kid. You shouldn't be tired. Go
out and run. Get into trouble. You're not really *tired* are you?"

"No."

"I know things have been different around here with me and your
mom, lately. Just checking up on you."

"What do you mean?"

"What do I mean? I mean things change with adults. Understand?
It's not always, uh, what do you call it, uh, fun. It's not fun. Just
checking up. How's school?"

"Fine."

"Fine? That's good. I hear things are good. You're really smart is
what your teacher tells me. She's taken notice."

"Does she send you away?"

"Does she send me away? That's an interesting, smart question. Why
would she send me away?"

I couldn't look him in the eye. "I saw mommy tell Ms. Kimbrel to
send you away."

"You heard that? When?" He waved at me, like never mind. "Don't
answer that. At the program, I guess. Does your mom talk about me and
your teacher?"

I shook my head and sat up. "I don't think so."

"At least she talks to *you*."

He thought there was somebody in the house who paid attention to
me, but there wasn't. I never forgave him for that oversight.

"You've been doing the crying thing a lot. What's going on?"

"She don't talk to me," I mumbled.

"What do you mean she doesn't talk to you?"

"She don't talk to me."

"Why not?" He gazed at the ceiling. "If she's been ignoring you then
I guess I've been ignoring you too, 'cause I didn't notice." He wrapped
his arm around me. "I'm sorry. I mean, I noticed but I didn't recognize
it, I really didn't. She's been ignoring you, I've been ignoring you, and
you've been crying a lot, hiding all of it at school. You're dying in there."
He tapped my chest. "We'll be better from here on out. I'll see that she
talks to you. How does that sound?"

"Good." I sniffed.

"That's something, then." He patted me on the head, stood, and left the room, not looking back.

That night we ate together, as a family. Dad brought home fast food. Here's what I didn't like about fast food when I was a kid: there never seemed to be leftovers. Never an extra burger or extra fries. No extra soda.

We all sat in silence with our burgers and cola in front of us, basically avoiding conversation.

I had almost finished eating when Bixby said to Mom, "So what's going on?"

"You're talking to me?" she responded. "*You* tell *me* what's going on."

"Don't treat him like you treat me."

"Who?"

"Arthur. Don't treat him like you treat me. Don't ignore him."

Mom set her burger down and wiped her hands on her pant legs. She looked over at me as if to say, really? Really?

"You're a lying sack," she said to him.

"A lying sack. I guess we're getting down to it. What am I lying about? Say it. What am I lying about?"

"You want to do this in front of him?"

He wanted me to see him stand up for me. He wanted to look like the good guy.

"Say it," he repeated.

"Say what?"

"You think I cheated on you."

"What?" she jerked her head back, pretending to be shocked. "You think I think you cheated on me?"

"That's exactly what I think. That's how you're acting."

"I don't think you cheated. Bixby, I *know* you cheated. You're cheat*ing*."

He raised his voice. "How do you know about something that isn't happening? How's that even possible? Explain that to me."

"I've met her."

"So."

"She's prettier than I am."

Mom froze and stared at Bixby, waited for him to say what he dutifully should have said. He should have said nobody was as pretty as her. He'd be lying, but still he should have said it. I knew that even then.

"There are plenty of people prettier than you," he said. "Did I cheat with all of them? Her being prettier than you doesn't mean anything."

"How do you know who I'm talking about if you're not cheating?

How do you even know who I'm talking about? You're a lying sack, that's how. You think you're good at it, too. You leave work early to go see her, not thinking I call to see if you're there. You leave from work early to pick him up, to talk to her, all the time. You ogle over her perky tits; you look at me like I'm a sack of friggin potatoes."

He yelled, "You being insecure doesn't mean I've been cheating."

"Did you fuck her?"

"Dana."

She raised her hands in the air and pulled them into fists. "Just answer the *question*."

He had that nervous look. "Why would I need to answer that? You know I didn't."

"Who do you think about more? Me or her? You fantasize about her more than you think about me, huh. She's always on your mind in some way. Tell me I'm wrong. I know you."

"I don't believe we're having this conversation."

"Did you do the damn thing?"

He took a huge bite of his burger and chewed. "Arthur," Bixby said in a soft voice, "go to your room, while your mother tries to get a rise out of me."

"Okay," I said. I pushed my chair away from the table as if to leave. But I didn't go anywhere.

"Dana," he started, "I don't know what to say. I've never put my penis or my confidence in anybody else. That woman is very pretty. I'm not going to say she's not. I'm saying you're my wife. I like you as my wife. Doesn't sound romantic. It's just a matter of fact. I'll be honest. You're not completely wrong. I've thought about her. I've thought about fucking her. More often than I want to say. The point is to be honest here, right? I'm going to be honest, then."

"You think about her more than you think about me?"

"It's like you're mad at me all the time. What'd I do? What did I do? You're suddenly, one day, mad at me, and there's no communication."

"You're saying it's my fault." She slapped her chest. "You want to make love to another woman, there's nothing I can do about it, and it's *my* fault. I get it. You're not here. It's just little ol' me in this relationship. You respond to little ol' me like I'm the great and friggin powerful. Well, I'm not in control. *You* are."

Dad smiled, a huge, blistering grin. He started for her, every step measured and calculated. "You act like I don't love you. I do. What's going on? Say something to me, already. Is it that you cheated on *me*? There's somebody else?"

"Who?"

"Whom."

"Who are you talking about?"

"Demetri. Don't act like you don't know. From the park. His daughter is in the program with Arthur."

"He's a hairy mess. Never even thought about it. You're out of your god damned mind. I'd never do that to you."

"Why do you think I'd do it to *you*?"

She turned her face away, shook her head.

"Honey?" He stroked her face, kissed her cheek. He pet her hair, brought her into his chest. Mom sat there, and suddenly bawled into Bixby's shirt. She nervously tapped her foot on the floor, tapped her fingers on the table. She pointed at me, pushed Dad away, not in a mean way. She turned her head at me, stood and gave me the evil eye, as she exited the room with my dad calling her name all the while. "Dana. Dana. Dana."

After she left, he asked me, "What the hell was that?"

Dad saw things in black and white. If things were in that forbidden gray area, he did everything he could to make it black and white. So, he asked me again.

I sat motionless.

He sat next to me, placed his hands in front of me on the table. His eyes softened, but his face held firm. "I think you know why she's mad at you. Honestly, she's mad at me for something you did, I'm certain. What'd you do? Be honest."

"I made a deer out of sand."

He frowned. "I've heard this story. Okay, try to make that story make sense. What else. You're missing something."

I shrugged.

"That's not going to be good enough," he said. "She's upset. Not a normal upset. She's pissed. What else?"

"I think I can make my teddy bear come to life." Admitting this aloud caused hot tears to roll down my face. I thought I was confessing to a doing something wrong. He wouldn't like me after, so everything I had would soon be gone.

"Shit. I put everybody into tears. No. I'm not cursing. Saying 'shit' is not cursing, for adults. Okay," he sighed. "You can make your bear come to life. How does that affect your mom?"

"She saw me do it," I mumbled.

"She's seen you do it? In addition to the deer you made of sand."

"Yes."

31

"You want to show me the bear? I want to see what Mom saw." How he said it, he didn't believe me. He was still only trying to get rid of the gray area. Knowing Bixby, he knew yelling wouldn't get the truth out of me. He wasn't a yeller. He would try to get down to the bottom of this, logically.

"My old bear won't come back anymore."

"Well, don't you think if you can bring it to life then you should be able to do so when you want to?"

"Yeah."

"Don't say, yeah. Say, yes."

"Yes."

"What's the deal? Let's go see that *bear* of yours."

"I can't," I said.

"Why can Mom see it and I can't?"

Again, I shrugged.

This time when he looked at me, he allowed for no gray area.

He leaned back in his seat, pursed his lips. "Well *fuck. Fuck.*"

He kicked his chair away from the table, caused it to fly against the wall. "It's okay, Arthur. Very little to do with you. Not you at all."

Looking back on that moment, I see that since I corroborated Dana's senseless story, Bixby saw me as taking her side and hiding things. One of the things he thought I hid was mom cheating.

He left me by myself in the dining room, fast food laid out. To make sure, I checked the bag for an extra burger. I was still hungry, tears streamed down my face. I couldn't put it all together. One thing was clear. For the first time ever, Bixby had purchased an extra cheeseburger. I unwrapped it, and ate it, alone.

The First Witnesses

The living room door creaks open, distracting Arthur from typing in his journal to Sandra. He pushes himself away from the computer, sets aside the memory of eating by himself during family turmoil.

He finds Glenda and Raheem lurking in his living room, draped in purpose. Raheem stands in front of him, shirtless and shoeless. Glenda changed her Rams jersey to a t-shirt.

Raheem stares at Arthur, picks him apart with his eyes.

Glenda moves to the side of Raheem but focuses on Arthur. "What's going on?"

"You tell me," Arthur says, suspecting an upcoming conflict regarding Raheem's experience.

She says, "He got himself together and insisted we come over. What the *hell* is going on?"

Attempting to control the moment, Arthur motions to his couch. "Sit down, 'Heem." Arthur sits on his couch in front of the glass coffee table. "Guys. Raheem, have a seat."

Reluctantly, Raheem does as suggested.

Glenda sits next to her husband, puts her hand on his bare chest, leans over and whispers in his ear, "What's going on?"

"That is not a man I'm looking at," Raheem says. "Or not *only* a man."

Glenda whispers to Raheem, loud enough for Arthur to hear, "Do you smell that?"

Raheem closes his eyes and purses his lips. "You can't be *Him*. Something…from *Him*?" He darts his index finger at the ceiling.

Arthur says, "I'm only me, always been me, am nothing else but me. It's just that I can do this…thing."

Glenda chimes in, "What are you guys talking about?"

Arthur hears himself say, "Your husband died."

"Excuse me?" Glenda says.

"I died," Raheem adds. "He brought me back. He's Him. I think we all have to come to terms with that fact."

"He's who?" Glenda's frowns.

"I'm not Jesus," Arthur says.

"No one's calling you Jesus," she says. "What's that smell? That stench smells crazy different in your house."

"Same smell that killed your husband," Arthur says.

Glenda replies, "Come on, Raheem. Let's get the kids. We're late."

"How long was I dead?" Raheem says to Arthur, matter-of-factly.

"Something like ten minutes," Arthur tells him. "She had to come over here, get me, then we had to go back over there. It must have been at the very least ten minutes, altogether."

Glenda lifts her chin. "Baby, the kids need to be picked up. I'll be out in the car."

"You won't listen?" Arthur says to her.

"Hell no. Not sure what the *hell* you two are talking about." She walks away.

Raheem stares at Arthur. "Was that really you over there?"

"Huh?"

"You wouldn't stop stabbing me. No, you don't understand. It's a good thing."

Arthur says, "I don't get it."

Keeping his eyes on Arthur, Raheem slowly backs out of the house.

***

About an hour later, Arthur sits on Raheem and Glenda's porch steps, hanging his head between his legs. The time may never be right to let them or the world know about his abilities. Still, he could feel the urge for revenge on the world for not being sympathetic to him for having his abilities. A childish feeling but the anger festers in his joints, regardless.

Raheem and Glenda pull up in their driveway, having picked up Tracy and Shelly from the after-school program. The engine cuts off, and the back doors of their sedan open like metal wings.

"What happened to him?" Tracy asks.

"Nothing happened." Raheem exits the driver's side.

"Kids," Glenda says, exiting the passenger side. "I want you to walk right on passed Arthur, don't say anything to him. Just go on passed, understand?"

Tracy says, okay. Shelly nods. The kids quickly scoot around the adults, wait at the front door. They're let into the house by their father. They know better than to pay too much attention to adult conversation.

"Stay right there on the steps, guy," Raheem says to Arthur after letting his kids in the house. "You don't have to move."

Glenda stops in front of Arthur. "You got something to say?"

Arthur lifts his head. "I want to show you something because you're going to find out anyway."

Raheem turns to Arthur. "Find out what?"

Arthur stands. "I'll show you."

He waves for them to follow, starts across their shared driveway. Seconds later, Arthur's on his front porch.

On his heels, Glenda follows Arthur into his house. Raheem is right behind them.

"Is the smell in here worse than before?" Raheem's nostrils flare. "What is that?"

"You ignored it earlier," Glenda says.

"Damn." Raheem tries to shake off the acrid smell.

The tap of their footsteps echo on the hardwood floor of the hallway.

Arthur pauses as he grabs the door handle to his bedroom.

"What's that smell, Arthur?" Raheem's hand goes over his mouth. "Rotten eggs in your sink?"

"You can almost taste it," Glenda whispers. "Friggin horrible. What *is* that?"

Arthur eyes his shut bedroom door. "I didn't know what else to do."

"What'd you do?" Raheem says, covering his mouth.

Arthur pushes his bedroom door open, leads the way in. Glenda and Raheem stop in the doorway, squinting because of the smell.

Glenda finds the courage to press forward. "Is that her? Is that her?"

Raheem says, "What the hell is this?"

"Lift the blanket," Glenda insists, pointing at Arthur. "Lift the blanket!"

"It's her, the blanket lifted or not." Arthur grasps the blanket above Sandra's waist. "I swear I was going to figure all of this out. That's all."

"What the *fuck*, Arthur." Glenda's hands turn into fists.

"I can still bring her back," Arthur says. "I just don't know how, for some reason. Need to adjust…something. *Something.*"

"Can't you do to her what you did for me?" Raheem says.

"No! No." Glenda swings her head around, so she faces Raheem. "He didn't do anything for you." She slaps Raheem's shoulder, her eyes fixed on the body under the blanket. "Lift it."

Arthur tightens his fistful of blanket and rips it off Sandra's body, like a magician who has unveiled the surprise in a newly learned magic trick.

Sandra lay on her side in the fetal position, her hands clasped together as if snuggled down for sleep. The sheets soiled with dark brown, almost black splotches, and streaks of dried blood. Deeper splotches of dried blood near her head. Her hair, still its usual burnt amber shade, curled over her neck. She lay in one of Arthur's baby-blue collared shirts.

Nobody should see her like this, Arthur thinks.

Sandra's stained teeth. Her sloppily hanging tongue. Her eyes blankly in her head, perfectly white. The side of her face basically shot off, but the mangled flesh partially healed. He expected to see the right side of her forehead shattered. Instead, pinkish flesh has grown in the area she had shot off.

A butterfly seems to flutter around the inside of Arthur's stomach. Perhaps he hasn't failed yet.

"She shot herself," Arthur says.

Her decomposition is less than it should be. Still, she's dead.

Glenda steps backward towards the exit, her hands over her mouth, in shock. "You can't do this."

A single, deep breath leaves Sandra's body.

Raheem gasps.

Glenda's fingers intertwine at her chin as if in prayer, her feet together as she bends forward, peers in at Sandra from across the room.

"Did we all see that?" Glenda says in a whisper. "It's all wrong."

"Is. She. Breathing?" Raheem gathers himself.

Arthur grabs Sandra's wrist, and then moves his hand to her forehead. He tilts her head back. With her head tilted, he splits her colorless lips with his thumb, index, and middle fingers. He leans forward and breathes a single breath into her mouth. "She's breathing again."

"911," Glenda says.

"Nobody's helping her but me." Arthur sets down Sandra's head. "I'm the one. I'm the only one for her. Always have been." He starts in Glenda's direction, meaning to make or let her understand.

Glenda backtracks to the door, sticks her arm straight out, gesturing for him to stop. "Stay the *fuck* away from me."

Arthur stops.

Raheem makes small steps in Glenda's direction. "It's okay."

She lowers her hand. "No. It's, not."

"It's a lot simpler than you're making it, honey. Arthur is curing Sandra, in his own way. That's what we're seeing. That's all. Baby, it's okay."

"Look at her," she pleads. She points to Sandra. "Does that look like curing to you?"

Arthur says, "Go ahead and be confused. It's why I showed her to

36

you. It's easier explained if you see it. It's my mistake. I really thought she was gone for good. She's coming back. She's breathing. Probably a mistake showing you."

Hands on his hips, Arthur stomps passed Glenda, and then out of the bedroom.

A moment later, Glenda and Raheem arrive in the living room, covering their mouths and noses, protecting themselves from the smell of Sandra's body.

Glenda raises her voice. "I'm calling 911."

Arthur hears '911', the threat in her tone. "She's coming back, the same way Raheem came back. Ask your husband."

"Baby," Raheem says, almost singing. "We can't deny any of this is happening. Look, Arthur might not believe it, but this is God working. This is how He does His work. People see it and don't believe it. I wouldn't believe it either except for what happened to me. You want me to come to my senses? That's what I've done."

"But Raheem," Arthur says. "It has nothing to do with God. I don't want someone thinking I had her holed up because of God. That's crazy. Not what's happening. People will be offended by what I've done."

Disappointed, Raheem drags his feet out of Arthur's house.

"You have to stay away from us." Glenda points at Arthur, as she starts for the door. "Don't come anywhere near me or my family."

***

Glenda strolls across the driveway to her front porch where she hesitates to walk into her home. *Check on the kids, call the cops. I don't know everything, just call the cops.*

When she finally enters, Raheem is waiting for her. "You're not turning him in."

"I don't see it as turning him in. You shouldn't either. You should look at it as helping Sandra."

"He's already helping her. You don't want to see it that way."

She throws her hands in the air. "This is too much. It's *too* much. What's he doing to help her? You saw what I saw. He's not helping her. I-I'm calling."

"Think about it. What's he doing to her?"

"There's blood all around her. Old blood at that. It's Sandra. Are you *crazy*? Are you friggin *crazy*?"

"You're the one treating her like she's going to die. Clearly she did something to herself and he's helping."

"What are you asking me to do? He-he's killing her, or at the very least not helping. I don't know how you don't see that."

"I'm begging you. Leave him alone for a night or so. Let him see it through. The truth lies in what if. What if she's better tomorrow than she is today? I want you to think to yourself, what if she's even better the day after. I'm begging you. *Begging* you…don't call anybody."

She smacks her thighs. "You don't think being over there earlier plus knowing what we know makes us responsible?"

"Responsible for what? We didn't do anything to harm anybody. I don't think he did either. He said she shot herself."

"You believe that? Is she someone who would do something like that? It's more like he did some crazy shit so she's barely hanging on. Don't you see that?"

"We're going to regret it if we turn him in," he says. "We're married. We're both going to own the actions we take against our neighbor. We do certain things as one person. This is one of those things. I can't let you call on him."

"I'm waiting, then, for him to, what, finish hurting her?"

"You don't believe that. If you stop his process right now, I want nothing to do with you. I'm being real right now. This is bigger than me or you. Let him finish."

"You'll actually leave me over this? Oh my God, what the hell."

"He's not hurting her." His tone is soft. "Wait one day. The end of tomorrow, not even through tomorrow night. After that something is wrong."

"Where are the kids?" She gazes up the staircase. "In their room?"

"She's going to come back healthy. He'll eat her pain like he did for me."

Her eyes close, her shoulders drop, as she hangs her head. In an amazingly short amount of time, she's lost her husband, and Sandra. Arthur caused both losses.

"You'll be in the room?" she asks.

"I'll be praying about all this. You don't have to join me. I won't ask you."

Fine, she thinks, before marching her way into the kids' bedroom.

The Real Ms. Kimbrel

Arthur rolls off the office futon, the sun yet to rise. He takes his usual walk down the hallway, cracks his bedroom door open, hopes for signs that Sandra has moved—her body in a different position, the blankets bundled in the wrong place, something that means she's come back to him. He doesn't mind the smell. It's temporary. Barefoot, he steps deeper into the room, ignores stained splotches of blood on the carpet.

He hovers over her, stares at her pasty skin and silently wishes for her to come back. He kneels at her bedside, then sits on the floor next to her.

The next thing he knows, he's waking again, the sun shining through the window above her bed; a sliver of hope beams in from outside.

Time to get ready for work.

After showering, he stands in front of the large mirror on the dresser.

"A long-term sub has so much stuff in her room that I can barely get it cleaned properly."

He can't pinpoint how talking to Sandra's body helps him.

"It's an unnecessary mess. Takes custodians for granted. Not going to get much respect leaving a mess like that. There's stuff all over the desks, stacked in corners. She has boxes of things on top of things on top of other things. Nobody knows what's in all that junk. It's the kids who suffer, I'm sure. It's a guarantee I forget to take out her trash tonight. I'm a custodian, not a servant."

In the mirror, his once flat belly is six months pregnant. He can't see the back of his head where his hair is thinning, but it reminds him he's closer to fifty than forty. The whites of his eyes have yellowed, partially from his recent bout of bad sleep. Since she killed herself, birds tweeting wakes him. His own breathing wakes him. He only sleeps a few hours a night.

The moment she shot herself replays in his head like a .GIF image.

***

This afternoon, Arthur doesn't bother rolling down his window on the way to work. No point in smelling the air. In the past, the stench had come and gone, arrived, and left on its own. Nowadays it lingers for days at a time. Sandra had once described the odor as dirty, iron ass-pipe. Somehow, it has progressed to where it can harm people, such as Raheem.

At the elementary school, his work site, Arthur finds his way to the Teachers' lounge twenty minutes early to meet with the rest of the custodial team. If you're not early you're late. Someone called in sick today, so they'll be dividing extra duties. Communication is thin, due to not all of them carrying walkie-talkies like they should.

Arthur starts his route in the bungalows, empties the trash in the classrooms and vacuums.

A few hours into his route, he opens the door to Mrs. Logan's classroom, the disrespectful long-term substitute who he told Sandra about, the one who keeps her classroom a mess. To his surprise, she's at her desk amongst disorganized student classwork on desktops, pencils, and crayons on the floor. Lids to glue lay on top of things, randomly. Nametags on the desks, hang, torn in half, or in shreds.

He's not the only one with complaints about her. Numerous faculty and parents want her gone, if for no other reason, her old age. Until now, he hasn't met her or seen her.

"I'll come back when you're done," he says, partially in the room. Her black-rimmed glasses go well next to her completely gray, short hair that is combed to the side. "I'll let you finish. Come back later, I guess."

"Young man," she says. "Young man, I've been meaning to speak to you."

She rises from behind her desk. She approaches in a white, flowing dress that comes down to her ankles. The vague scent of roses is familiar.

"Young…man."

"Arthur."

It must be uncomfortable to be her. Her skin looks tight, especially on her hands. She has liver spots, especially on her face.

He smiles, if only to placate. "What can I do for you?"

"Arthur Lowe." The name rolls off her lips, as if she has a right to it. "I thought you were avoiding me. You don't remember. You were so bright. So quiet. You were confident. Cried a lot. Not a usual combination. I always wondered how you were so well-rounded, so smart, got along with so many people, so many kids, but cried so often."

Arthur involuntarily throws his head back, realizing the person in his presence.

"Oh, you remember," she says. "I was prettier back then."

"I actually haven't seen you around. I would have recognized you, no doubt. You recognized me."

"Not at first. You still have that certain something about you."

"What thing?"

"I don't know. Something. A kind of sadness follows you. It helps that you have the same name." She moves back to her desk, favoring her right side. "When you first walked into my life, you had your dad with you. I leaned down thinking you were a scared little thing in the wrong place. I thought I could make it right. I think I did, too. You had so much going on."

"Ms. Kimbrel."

"Yes, yes, how are you, young man?" She holds her hand out.

They shake.

"You're Mrs. Logan."

"Married. A few. The last marriage with Mr. Logan… I kept his name."

"I don't know what to say."

She rubs her eyes with her palm. "You're a man now."

"I'm old."

"At some point, age speeds up. It comes at you." She blinks, still in wonder of the moment. "I'll be gone in a few, if you don't want to work around me."

"I'll finish up wherever else. Come back when you're gone."

"We should talk."

"You're on my route every night."

"How are your parents?"

He thinks back to her grabbing Bixby's elbow, and flirting with him for the entire class to see. "They're not around. Haven't seen them for a good minute."

"Did they make it?"

"Excuse me."

"Are your parents together?"

"Truth be told, I don't know if they're alive. They divorced, if that's what you're asking."

"I'm so sorry to hear that."

"Well…"

"Who had custody, if you don't mind me asking?"

"You know what—"

"—I understand. That's too much." She loses her eyes, ponders something. "We should talk. Not if you don't want to."

"I don't mind. Like I was saying, you're on my route. I'll stop in."

"I wish you would."

"I'll come back after you've left."

She steps backwards, looks him up and down, and then turns and finds her seat at her cluttered desk.

About an hour later, Arthur returns to her classroom with more than enough time for her to have completed her tasks and gone home. He opens the door, pauses in the doorway, and again sees Ms. Kimbrel at her desk.

"I've got something to tell you," she says, tapping her desk. "I think you should listen. About your dad and I."

"Bixby's not my dad."

"He was your biggest advocate. Why don't you grab one of the chairs from the kidney table?"

As suggested, he grabs the only adult-sized chair from the arts and crafts table that is shaped like a kidney. "You have a lot of stuff. Is it all for the kids? A lot of random stuff for a classroom."

"It's good I have it, to let the students be as clean or as messy as they're going to be. Not a goal of mine to teach kids about neatly stacking paper. That's the job of someone at home. I'm none of their mothers."

Setting the chair down in front of her desk, he leans forward with all his attention. "I vaguely remember you always letting us do our thing."

"You were definitively bright."

"That's what my dad thought. I turned out to be an ordinary man. Ordinary kid. Same issues as anybody. Grew up with the same problems as anybody else. Got an ordinary life. Ordinary job. Here I am as a normal custodian."

"Nothing wrong with that."

"Nothing wrong at all. I lend a hand to about a thousand people a day. About 870 of them are kids with no idea of the world around them, and then all the teachers and administration. I feel helpful."

She leans on her desk. Her palm props up her chin. "Because of your dad, I know you can do special things."

His eyebrows raise. "What are you talking about?"

"I mean to talk to you about what your real father said about you. It seems more important now than thirty, forty years ago. Do you know what I'm talking about?"

"My biological dad is a myth."

"I met him, briefly. Regardless of how brief, he feels like an old friend."

"My *actual* dad?" He leans back in the chair. The front two legs lift off the floor.

"He said you were special like him."

"Special like him?"

"He proved it to me. He proved he was special."

Biting his tongue, Arthur contemplates the point to her words. "How'd you meet him? Why would you have met him?"

"He didn't want you to know about it. He said that for the amount of time he would be in your life, he didn't need to bog you down with his presence. I never saw him again. Never met anyone like him after that, or before that. You're the closest thing."

"What you're saying is kind of hard to follow. You met him one time or a few times..." He opens his palms to her, like, what are you talking about?

"If I tell you that he could do things, would you know what I was talking about? He could do *amazing* things." She gives him the look like she wants him to say something. "He said you could do what he did. You're his son. This was when you were in the third grade, not my direct student anymore."

"I was in your program."

"That was our connection." An assertiveness presented itself, in the lines in her forehead, in the wrinkles of her cheeks. "Can you do like your father?"

"I don't know."

"I think you do, I really do, young man."

It's as if she's accused him of something.

"You don't have to lie to me. You don't need to do such a thing, not with me." She sweeps her hand over her body, as if to say, look at all this. "I'm old, Arthur. Understand? I'm not what I once was. You being here is meant to be. I get displaced from my old school. After decades of service I don't have a job, which is shocking at first. I move on. Find myself here, don't know what's going on. I don't have kids of my own. I'm married, but I'm not in love." She covers her mouth with her hands, hides whatever expression she may have.

He squirms in his seat, finally sees her as an old, bitter person. She thinks she can be fixed.

"Don't tell him I said it's not real love. If you tell him, you'll kill him. Literally. He's so old. He's not old like me; he's old like... Anyway. I find myself here, and then I see you. You must be back in my life for a reason."

"You think I'm going to help you?"

"Why else would you have such a gift?"

Arthur cups his chin. "This person you say was my actual father must have told you something—I don't know what—for you to have this idea of me. I'm curious as hell, what did he tell you, or show you?"

She lowers her voice. "I thought he was a pedophile, at first."

"—This person you're calling my actual father..."

"I thought he was a pedophile. It's because of how I met him. At Kennedy."

***

I saw him at the opposite end of the playground one recess, outside the gates, staring at all the kids. He left before I said anything to him. The next day, while on playground duty, I saw him, although outside the gates, still heading towards you and your friends. I yelled to him. Although I didn't say anything to him the first day, that second day was wasn't tolerable. I couldn't chicken out and leave it up to a report. I had to approach this individual. A Black man, just watching at first, now approaching you guys. When I yelled to him, he ran off. He didn't actually, run. You know what I mean. He fled. Scared me to death. He was the nightmare of a child stalker come to life. I went home mostly sickened that the worst kind of person, the enemy had shown himself. I told the faculty about an awkward man lurking about. They knew what to look for. I dropped a description of him in all the teacher's boxes—a tall Black man with dirty hair and raggedy clothing. A sweater for no reason. Jeans and tattered tennis shoes. Him being around was a big deal. A child predator of all things.

A few days later he returned. I approached him again with threats in mind. Police. Prison. Hell.

Instead of running off, he waited for me at the playground gate. He said he was fine where he was and that he wasn't a problem.

"You're most definitely a problem," I said. "If you don't leave on your own, I'll be the most likely solution, when I call the cops."

"The police, for standing on the sidewalk, looking at kids? The police?"

"I'm calling the police no matter what."

"I see what your mind is up to, but the real world has other things going on. See that little boy over there?" He pointed to you, his dirty fingers intertwined in the fencing. He smelled like neglect. Body odor. His uncombed hair hadn't been washed in I don't know how long. "That little boy is mine. My son."

"Which little boy?"

"The only one over there who looks like me."

44

I looked him up and down, made sure he saw me do it. At the time, there was only me out there with this man. No other teachers on the playground.

"I'm taking a look at my kid," he said. "I don't see any other parents out here trying to look after their kids."

"When they come, they visit the classroom. They check in through the office. They don't stalk them at the gate. They don't run off when approached."

"Arthur. That's my boy." He was so proud when he said it.

I wanted to take him over to you, to see if you recognized him. He said you wouldn't recognize him. It all added up to the fact that he shouldn't have been there. With that in mind, my gut still told me he was harmless.

"What's his room number?" he said.

"No."

"You're his teacher?"

"I can't give you that information."

"You're in charge of him at other times, right? What about after school?"

Although it was alarming that, apparently, he had been watching you, it didn't come as a complete surprise. I'll admit, it made me more curious than frightened. I knew, in my gut, he was telling the truth.

"How can I visit him in class if I don't know his room number?"

"Go to the office, tell them who you are. They'll give you a pass. Until then…"

"I can't prove he's mine. See what I'm talking about? Maybe I could stop by after school."

"You can't prove it to me either."

"What's your name?"

"I'm Ms. Kimbrel."

"Not Mrs?"

The bell rang.

We watched you and your friends run off to your class lines. He knew I wasn't married to begin with.

Feeling I may have misjudged the entire moment, I told him the police would be along shortly, and then I walked away.

Regardless, the administration and myself told Bixby and Dana he was around. Bixby and Dana took it in stride. They debated whether or not to pull you out of school for the time being. Ultimately, the principal left it up to them. Langston's presence caused a stir with other parents once they heard about it. Nothing like that ever happened.

Your biological father turned up two or three times a week for a few months. We always engaged in small talk. Never about me, never about him. A few times we met after school. He wanted to get a closer look at you, but we couldn't keep that up. Too much hiding. Too much thought, especially since it was clear that he didn't want to engage you. That and I became concerned he had a crush on me. I had to insist we discontinue our arrangement. I did feel better once it was over, kind of sad at the same time. We weren't our best selves at the wrong time. That's a way to put it.

A week or so later, he showed his face again—on my front porch of all places—with brown work shoes and slacks. A very physically tone person. Not, as they say, buff. His arm muscles were defined. I could tell since he wore a short-sleeved work shirt, like a fancy Mormon. His facial hair, which had been growing like a weed the previous time I saw him, was neatly trimmed into a thin beard. His hair had been cut short. He hid his eyes behind a pair of sunglasses—something Officer Ponch might wear, only fancier. Remember that show? I didn't recognize him, at first. He stood on my porch with his hands on his hips. In his hand he had three withered yellow roses.

At the front door, he handed the roses to me without looking me in the eye, without saying anything. Right before he spoke, I recognized him.

"I can come in?" he said.

"You're disguised."

I thought it was cute of him to work so hard to change his appearance for me. I can admit, I was slightly flattered at his ambition towards me. No doubt he had come to impress me in some way. Why else such a change? This is how he wanted to convince me to let him see you after school.

I waved him in.

The roses weren't pretty, didn't smell nice, but they were meant to impress me. A debonair gesture.

He looked around my place, unmoved by the surroundings.

"How did you know I lived here?" I said.

"Been spying on you."

"You followed me home?"

"Phone book. I've never been to this place. I've been to Arthur's house, doing my spying. Kept up with him."

"You say that to scare me?"

"Why would I offer you roses and mean to scare you?"

"They're dead."

46

He said, "You're thinking, why didn't I introduce myself to Arthur if I've been spying all this time? The answer is, I did. I told his mom he was special. Not how special. By looking at her she already knew. By how she talked about him she already knew. She asked her questions. I didn't give her any answers. If you're me, you learn scared people defend first and appreciate later. I could hear it in her. She's going to get rid of him."

"What do you mean?"

"I don't know how, but she will. It's in her nature to defend herself. You can tell."

"Rude to say about a person, about a mother. I don't think you know her well enough to speak to how scared she is."

He had his hands at his sides, appearing nervous. "I gave his acting mom the heads up. I can't have her for a mother. Wouldn't have told her if she wasn't so scared of him. More scared than she looks. Like a little girl, how scared she is."

"What did she say?"

"She didn't want to be around anyway. To be honest, I myself don't want to be in his life right now."

I couldn't believe what I had heard. Why would he announce himself just so he could leave? "There's shame in what you're saying. Making a life out of abandoning your son."

"That's not how I see it. In the end I won't abandon him. It won't be the case at all, is what I'm saying. I came back for him…but I met you. Understand?"

"I absolutely don't understand." I very well understood what he was trying to say. I just didn't feel that way. I couldn't. It wasn't possible.

He said, "Aren't you getting in good with his dad? When he picks Arthur up, you're happy to see him. You know what I'm talking about."

Him saying it threw me off. Bixby said his wife couldn't know about us. I didn't think we were doing anything wrong. Bixby always said if Dana thought something was going on between us then something was going on, no matter if nothing had been. Having Langston say he knew we still met after school concerned me. If something had happened between your dad and I, I wouldn't tell you, but nothing was happening. I wouldn't be with a married man. That kind of relationship can't possibly go anywhere.

Langston said, "You're silly to think she doesn't know. She knows."

"Do I have to ask you to leave?"

"You would be a better mother to him than his current one. Bixby would do better with Arthur on his own, until me and you worked it out. Then he could hand my boy over. I'd like that."

"That's just crazy."

"Me and you could raise that boy from the ground up."

It was the oddest thing anybody had ever told me. "You're here to propose marriage?"

"A kid, too."

I laughed out loud, not because his proposal was silly, but because I immediately considered it, pictured it. It didn't make sense all the way.

"What you're saying is too much," I said.

"Here's to happiness. And love." He raised the roses up to his forehead. Held them there. "And to the people we should be with." He pulled the roses down to his mouth. He whispered something to them, like they were old friends.

From there, I couldn't believe what I saw. The withered yellowed petals slowly turned deep yellow, and soft. They began to smell fresh and airy. It gave me the impression I was watching life move at a pace I could see, right before my eyes. Watching it happen made everything else seem, I want to say, smaller.

I didn't know anything about what he had just done; I could feel it, somehow, emotionally. *So* amazing. In my heart, I knew what he had done. Up here, in my mind, is where I had questions.

"What is it that you just did?" I asked.

"I can't explain nothin."

"Is this how you get by, doing these magic tricks?"

"Is it a trick you do to make dudes fall for you right when they see you?"

Yes, he said that. Rolled right off his tongue.

"You don't feel something between us?" he said. "How do you not feel that? It's you I want as part of my son's life. Shit, you don't feel that? He's special, can do what I do. It'll be a hell of a ride. These are for you." He handed me the roses, now all fresh and new.

I inspected them for a trick, to see if they were fake. "It's not possible."

He thought I was talking about him and me being together. I was talking about the roses.

"Didn't think it was possible this very moment. What if I told you I can make you young again, like I did the roses? When you're old I can make you young. How 'bout then? Then, you won't need to love me or even like me, but would you be with me?"

"That doesn't make sense. Does it?"

"Not yet. Not all the way, no."

What he said didn't seem real enough to act on, or not to act on. So confusing.

"Pay attention to my son."

I sniffed the fresh rose petals.

"They smell like that pretty perfume you wear," he said.

I sniffed them again. They smelled much better than my perfume.

I watched you the first chance I got. I never saw what he wanted me to see.

***

Ms. Kimbrel says, "You're in front of me now, and I'm asking: I want you to make me young again. Can you do that for me, Arthur? Can you do that?"

"No, I can't. I'm actually not capable."

She lowers her head in disbelief, looks up, shoos him away, and sinks into her seat.

The Friction

My Sweet,

Seeing the sun rise from my office window a while ago got me thinking of how I've been waiting to disappear, like a slowly sinking sunset. I've stopped asking *why* I want to die and started asking *when* I want to die.

At about two o'clock this morning I saw your legs cross under the sheets. I'm not going to last another week without you. However, seeing you've changed position, I'm almost sure you'll be back with me soon. Your possible arrival doesn't lift the fog from my mind like I thought it would. It's as if my own self won't let me be happy or excited.

My life may have stopped. The world hasn't. That's what I tell myself.

I need to get to work right now.

***

Arthur peeks into Ms. Kimbrel's class on his way to the teachers' lounge before starting his shift. She reads something at her desk while her class quietly works. She looks up from her reading, smiles at him, as if he is Santa Claus concealing her gift.

"Should I clean your class later tonight?" he says, risking disturbing the class.

"Please do."

***

He knocks on her classroom door.

She doesn't say as much as hello before she lets him in and limps back to her seat. Her long, flowing red dress waves around her ankles.

"Are you okay?" he asks.

"I'm fine, why? You think I'm crazy to think a person can make another person young again?"

"What happened to your leg?"

"Not my leg. My knee. It's time reminding me of itself. It'll probably be better tomorrow. If not…" She takes a seat behind her desk. "Are you going to sit or clean?"

"I do have a job to do."

"This isn't the end of your route?"

"It is. I still have to do it."

"Grab a chair from the kidney table."

As instructed, he fetches a chair, starts back in her direction.

"There's something I want you to tell me." She places her fingertips on her desktop, presses down, angles her body in his direction.

He flips the chair around and sits in it facing the wrong direction.

"What became of you?" she says. "Did you ever leave town? Did you go to college? Did you do those things? What have you been doing all this time?"

"What have *you* been doing is a good question."

"What have I been doing? Alright, why don't we catch up? Me first, I suppose."

"You, first."

"I got old." She laughs. "I got laid off from your old school, Kennedy, inevitably, like I told you. Got my masters. For a while I thought I wanted to be a college professor. That didn't pan out."

"Why not?"

"Life happens."

"Life is why you didn't become a professor?" he says.

"You're going to push this aren't you. You know why. A man, of course. Why else do women not succeed at their goals? I followed him to Arizona, of all places. Not for the money. For the flexibility." How she said flexibility, she might have said friendship or family or future, but she meant money.

"I don't mind Arizona," he says.

"We had a child, the child died, and then our relationship ended." Her hands clasp. "It's one of those things you look back on… It all happened so fast it didn't matter. It's one of those, he worshiped the ground I walked on. It died, and then, I don't know, I didn't need someone to worship me like that."

"It was an it, not a he or a she?"

"The point is I went away, came back, got back on my feet and couldn't… In the end, we ultimately don't care anymore. *You* care, I can tell."

"Things don't roll off me like they used to. The love of my life committed suicide," Arthur says. "I'll be okay. I think about what I would say to my wife if she somehow came back. What would I tell her?"

"What's her name?"

"Sandra."

"Anna. That was my girl's name. Anna."

Arthur rocks back and forth, uncertain in how to proceed in the conversation.

"I can hear that child in you. I'm ready to listen this time." She bats her eyelids. "If I had my interesting moments, I'm sure you've had yours. Tell me about them. Tell me about this love of yours. Damn the tragedy. Tell me about the good times."

"The good times with Sandra."

"Yes. She must be a wonderful recollection. I don't see how there's anything else to talk about. I bet neither me nor you are nearly as interesting on our own."

A string of moments come to him, but none that feel natural enough to talk about. They're secrets about when people died, and he made sure they lived again.

"I have a job to do." He stands, pretends to look for a clock. "You have someone waiting for you at home. What time is it?"

"Barely seven."

"I guess it would be weird to up and walk out right now."

"Very much so."

"Maybe I'm not quite ready to talk about her."

"I'm sorry, I shouldn't have even asked."

"I actually want people to know."

"Arthur. Call me Trinna."

"Fine, Trinna." He sits. "There is a hell of a story."

***

So, Trinna.

I can tell part of the story.

I stepped on campus at Centennial Junior High and saw kids who were older and bigger than me. The world had become incredibly large. Me and Sandra didn't really talk in elementary school, so we went into the next level propping up two different cultures. She was in a culture of popular people; I was in a culture of loser people. She had her friends, I had mine.

I had only seen my friends Charles and Justin a few times over the summer. It was perfect running into them in the gym on the first day. Since we hadn't been completely sorted, a ton of us scrubs' classrooms met in the gym on the first day. We weren't assigned classwork or anything. No teacher. We were supposed to simply not get into trouble.

I spotted Justin and Charles at the top of the bleachers.

Charles had put on a little weight over the summer, in a good way. He had filled out more than me and Justin. His hair looked manicured if that makes sense. He had gotten rid of his glasses. He had on all new clothes, like we all did, but his new clothes were nice.

"What. Is. Up," I said to them.

They stood to greet me. We did the whole handshake thing.

Charles said to me, "I'm getting me some pussy."

"Wow. What?" I had never heard him speak like that.

Justin added, "His sister's been working with him over the summer. She says the only thing he needs to be thinking about in junior high is getting laid."

"Isn't that a high school thing?" I said.

"If you want to wait till then," Justin added. "Man, pussy."

Justin had changed as well. His hair was so nicely trimmed, one might think the gardener got to him. He dressed himself these days, and it showed. He had shorts and purple socks and yellow high-tops. It would have been better if his parents dressed him.

I had my hair grown out into a huge afro. For style points, I had a pick with a fist on the handle stuck in the back of my head. My hair was so thick, the comb stayed in place well enough that I didn't need to think about it. Mostly everything I wore was jean. My pants. My jacket. Not my red t-shirt.

We metamorphosed from some kids who hung out at the back of the playground for a few years gathering dirt, to the kids who pretended to play kickball, to the kids without classrooms at Centennial talking about pussy.

Junior high meant academia would take a break for a few years; the goals in junior high had nothing to do with learning and everything to do with not getting embarrassed. Being embarrassed was the source of fear for nearly all of us.

"How are you going to get pussy?" I asked.

"She told me things," Charles said.

"Tell him what she told you," Justin said. "Tell him."

Charles nodded. "It's about impressing with your junk."

"Say what?" I replied.

We all took our seats on the wooden bleachers.

"First off," Charles began, "let them know about your cock. Girls are cock-aware, at all times. Make them curious about the cock. See, now that I've mentioned cock, you guys are thinking about mine. It works the same for them."

"Does that make sense?" I wondered aloud.

Justin tugged his belt. "It doesn't need to make sense if it's true. It's what girls—deep down—really want from a guy. Tell him, Charles."

"Okay, look," Charles began. "It's all about making nice friction for the female both inside and around the snatch area. The larger the wood, the more the friction. From what I know, the more friction the better."

"Does your sister like the friction?" I said.

Charles replied, "I didn't ask. Won't ask. You won't either."

"She likes the friction for sure," Justin said.

"Man," Charles said, "they all like the friction, even if they don't know it yet." He flipped his hair behind his ears. "Girls love hair. I've got a lot of it. It's a really good thing."

I scoured the bleachers for prospective girls who might want me to give them the friction. It's kind of funny now, but back then I wanted to, basically, find a pussy to light on fire with my dick.

***

Physical education was a hub of embarrassing moments, a source of some serious fear.

The Physical Ed teachers wanted us to shower after class. Instead, we ran through the showers, naked, holding our junk. On the other side of the showers we were handed cotton towels that weren't big enough. They broke if you got them too wet. The point of showering, for most of us, was to *not* shower. The last thing any dude needed was to have girls hear about his dick before you showed it to them.

You had people pointing and laughing at your junk, no matter what. "Scrub cock!" they'd yell and then make chicken sounds. These were things we didn't have to deal with in elementary school. Junior high filled me with enough fear to last me clear through college. With the exception of a few friends and Sandra, I still think of it as a rather horrible experience. You think the bathrooms in an elementary school are bad? Try a locker room in junior high.

We were all scared, including those who pretended they weren't. The bully types were as scared as us, looking back. Everybody might have been scared except for this one guy who, for whatever reason, was never part of the group, though he hung out a bunch. We all knew him.

Quincy.

After "showering" we all waited in the toweling off area, with those thin towels that could tear easily upon getting wet. A large gate sat in front of us, closed. We were trapped, naked in a cage.

Some kids wanted power over the rest of us. To do so they had to pull our towels off our waists or tear them from our bodies. Exposing someone was a typical thing to do. No doubt, always embarrassing to the victim. Sometimes you did it to somebody else because it happened to you a week or a day ago. School is about education. Not only the kind in the classroom either. You know what I'm talking about.

So here comes Quincy out of the showers. He took a shower, and slowly walked to get his thin, white towel. He didn't wrap it around him. Instead, he dried off. His junk swung from left to right for everybody to see. A giant smirk on his face. At the gate where those most eager to get the hell out of there were, he said, "You can look. Yeah, you can look. There it is. Don't lie to yourself. This shit is happening."

The gate opened.

"Whatever," he said, as they ran off.

Quincy refused to be scared. He created fear. He owned the entire P.E. period.

Quincy seemed older, like he had been through a bunch more than we had. For instance, he had a brief and shaky history with a bunch of girls. The rumors were saying he'd been giving out massive amounts of friction. We shouldn't have been listening to Charles about that sort of thing; we should have been listening to Quincy. Hell, Charles shouldn't have been listening to himself.

After P.E., myself and Charles cornered Quincy, who we later started calling Q's, with one thing on our minds.

"What's up fellas?" Quincy said on the way to nutrition. "Please don't ask how big my dick is. I'm kidding, y'all. What's up? What's up with you, Arthur?"

Charles pulled his hair behind his ears. "How'd you get the girls to…" He looked around to make sure nobody was eavesdropping. "How'd you get them to have sex with you?"

"Who?" Q's said.

"The girls," Charles responded.

"You want to know right now? Like I'm going to teach you about the birds and the bees on the way to nutrition?"

"Tell me about one," Charles said. His tongue hung out, his fingers extended. "What do you do?"

"All right," Quincy said to Charles. "I'm going to help your desperate ass out. I'm going to tell you what grown men know."

The desperate search for knowledge all over Charles' face is what you teachers wish from your students.

"It'll be quick," Q's said. "You know, without the proper oversight this information could be dangerous. Ready? This is what you got to do. First off, lie to yourself. Convince yourself you care for her. Girls, they all want to be special. When they hear you say they're special, authentically, they think it's the only chance they're going to have at love. They most likely won't pass it up. Real women won't necessarily give a shit. These little girls, man, they don't know. To make it good, you might have to lie to yourself to make you believe it. Say something simple and use their name the right way. Address them how they want to be addressed. Y'all know Gloria?"

"You gave her the friction?" Charles asked.

"I lit her vagina on fire, and then split. She hates me."

Charles said, "I thought they liked the friction."

"Man, they think about you differently after that. It's a respect level. I didn't do all that. She's pissed."

"Jesus," Charles said. "Gloria?"

Q's said, "You can't tell anybody. *Anybody*."

We nodded.

"I knew she already had experience," Q's said, "so she wanted somebody with experience."

"Wow," Charles said. "How'd you know?"

"'Cause I looked at her like, let's me and you do this. She looked at me like, why haven't we yet? So, I walked over and tested it. I told her some stupid shit. Told her how fine she is, that she's the prettiest person I've seen. Like, 'You going to be in this spot tomorrow?'"

"That did it?" Charles said.

Quincy put his hand on Charles' shoulder. "I, my friend, was authentic. She looked good. She's fine, right? Have you guys met anybody like her? See, I was honest. About a week later I went to her place after school. Her parents weren't home. I gave it to her on her living room floor. Not her first time."

"How do you know?" Charles asked.

"It *wasn't*," Q's said.

"Whaaaat?" Charles exclaimed.

"Don't tell anyone this," Q's said. "Don't tell *anybody*. I never said shit to her after that. It's why she's so mad at my ass."

"She didn't tell anybody that you ditched her?" Charles asked.

"Nah, man. Well, she might have. She's a respectable person. It happens that she took a risk with me. And lost. Don't go mouthing her business. I'm only telling you guys, because, this is man stuff, right? We all need to know. Don't disrespect her. Keep your mouth shut."

***

Charles and Justin could always tell when I had been thinking about Sandra because when I did, I'd get so distracted I'd stutter. I'd be thinking about the friction far too much, to be honest. Added to that fact, she became too pretty to approach. Everybody wanted to talk to her, so approaching her became a political endeavor. She had wide hips for someone her age, and older guys were always around.

Even before we hung out, I felt better when she was around. I had become infatuated with her. When I hadn't been around her for a while, I felt inadequate, awkward, and powerless. That's what love feels like in junior high. Inadequate, awkward, and powerless.

One day in P.E. we had to run or walk the mile. Our choice.

"Why do you get so nervous around her?" Justin said, walking next to me on the grass field. "You've known her for years."

"Because he wants to give her the friction," Charles said next to us. "We know this."

We were in our burgundy shorts and white t-shirts for P.E., kicking up grass as we plodded our way along the course.

"You're planning on giving her the friction?" Justin said. "I mean, you're going to try and give it to her?"

"Hell, yeah, I want to give her the friction. Why don't you want to? She's hot, right?"

"True," Justin replied. "I've got to say, it's not going to happen. She's got a nation of friends around her. Look."

Sandra walked the field with a set of girlfriends. She never seemed to be around fewer than four of them.

"You have to make them want you." Charles cupped his chin like a sleuth. "You have to make her want you. What you got to do is demonstrate friction. My mom complains my dad won't give her enough of it. I hear them argue about it. It's important. Friction, penetration. It's the only thing that matters."

"Other things matter," I said.

"Like what?" Charles said, looking at me like, what the hell?

I laid it out for them. "My parents didn't break up because of sex."

"No offense but you're adopted," Charles said. "Why did they adopt you if they were having enough sex? Think about it."

"He's got a point," Justin said. "Slow down, slow down. Let them catch up."

There were one of two reasons for us to wait for Sandra and her crew to catch up: Justin and Charles wanted to find a way to embarrass me in front of Sandra, or they wanted to attempt to flirt with her or members of her group. Either way, I didn't want to be around for it.

"Let's just ask her if she wants the friction." Justin stopped walking, had his hands on his hips.

"What the hell? Hell no." Although I wanted to keep going, I found myself waiting. "Nobody is asking her if she wants the friction. *Nobody.*"

Charles said, "Not a good idea. If you ask out of the blue, it will never happen."

Justin retorted, "I'm not saying it's a good idea. I'm saying it'll be funny."

"That's true," Charles added.

Charles waved to her group. Then something happened as they approached that I didn't see coming, although I should have. Charles and his long hair, confidence and smile got Sandra and her group to stop, by holding his hand out like a crossing guard.

He playfully said, "Stop."

It was the moment I realized Charles had something going for him as far as girls went. They giggled at him. One of them kept walking right on past.

Charles said to them, "I have a friction making penis, yes, I do. I make friction like hard rocks make sparks." He had one hand over his heart and the other in the air as if reciting Shakespeare. He even had the cheesy cadence. "I will create a fire in you so deep, so deep you will piss hot water. Excuse my rudeness. You will urinate soothing warm water."

"I like your hair," one of them said.

"You can touch my hair, my less than frictionful friend."

She reached out and touched his hair, giggling.

Then I asked Sandra, "Do you want…the friction?"

Her shoulders sunk as she sighed. She jogged off, I thought, pretty damned mad.

The girl petting Charles' hair said, "What are you talking about, the friction?"

"I'll be happy to show you," Charles said to her, as she giddily jogged away from him. "Seriously, I'll show you!"

As bad as that moment went with Sandra, it led to a much better moment.

A few months after that we were at P.E. again, instructed to play soccer. It's the first time in school when she didn't ignore me. Keep in mind, deep down I thought she would probably always ignore me because her dad and my mom became decent friends before Mom left us. I've wondered if they hooked up. Sandra said they hadn't. I have my doubts. Anyway, the thing is, nobody wanted to compete in soccer with those who could actually play. Again, why be embarrassed? Instead, Charles flirted with girls behind the backstop. Justin observed Charles' lessons on flirting. I wasn't too far from them, on the fence, watching Sandra hang with her shallow friends.

Then it happened. Sandra started over to me all by herself.

"What's wrong with you?" she said, upon arrival.

"I don't know what you mean."

"If you're going to stare at me, you might as well come on over. Everybody else does. Something wrong with you?"

"I have no idea."

"Wait," she said. "You're not going to pretend you don't know me..."

"I wouldn't do that."

"Okay, then. Is it because I'm around them?"

"I don't know."

"A bunch of people you don't know? Is that it?"

"I hadn't thought of it like that." She had given me an out. "Kind of weird to just walk up to people and say, what, exactly? You know? That might be it. Yeah, that's it."

"I'm going to go back over there."

"Alright," I said.

"You know, I remember that day in the park, way back when we were small."

"Really?"

"My dad and I still talk about it, sometimes."

"Really? That was a long time ago. Which time?"

"You don't remember?"

I wasn't sure what she was talking about. I didn't realize she saw my sand deer.

"You never say hi." She grimaced as if reacting to being kicked in the stomach.

"Are you okay?" I said.

"I'm going back."

I thought of something to say off the top of my head. "Did you mind I asked you about the friction? I didn't know what to say, so I was just talking, I guess."

"I don't mind. I have no idea what that means. What does it mean? I'll tell you if I mind."

"If you don't know what the friction is, then I probably shouldn't tell you."

"What's the friction?" she asked.

"What's the friction?"

"Yeah, what is it?"

"Fine. Okay, here goes." I took a deep breath. "The friction is when a proper, hard penis goes up in you and grinds up in there."

To my surprise she didn't spit on me.

"So, you asked me if I wanted the friction?"

"Shit. I guess I did. Yeah."

"I'd be getting it from you?"

"I mean, I asked it as a general statement. Kind of like do you want to eat apple pie? Do you want the friction? This isn't the conversation I thought I'd be having."

"Me neither. Do *you* want the friction?"

When she said it, blood rushed to my dick.

"I don't want cock," is what came out of my mouth.

"This *is* awkward. Maybe don't ask penis questions."

What I took from the exchange was this: she didn't say no to getting the friction from me. In some ways, she said, yes.

***

Trinna, I'm going to tell you, there is a moment in my last year at Centennial Junior High School when I knew I could make Sandra my girlfriend. She had stopped by my house. She never stopped by my house. Stopping by meant she had been thinking of me.

Before I realized she had stopped by, I was hanging in my room, not doing a whole lot, watching the boob-tube.

All through junior high I kept my bedroom mostly the same as in elementary school, except for a few tweaks. I didn't have a use for any of the stuffed animals. I covered the main wall with pictures of skateboarders. Same room, however, filled with ghosts of Mom and old times.

Even with the good times, mine and Bixby's relationship deteriorated. We wound up being too different. Bixby didn't look like me, didn't care to know where I came from. Despite all that, he expected me to go forward, somehow. I wanted to love him, and I did, but, man, I *didn't*. He was a good guy, just not my real father, whatever that means.

So, I'm watching the idiot-box and Bixby came in without knocking or asking to come in. He stood in the doorway before finally asking me how things were with me at school. Keep in mind he already knew how well I did in school. He knew I had good friends, a decent social life. If there were issues, he'd know about them. He was talking himself into what he really wanted to say. It's a bad habit he picked up along the way.

"Arthur," he said, leaning on the door jam.

"Uh huh."

"Could you turn it off for a minute?"

I turned off the television. I came back over and sat on the bed and faced him. "What's up?"

"I have a question I don't think you want to answer but I'm going to ask it anyway."

"What's up?"

"I take this seriously."

"Okay."

"Have you had sex?"

"*Hell* no."

"Perfect. Perfect." He dropped his shoulders, in relief.

"Do I look like I'm having sex?"

"You look exactly like someone who is having sex."

"No sex, swear to God."

"Sandra came by today."

"Dad. *Dad*, what did she say?" It was like I won the lottery, but he wouldn't let me see the winning ticket.

"We'll get to that."

"Get to what? What did she say?"

"She's not allowed in this house for any reason."

"What do you mean?"

"I don't want you to see her. I can't stop you from being her friend, but it'd be nice if she wasn't in our lives in that way."

"In what way?"

"If it's going to be her, I don't want her in my house. I don't want you going over to her house, and I had better not hear about you going places with her. Pay attention to what I'm saying because I'm serious about it."

"That's the stupidest, dumbest thing—"

"—How old are you now? Fourteen? Do I need to draw this out for you?"

"Draw what out?"

He paced across the room. "Your mom left us because of Sandra's dad, to be straight-forward. You know what I'm talking about. Why would I want his daughter over here? What's that say?"

"You should have given her the friction. You were probably giving it to Ms. Kimbrel."

"Your mom got you stuck on that crazy idea. The point is, Sandra being over is like him being over."

I didn't know what to do with that.

"Most likely there's a better way to talk about it," he said. "I don't know anything about that way. Listen, you're Black. I'll start right there. Your mother and I aren't, if you hadn't noticed. At some point, she decided she couldn't love someone with your skin tone. No, she never said it; it's how she acted."

He suddenly seemed like a sad, bitter person who found a way to finally lash out. The reasonable Bixby had bounced out of there.

"Come to find out," he said, not making eye contact, "to this day, you think I cheated on her. Why would I cheat on her and then have *her* leave? Wouldn't it be the other way around?"

I sort of believed him. Not totally. She had become too scared of me, too angry with me to have not cared. Still, wherever she is, I don't want to find her. Any mother who leaves her kids, I don't give a shit where they are. That's what I tell myself when the subject comes up. The truth is, my ability is at least partly why she left. I still don't give a shit where she is.

"I'm sorry," I said. "I swear I'm sorry."

"You understand I can't have that girl in my house."

"We're in love."

"No, you're not."

"Why not?" I thought being in love would be a valid argument to sway his position. I thought it universally known that being in love meant I had no choice in my actions. Because I didn't have control of my actions, he'd have to make concessions. I laugh at the idea now.

He said, "At your age, I'm sure you feel something. Love isn't it."

He couldn't have been correct, I thought. We had to have been in love. Why else did she stop by my house?

***

Trinna Kimbrel cranes her neck in Arthur's direction. "You're passive-aggressively saying I was part of the reason your parents broke up."

"They broke up because of me. My mom couldn't communicate with him because of me. I was the distance between them. You fit yourself between that distance."

She scrunches her lips. "I partly want to apologize."

"Do you?"

"Nothing real happened between your dad and I."

"Don't worry about it. I have more of an issue knowing I grew up as a statistic. Little Black kid with no home, out of his element, father dumped him. Adoptive mom left him. What I did to survive is bury myself in deep with Sandra. She is where I belonged."

"There's a type of wonderful there, I'm sure."

"The thought of her kept me going. My freshman year of high school, I did manage to get *off* track."

Quincy

For a stretch in high school, I kept getting detentions for being late to school. While there, we weren't supposed do anything but be punished by being bored. I didn't want detention, but to be honest, being there or in first period didn't matter. The real difference was that in detention you didn't need to listen to the teacher lecture. I'd rather take my lumps in the cafeteria, half bored to death.

They wanted you bored. They didn't even let you do homework.

It's in that detention that I reunited with Quincy, one of the few Black friends I had. Hadn't seen him all summer.

We all have someone who impacted us more than we realized. It could be a teacher, an ex-girlfriend or boyfriend, a doctor, a relative. For me it was Quincy.

That day in the cafeteria he says, what's up? Then he tells me this: "Man, you ever wonder why they don't just make school open later? I'm not saying don't show up on time, but fuck this for real."

"I deeply friggin agree."

"My dad would tell me they should tell you what you're going to learn ahead of time. If you can learn it on your own, then you don't need the class. School is stupid. It won't teach you what you already learn on your own. Just have a bit of that discipline. A little muffuckin discipline. Teachers aren't the only muffuckas who know shit."

Some adult running detention spoke up saying, "Quincy, Arthur. Not talking right now. Mouths are closed."

After that day, I kept running into him at school. His reputation had followed us into high school. Guys would bring up his name because Quincy said something in class that got them going, or he said something to some girl that caused a stir. The girls loved to hate him. Regardless, they paid him so much attention, he didn't have to pay them any.

The three of us—me, Charles, and Justin—lucked out. Quincy liked kicking back with us for a few minutes each day. He'd run track with us or shoot hoop at lunch. Both Charles and Justin mentioned him hanging out was because me and Q's were Black and had to stick together.

On a day when we were running the mile for P.E., Q's came on over and ran with us.

Q's said, "What up?"

We didn't say much. Small talk. What's up? Then he jogged next to me and said, loud enough for Charles and Justin to hear, "We have to stick together."

"*I...told...you,*" Justin said.

"Told him what, muffucka?" Quincy said.

"You like him more than us," Charles said. "Since, you know, he's like you."

"What the hell do you mean like me?"

Although Q's words made him seem intimidating, he didn't look as intimidating as his talk. By high school, we took on similar features. He was skinny like me and kept his hair short, unlike me. We were about the same height and had similar noses. People said we looked the same in the face, had similar gestures. Charles would always correct them by saying all Black guys don't look alike. However, in this case, we kind of did.

"Why do you guys act like you don't know?" Quincy said. "He *is* more like me. Adopted. Me and him are adopted. You two have mommy and daddy at home. We don't have shit. I'm right, huh?" he said to me with a nod.

I had Bixby but I knew what Quincy was saying.

"We have to stick together," he said. "Stick muffuckin close. Hey," he said to me, not them, "when everything goes to crap for you, these dudes won't have nothin to do with you. They don't know about the wind inside a person. You know what I'm talking about?"

My heart stopped beating for a second. Did he know about me? I should have seen it coming, right there.

"Did you say we don't know about the wind in a person?" Charles said. "That much is true."

"That's what I'm trying to say," Quincy said. "My man knows what I'm sayin."

I knew what he could have been saying. Didn't know the purpose for why he would be saying it.

***

Trinna, you wouldn't be surprised to hear Bixby realized my mom had left for good long before I did.

Bixby adjusted to day-to-day life by subtly developing a normal routine that went like this: in the morning, wake me up, we'd get ready together. He'd leave for work long before I left for school. His hours were from about seven in the morning till about nine at night. He never helped me with homework, not that I needed it. Money became a little bit tighter for a while after she left. We didn't eat out as much. He bought stuff I could cook—beans, rice, cheese, pasta, and microwave stuff. Domestic things we got down, or we did the best with the parameters our egos allowed. We didn't have the family part down.

A broken home wasn't new to me. It was to him. It just so happened I wasn't qualified to teach him about it. Through his entire sheltered life, he hadn't figured out how to learn from someone younger than him. Up to Mom leaving, Bixby had a normal life. He did well in school, loved his deceased family—his dead dad, dead mom. He was an only child. The dude married while in college to his high school sweetheart. Come to find out she didn't want kids. They adopted me, and then she walked out on him.

I know now that the time he spent at work supporting me kept him from knowing me as an adolescent. He knew me as a child, not as a teenager. Even knowing what I know now, I still see him through those young teenager eyes, the ones that saw him as out of touch and out of place. He knew we didn't see eye to eye, which meant he lacked the skills to bring us together, which made him that much more pathetic.

It was no wonder I did the opposite of what he wanted and dug in deep with Sandra. I thought about Sandra, called Sandra, hung out with Sandra, and thought about how to make her my girlfriend. When someone asked her if I was her boyfriend, knowing they'd be confused about us, she'd say, yes, but she meant boy-as-friend, not boyfriend as in we were kissing and fondling each other.

Our newly discovered relationship took nearly all summer to develop. On a huge, unsubstantiated level, I needed Bixby, especially in my relationship with her. I needed someone to help me figure it all out. I horribly, terribly needed my dad.

Instead, I got Quincy.

This is in the summer after our freshman year of high school. Late one night me and good ol' Q's were skateboarding near a curb in a shopping center. Quincy skated faster than I did. The parking lot had our beads of sweat all over it. The big thing we were trying to do was a handstand on the skateboard while moving. He did it better than me. While he practiced, I watched him, thought about how to do it better. I couldn't quite pull the trigger in trying my best. Part of my mind had been hung up on Sandra, as always.

"Why don't you have a girlfriend?" I asked him.

He jumped off his board and kicked it into his hand. "Five are enough."

"No, a *girlfriend*, girlfriend."

"You mean *one* girl?"

"I mean someone like Sandra."

He jumped on his board and cruised in a circle, glided back over near me, and kicked the board into his hand again. "I like someone way more than you like Sandra."

"Who?"

"I can't tell you. Maybe in a few years I can tell you."

"I might not even know you in a few years."

"Whenever you don't know me, I'll come back into your life. We're cool like that, without question. More than brothers."

I thought about that.

He disappeared one day. Just gone.

"Okay," I said. "You like her and you're messing with five other girls?"

"You're saying you seriously like Sandra, like you're in love with her?"

"You're going to make fun of me?"

"Why the hell would I do that? I'm in love with the person I'm in love with."

"Does she know you're in love with her?" I said.

"I can't know for too damned sure. I pretty much told her without saying the three words."

"You can't lie to her? I mean lie to yourself, so you can convince her like you told us."

He drew his head back. "You have the wrong idea. I don't want to just make her feel the friction. I do, but that's not what's going on. I hope that's not all you want from Sandra. If all you want to do is rub your dick all on her and in her then I can't say that's love. You're not in love then."

"I didn't say that's all I wanted. I want to be with her."

Q's turned his skateboard upside down and kicked it away from us. I dropped my board. We both had a seat on the walkway to the closed supermarket. It must have been after midnight.

He said, "She loves you, man, is what I see. She's waiting for you to make a move. You have to jump in. Need to take a leap, eyes closed and flailing."

"What?"

"Let me bring it down a bit so you can understand."

"Bring what down?"

"Listen. You're a kid. You have to do something to open her eyes to you. You want her to focus on you. Not so that she sees you, 'cause she does that already. It's like if you're watching a movie, it has to have a good scene for you to tell your friends about. You have to have something like that about yourself. You have to do something that makes her think you're better than the guy who looks better than you. You have no idea what I'm talking about. It's why rock stars get all the pussy. They play a guitar. Or the quarterback on the team in high school. You have no idea what I'm sayin'. Everybody has something that makes them a quarterback or a rock star. What is it for you?"

"I get it. What is it for *you*?"

"For me? It's personal."

"Huh, what is it?" I persisted.

"Fuck it. I have a big-assed dick. *What*. Now what's yours?"

"I got something, for sure."

"I know you do. Most dudes do, is what I'm getting at, and being honest, you can tell she's into you, just needs a reason to let herself go."

"She's into me?"

I felt this and knew this already. I could feel energy moving through me when me and Sandra were near each other. I could feel a different energy when we were apart. Either way, I couldn't imagine her not feeling it. So, like he said, according to him, she had been waiting for me.

"My goal is to convince her she's in love with me," I laughed.

He didn't find it funny. "You think she's stupid? Don't treat someone who is important to you like they're stupid. Don't treat someone who loves you as if they don't."

"Sorry. I didn't know you took love this seriously. You have five girls, right?"

"Could have more."

"You love all those girls?"

"Man, no."

"Then why have them?"

"Because I don't want no VD. I want a woman who is loyal."

"But—"

"—They don't all know about each other," he chuckled, "unless they do. Damn, unless they do. If they do know, I'll have to break up with whoever knows. If they don't respect themselves enough to break up with someone who is cheating on them, then I don't want them around. Know what I'm sayin? They need standards. Sandra has standards."

"I hope so."

"Love does not compromise," he said. "Relationships do. Love doesn't. I'm in relationships, so whatever about that. You're doing something else."

"Why don't you get with the person you're in love with?"

"She's not available. Yet. Hell, man, I barely know her."

"How are you going to claim you're in love with someone you barely know?"

"I know me and trust myself. That's what you need to be in love. Know more than a little something about yourself. Love yourself. That I do, son. That I do."

***

Ms. Kimbrel said, "Quincy really holds a place in your heart as one of the few people who nudged you in the right direction with your future wife."

"It's the whole thing. When your family isn't there for you, your peers are. One of them is, at least. Friends and family, in the same breath."

"I have none of that. No family. No friends."

"You were really hoping I could do that thing. Make you young again."

"Not so much. When I transferred, I thought, wow, this could happen. A second chance. People say everyone needs a second chance. Nobody actually gets one," she says with a sarcastic chuckle. "You agree, relationships compromise and love doesn't."

"I can still hear him say it in the back of my mind."

"You ever use that advice? It makes me think of my current marriage. The relationship works." She mumbles, "I don't know if the love does."

The idea of such a relationship as hers, one where she might not be in love, causes his stomach muscles to contract. He stares at her, wondering if he loved Sandra but had compromised their relationship. Maybe relationships were only compromises to keep love upright.

My Rock Star Quality

When Quincy told me that stuff about love, I think he was specifically talking about something he had been going through. Let me ask you this, Trinna: At the time, why would I take anybody except Quincy's advice on the subject of the heart?

We were kids with silly ideas. I figured Quincy's ideas on love and relationships made more sense than, let's say, Charles's. Unlike Charles, I thought a guy could have a perfectly fine, passionate relationship without igniting someone's vagina. Then there was Bixby, who advised me to stay the hell away from Sandra. That couldn't have been the right thing to do, no matter his reasoning. What did my own gut say? Really, nothing. I froze at the thought of her.

I went with Quincy's advice of becoming a rock star in her eyes. If I showed her how amazing I was, I'd stand out.

No matter how unique, if you do normal things long enough, you become normal. If you do what most people do on the regular, then it's normal. Go to school, get good grades, make friends with people who probably don't care for you, get a job millions of others have, pretend bad jokes are funny. If you do what I can do, there is probably no place in any of this for you.

My mom left because she found out I wasn't normal. She left because of my rock star ability.

The truth is, you aren't always what you do or don't do. Most of the time you're what people see you as. I'm normal, as long as nobody knows me.

Despite being afraid to scare her off, I called her up.

She answered as if it was a business call. "Hello. Dunbar residence."

"It's me."

"I know."

"Just saying what's up. Maybe you want to meet up tomorrow night."

"Tomorrow night?" Shocked like she didn't know I wanted to hang out. "Why night?"

Because in the afternoon there would be too many people. "I've got something to show and tell you."

"Don't know. I might be busy."

"Make it so you're not busy."

"I don't know if I can," she said.

"What are you doing to make you busy?"

"Family stuff. I can get out of it. Where do you want to meet?"

"My place."

"Your dad doesn't like me."

"Your place," I said.

"I don't think that's a great idea either. The family stuff."

"What's wrong?"

"Nothing."

"If nothing's wrong, then what's wrong?"

She said, "You sound funny."

"What do you mean?"

"I don't know. You sound different."

"I had coffee at dinner." I was nervous to ask her out.

"I don't like the suspense. Why don't we meet tonight?"

"Oh shit. Tonight? Can you do that?"

"What time? When?"

"How 'bout at the park after it's dark."

"That sounds...smart?" she said.

"We'll be fine. Won't be there for too long."

"What time? I'd rather have a time."

"Let's meet down the street from your house in two hours."

"It's a date," she said.

I had the date.

***

We met on the corner close to her house. We lived a few miles from the park. It'd be a good walk.

How she dressed, it could have been an actual date. I had shown up in shorts and tennis shoes. She had her hair brushed all to one side, and wore a formfitting but loose, sky-blue dress. I can see it like it all happened moments ago.

Quincy had advised me to be honest. So I was. She was pretty as hell. I told her exactly that.

She walked with her hands behind her back, hid them from me.

"What'd you want to tell me?" she said, averting her eyes.

"It's more show you."

She looked me up and down and around my back, as if I kept a secret behind me. "What'd you want to show me?"

"You'll see."

"It's not your penis, is it?"

"Huh."

"Just checking. They say guys won't stick around unless you give them that one thing."

"What thing?"

"You know what I'm talking about. Don't make me say it."

I knew what she meant. "That's not what I want to show you."

"Uh huh. You didn't want to give me…the friction?" She used air quotes when she said it.

It took me a second, but I caught on she had been kidding with me. "I'm cool frictionless."

"You can be the frictionless boy I know."

We were less than a block from the park.

I took my hands out of my pockets, got close to her, and gently grabbed her hand. I had never romantically held a girl's hand. In my mind, we would soon kiss, deeply gaze at each other, kiss some more, and then somehow end up in Bixby's bed having sex.

At the park, I ran ahead to the swings where she had sat years ago when I made the sand deer.

She said, "As much as I love the swings…"

Streetlamps dimly lit the park from the walkway that divided it. Parts of the park was mostly in shadow. Although our neighborhood hadn't been known for its crime, it had its share of homeless, its share of gang members. It couldn't have been the safest place at that time of night.

"You said it wouldn't take long." Sandra looked paranoid as hell, searching in the darkness for muggers.

To calm her, I grabbed her hands, told her nobody would do anything to us if I stood with her, because of my guyness.

"Let's not be too long, anyway," she said.

Clouds hovered over us like soft, invading spaceships. A breeze kicked in, blowing her hair, exposing her neck.

"Do you remember the day we first met?" I said.

She closed her eyes. "Do I remember? Hmmm. Maybe. Your mom was panicked about something. I think I saw what you did. I think. Did you… I don't know how to say it."

She had known all along.

I thought back to all the times I was too scared to talk to her, all the wasted time. I thought of what a relief that she had always accepted me. She was home, as I always felt she had been. A certain gravity instantly removed itself from my body.

"I thought you'd be afraid," I said.

"I am afraid. Not in a bad way."

72

"Are you for sure?"

"I get scared before talking to important people. It's the best part about meeting them. I was scared to come out here with you. That's the best part."

"You're important to me too."

Then we held hands.

"A lot happened that day, you know." I told her, "My dad heard about your dad being with us at the park. Made him all kinds of jealous. It's basically why they broke up."

"Why who broke up."

"My mom and dad. Dana and Bixby."

She gazed at me. "My dad is not why your parents broke up."

"After we left the park that day, my mom told Dad about what had happened with my sand deer—"

"—That's what it was? A deer?"

"Was supposed to be. What she told him about me at the park was so crazy that he focused on the only thing that made sense about her story—the fact that another man was at the park with us. Your dad. Something that small, in the long run, broke them up. Not anything to do with your dad, really. He seems really cool."

"I'm sorry."

"What freaked my mom out was I took sand," I leaned over and lifted some sand into my hand, "and molded it into something." I stood, held the sand in my palm. A bunch of it blew away in the breeze. "What I molded shocked her so much that she jumped to her feet in a panic."

I tossed the rest of the sand into the air. We watched it slowly descend on the ground in flakes of sparkling dust. Gradually, the sand remaining in the air morphed into silhouettes of me and her as small kids. The sand versions of us became dense, dirt individuals. In the details, even in the little light we had, a person could tell, it was us sitting next to one another, in sand form. Those were my sand cheeks, and that was her sand dress. From about ten feet away, we listened to the sand versions of ourselves whisper something we couldn't clearly hear.

Looking at them couldn't have been more amazing. I had no clue what Sandra's expression meant: her mouth open, eyebrows raised, fingers outstretched. She stood with her hands to her sides, her lips pursed, while she squinted at the sand versions of us.

"Is it magic?" she said.

It was the first time someone referred to my ability as a good thing.

It was magic.

"You look freaked out."

73

"I'm freaked the fuck out. Not a bad thing." She mumbled something to herself, took a step away from me. She reached out and grabbed my hand, again. She offered them, because of my rock star.

"I can feel something here," she said, in a joyous tone. "Can you feel it? Can they see us?" She whispered, "Can they hear us?"

"Arthur!" I yelled to my sand version.

"Huh," my sand version replied.

I didn't know what to say after that.

"Sandra!" the real Sandra called out.

"Yes?" her sand version replied.

"Is it really me?" Sandra asked.

I answered the best I could. "I. Don't. Know."

I let the sand versions of us dissipate into the rest of the park sand.

"Where'd they go, where'd they go?" Sandra's eyes searched, her mouth agape.

"They're around."

One thing I learned is, the more I matured, the more I could control my ability. If I wanted my old bear back, I could have it back. I don't want it back. If I recalled the sand versions of us, would I be recalling the actual me and her from the past?

She said, "Me and my dad talked about what you did at the park, off and on, for years. Whenever I brought it up, he assured me it happened. He said people can do things sometimes, especially when they're kids. You must have a good, nice, pure, child heart, in there." She swung our hands.

"Yeah, I'm just a big kid."

"He reminded me in kindergarten and in first grade, and in second grade. Magic happens with a big heart."

"If you mention it to anybody, no one will believe you."

She stopped swinging our hands. "I won't tell anybody."

"I'll walk you home."

"Are you okay? Does doing it do something to you? Are you okay? You feel alright? Are you mad?"

"I don't know what I am."

***

It's odd to call you Trinna instead of Ms. Kimbrel. It's kind of like we're old friends who haven't talked for years. It's kind of how me and Sandra turned out towards the end. We didn't talk after a while. I wonder why me and Sandra didn't talk more through the years. We worked together with basically no conflict. Most people would look back on how well we got along and appreciated it. Our circumstances are different. Getting along and not arguing didn't stop me from being depressed, didn't stop her from killing herself.

On any level, opening up to her gave me half a mind to open up to Bixby as well. Him knowing could have helped him understand what Mom had truly been through. Sandra and her dad knew, come to find out. They knew, and it didn't matter. For me and him to get along, he'd have to know all of me; he'd have to see my rock star.

It's my opinion that Bixby couldn't show Dana his true self. He and Dana had issues long before the day I made the sand deer in the park. Some relationships are kind of like the government. You can sustain it, but how well does it actually work? Does it make all parties involved better? Is it flexible enough to change if it needs to; can it grow into something better than what it is?

Realizing my mom and dad were going to break up anyway, and not because of me, I didn't see the need to help Bixby out. See, half my mind said to work with Bixby. The other half wanted to tell him to suck a dick. On one hand, Bixby had been one of the nicest people I knew, someone who had always supported me. On the other hand, I didn't feel a bond with him at all. History but no bond.

The same night I showed Sandra my rock star, the phone rang in the other room. My digital alarm clock read 11:15 p.m., way too late to get a phone call, but I was hoping Sandra would call.

I hurried over and flicked off the ceiling light. After kicking off my shoes, I jumped into bed, now prepared for Bixby to enter.

He knocked and then entered my room without permission. When he flicked on the light, he saw me under the blankets waking up from barely getting to sleep.

"You want to talk to her?" he said with his palm over the phone's microphone.

"Who is it?"

"Arthur, do you want to talk to her or not?"

I sat up and reached for the phone.

He took a few steps in my direction, handed me the cordless. "Not all night."

He lurked around for a moment.

After he left, I said, hello, into the receiver.

"Arthur," Sandra replied.

"Uh huh."

"I can't sleep."

"Me neither."

"I meant to tell you earlier," she said, "my mom and dad aren't together either. They still love each other."

"That's good."

"It could be the same for you guys."

"I don't know. I don't know how necessary it is."

"You know, your mom used to come over talking about you."

"Not in a good way."

The dead space on her end said I was right.

She said, "She tried to convince us of what we already suspected. Dad said he didn't think it was good to get into it with her."

"Too weird?"

"*Really* too weird. I don't know how to say this without hurting your feelings. She kind of thought you were evil."

"She used the word evil?"

"She loved you but didn't trust you."

"She wanted to love me but couldn't."

I think the same about myself most of the time. I certainly don't blame Dana.

Sandra said, "Originally, she thought you would bring them closer."

"I'm this thing."

"You're not a thing."

"I should find my real parents. My real dad, not this stand-in. My actual dad would know something about me."

"I have my real dad. He doesn't know jack about me."

"Is it parents that don't know shit or adults?"

"It's that they get old and get to paying bills and being all responsible. They forget about normal stuff. You're amazing. I swear I won't tell anybody."

"You won't?" I said. "I, for one, wish I could tell everybody. Not a good idea."

"You could make a lot of money. Magician. You could be a magician."

"I don't want people staring at me and applauding. Why would someone want to be an act?"

Bixby reentered the room, unannounced. "Not all night."

"I'm getting off right now."

"Arthur. I *am* your real dad."

He slinked off into the other room.

"I have to go," I said.

"Me too, Arthur. I think I'll sleep better now, Arthur. Good night,

Arthur."

"Okay, *Sandra*. Good night, *Sandra*. *Sandra*."

"I like hearing my mouth say your name," she said.

Another awkward silence on her end.

***

"You showed her your rock star?" Ms. Kimbrel says, placing her fingers to her mouth in awe.

"I trusted her." Arthur stands, lifts his chair, and walks back to the kidney table. He pushes the chair underneath.

"I had it wrong," Ms. Kimbrel says.

"What wrong?"

"Your ability isn't making things young. You animate things. You animate people."

"Animating people and things are two different abilities."

"Is that the word you use? Or do you call it a power?"

"*Are* they different?"

What she said flicks on a light bulb, a small epiphany—the wind has never left him. Bringing Raheem and Sandra back to life is no different than animating the deer or his old bear or the sand versions of himself and Sandra in the park.

"What does it look like for you to animate a person?" she says. "What's that like?"

The question makes him turn his head to the side in thought. "It might look like raising the dead."

She mouths the word "Wow," leans back and folds her arms.

"It's getting late. I've got a bunch to do, if I don't cut corners, which I will."

"Every day I wonder about that rose your dad gave me. I could be that flower. Beautiful yet dying one minute. Colorful and new the next. And you're right here in front of me. Can't get past that."

"I can't say it enough. I can't make you young again."

She places her elbows on the desk and her chin in her palms. "You don't talk to many people, now do you?"

"Not about animating."

"Keeping a secret that long probably takes a toll on a person. A secret that big." She bites her lower lip.

"I'm not high on myself right now. I should be going. I've got to get gone. I'll come back tomorrow."

"I wish you would."

By the look in her eyes, she's ready to forfeit her life for a younger one.

The Gatekeeper

Tonight, Glenda can't sleep.

She can't help but to picture Sandra, mostly dead, holed up in Arthur's room.

Cautious not to wake Raheem, Glenda slips out of bed, steps into her slippers, and strolls a few blocks from her home to a twenty-four hour convenience store where she bums a menthol cigarette off a heavy-set woman who has just bought a fresh pack. She pictures herself with a cigarette between her lips, inhaling, being confident and whole. Although she hasn't smoked for fifteen years, the situation calls for a god damned cigarette.

She ventures inside to get matches. The cashier, a heavily tattooed, twenty-something year old boy, says the store doesn't carry matches. Things have changed since her last smoke. The cashier lets her use one of the lighters on sale. She lights the cigarette and drops the lighter on the counter.

"Thank you," she says, and races outside to exhale.

She coughs, chuckles at herself through teary eyes, all by herself near a trashcan brimmed with used napkins, hot dog cradles, drink lids, ash, and other litter from store products. After taking a larger drag, she exhales again through her nose, lets the toxicity of the moment engulf her.

She walks the few blocks back to her house, puffing on the cigarette. She stops in front of Arthur's house and stomps out the cigarette. Arthur's vehicle isn't in the driveway, meaning he's not home from work yet.

His living room blinds are open. Thinking nothing of it, she stares through his window. The fact that Sandra is inside, dying, makes her complicit. Her feet can't move under the weight of her guilt.

Someone moves inside the house.

Sandra?

She approaches the front door. It's been pulled ajar, probably to get some air into a house that has been closed all day.

Glenda quietly steps inside. "Sandra?"

Somebody's footsteps tap on the kitchen floor. Bare feet, it seems.

"Sandra?" Glenda follows the sound of the footsteps.

As she arrives in the kitchen, the footsteps elude her, plod through the opposite end of the kitchen, down the hallway. The bedroom door creaks open, softly shuts. Glenda follows the steps to the room, turns the knob, then presses the bedroom door open. She steps into the room, switches on the light. Sandra is barefoot, sitting on the bed in an all cream robe.

"Glenda," Sandra says, exhaling in relief.

Sandra's skin looks smooth, and, albeit tangled, her dark brown hair is full and beautiful.

"I thought you'd be him." Sandra's voice is feeble.

"You...okay? I thought he...did something to you."

Sandra clenches her hands into fists. "Don't know if I am."

"Can I get you anything? Is the light too bright for you? You had them off."

Sandra rises to her feet. "You have to drive me away from here."

"Hold on. Where are you trying to go?"

Sandra aggressively rubs her arms. "I can feel him all over me."

"Shit," Glenda says, thinking she should have already called the authorities to report Arthur. "I've seen the blood. We can put his ass away."

Sandra purses her lips. "We can't do that."

"Why in the world not? Honey, he's saying he's healing you. It's— it's insane. Turning him in makes more sense than running."

Sandra brings both of her hands to her face, begins to weep into them. "Oh...my... He," Sandra says through tears. "He swallows you. Whole."

"We should get you out of here."

What Sandra said reaffirms she needs doctors and nurses, and medicine. "Grab some things and let's go. Can you do that?"

Sandra gasps, her face solid, expressionless.

"You grab your things. I'm going to go get my car keys. I'll meet you out front." Glenda pictures pulling into a hospital, sitting in a lobby, gripping her friend's hand. Maybe Sandra will go away for a while. It'll mean Arthur will be out of her life. It'll mean she'll somehow get better.

Glenda leaves the bedroom and heads for the living room. Entering the living room Arthur stops her. He takes a few steps to the side, and shows he is more than happy to let her leave.

"Did she let you in?" he says.

"It was open."

He dips his eyes.

Glenda says, "She's confused. I-I-I don't think she wants to see you."

Arthur straightens himself, politely waves his hand towards the living room and out of his home. "Get out of my house."

"There's nothing wrong with leaving her alone."

"'Scuse the shit out of me." He starts towards Sandra's room.

"Wait, wait, wait." Glenda grabs his arm.

He rips his arm away from her. "Thank you, Glenda. I'll call if I need you."

Not willing to escalate the situation, she keeps her mouth shut and hurries to her house.

***

At home, Glenda stomps into her room.

Raheem flicks the end table lamp light on. "Where'd you go?"

"For a walk. Ended up next door. Listen—"

"—That's cigarette smoke."

"Sandra's awake."

He purses his lips. "She is?"

"She's different."

"Come here, baby." He pats the sheets next to him. "Come here."

She does as he suggests.

"Does she look alright?" he says. "She's good?"

"She's saying weird stuff I can't wrap my head around."

"She looks, okay? I remember her dome, and the—"

"—All healed, somehow. All freaked out. Arthur didn't seem right either. We can't leave her there with him."

He rubs her back, massages her shoulders.

She pulls herself away from him, bounces off the bed. "You're not understanding. She's not safe."

"It's fine."

"No, it's not and you know it."

Raheem hurries out of bed, steps around the far side of it, and juts his finger at her. "Now, listen. The only person who should be around her is him, straight up."

She sidesteps him, starts for the door. "*Pussy.*"

"On the other side, Arthur does something to you. He did something to me. I'm not a *pussy*; I'm confident in what he can do for her."

"What's this other side talk?"

Raheem closes his eyes. "I'm going to come straight out with it. He ate me."

Hearing him seemingly affirm what Sandra had said sends a jolt into her. "What are you *talking* about?"

Raheem sets his hand over his heart, as if about to recite the flag salute. "We should all want to be swallowed by him."

A woman's scream from next door.

Raheem leads the way, rapidly through their living room, then outside, and finally to the front door of Arthur's house where they pause for a breath before stepping into a smothering silence.

"Where are they?" he whispers.

"Arthur's room."

Another scream, and then the bumps of a domestic dispute.

Raheem rushes towards Arthur's bedroom with Glenda on his heels. He turns the knob, pushes the door open.

"Get her arms," Arthur shouts to Raheem.

Raheem struggles to keep hold on Sandra's wrists.

Arthur yells, "Get her feet. Get her feet. Grab something."

Raheem pounces on her, straddles her legs, presses on her shoulders as Arthur grips a wrist above her head. With her free hand, Sandra repetitively smacks Raheem in his side.

Glenda speaks to Sandra in a soft tone: "Honey, it's best to not fight right now. You need to calm down, honey."

"Get him away from me!" Sandra struggles. "Get him away!"

Raheem levels his gaze on Arthur. "Go. Get out, man. *Get out.*"

Arthur releases her, jumps to his feet, and inches towards the door.

Sandra grinds her teeth. "Get him away from me!"

Glenda shoves Arthur towards the door.

Arthur nearly loses his balance.

Once Arthur is outside the room, Glenda slams the door behind him. She turns and sees Raheem backing away from Sandra.

Sandra spits, and pants, her chest heaves, as she stands.

"I'd bet you'd be doing us a favor if you followed Arthur," Glenda says to Raheem.

"I'm supposed to leave you with her?"

"A big favor. Why don't you go hang out with your boyfriend who swallows?"

"I'm not the issue. I didn't do shit."

Glenda cranes her neck at him. "That *is* the problem. You chose to not do anything. If anything happens, I'll whoop her ass. Get gone."

While focusing on Sandra, Raheem flees the room, closes the door behind him.

***

Glenda meets Arthur and Raheem in the living room. They eye her as if she's withholding a verdict.

"I think she's fine," Glenda says.

Arthur points towards the bedroom. "I can go in?"

"Why can't you wait?" she says.

Raheem's nostrils flare. "Do you guys smell that?"

The same stench that killed Raheem crept into Arthur's house, again. The three of them cover their mouths, their noses. They head from door to door, from window to window, trying to keep foul air out of the house.

Arthur bursts into his room to close the window in there that he knows is open. The stench dries the back of his throat.

He says, "You have to close the window."

She makes her way to the window. "I can feel you all over me."

"You're alive."

She closes the window. "I don't think you know what you did."

Glenda and Raheem enter, holding paper towels over their mouths and noses. Unsure of what conversation to have, Arthur exits, to think of a way to reconnect with his wife the right way.

Raheem closes the door behind Arthur.

Sandra says from the back of her throat, "He doesn't understand that—"

"—You need to be swallowed," Raheem says the remainder of her thought. "The pain he gave saved me. You can feel the pain healing you. Tell me you didn't feel it."

"I killed myself to escape his abuse. Now he can keep abusing me."

Glenda gasps. "You're saying you *did* kill yourself?"

"I was dead," Sandra says. "You don't believe it, I can tell, but *he* does. If you ask your husband, he'd say that while being swallowed, you can feel yourself coming back here. Right, Raheem? Arthur swallows you."

"All of it is part of the pain from the moment," Raheem says, "which, I'm learning, is the only real thing in this world. There's no perspective to pain. Pain just is. It's true. Pain is all we have. That's why he can bring you back by using it. He doesn't bring you back through your contentment, or your happiness. It's your pain that has the energy to make you whole again."

Sandra shakes her head. "Pain is what put me there."

"You reached the truth. Couldn't handle it. That's what got you there. Pain is the truth. How else do you explain what happened? The truth is you learn everything through pain. We find the center of ourselves through overcoming some form of pain. In this case, Arthur's."

"That wasn't my experience." Sandra stares at Raheem. "No, no, no that's not right."

"I think," Raheem says, puffing his chest out, "that's why we have to die to move on. We have to die to be cleansed by pain, on our way to a better place. We get a sense of it here to prepare us. We need to stop closing our eyes to all that wonderful pain."

"Raheem," Glenda says, "that's absolutely stupid. Stop talking. You want to hurt our kids to make them better? You think people are better off, what, raped? Um, shot and stabbed. You think they're better off as addicts? What the hell, 'Heem?"

Sandra frowns. "Where I went, I was repeatedly murdered. Stabbed to death. Again, and again. That's what you find so appealing?"

Sitting cross-legged on the floor Raheem says, "No. Oh, no. He swallowed me, from that darkness. The pain seemed necessary, somehow."

The bedroom door creaks open.

Arthur stands in the doorway, arms hanging at his sides. "I can tell you about dying. I've watched people die—get hit by cars, have heart attacks. I've *helped* them. Never hurt anybody."

"You stabbed me, in a dark, pitiful place, after I shot myself." Sandra stares at him, a challenging gaze.

"I'm sorry, "Arthur says. "I don't know what happened to you. It wasn't me who did it." He moves his arm up and down his body like a wand. "Believe me, it wasn't me."

"It's you. There's no way it's not."

"Baby, I don't know what you're talking about."

"You're inside of me, again, Arthur. You're on me, seeping into me. Get out of me, get off me!"

Arthur leaves the room, shaking his head.

"Are you okay?" Glenda says.

"I think we should go," Raheem adds. "We're not helping."

"At this point, you might as well," Sandra says. "It's probably too late."

Glenda starts in Sandra's direction. Thinks better of it. "We're right next door."

Glenda and Raheem leave Sandra alone. They find their way back to their house. They both check upstairs to make sure the kids aren't awake this early in the morning.

After deciding the kids are safe, Raheem finds his way into his and Glenda's room. While she paces around the living room, he lies in bed, alone and in the dark.

The smell sits around him, sticks to the hair in his nostrils. It won't kill him twice, will it?

In the living room, the back of Glenda's throat begins to close, probably due to the smell, she figures. She starts to choke. She briskly steps into the kitchen, turns on the faucet, and dips her head under it. After a few gulps she wipes her mouth with a paper towel, then uses that same paper towel to cover her mouth and nose.

Still thinking about the events next door, she joins her husband in bed.

"I love you," she says, getting comfortable under the sheets.

"I don't have a life without you."

"He saved her from suicide."

"Postponed it."

"She's not going to make it." Glenda freezes, thinking of the implications of her own statement. She repeats her own unbelievable words to herself. *He saved her from suicide.*

Raheem says, "The only way she doesn't kill herself is if she finds the pain of him bringing her back to life worse than the pain of her staying alive."

"She'd be better off killing him." Glenda senses a type of gravity, after she says it.

"You mean that shit?" he says.

"No matter the situation, it sounds like abuse to me. If he's done something that makes her want to kill herself, it's abuse. If she doesn't feel safe, and is trapped, it's abuse. If he doesn't know about her mental state, it doesn't make it better. I wouldn't harm him, but I wouldn't stop her."

"You'd do nothing."

"You won't even acknowledge he did anything to her, will you?" Raheem rolls his eyes.

"That's what I thought," she says. "You and your pain."

Bringer of Pain

Raheem wakes with his throat so dry he can't stop coughing. The stench in the morning air, a culprit to his condition. He hurries to the kitchen, hopes water will be a remedy.

It is for now.

He makes his way back to the bedroom where he collects himself before Glenda wakes.

Time to get his kids ready for school. He himself has to get ready for work. No. Screw that. Nobody will leave the house today. He had a few snow days as a child living in Washington. Today is a bad air day. No school.

He ventures upstairs and wakes the kids, tells them they aren't going to school. He tells them to go back to sleep. As he shuts the door, he hears Shelly cough.

Raheem whips himself around. "Are you okay?"

"I'm okay," she replies, in her small voice.

"Why don't you guys come on downstairs? Get some breakfast."

They jump out of bed, both Tracy and Shelly wearing cotton pajamas, hers pink and his blue. They hurry downstairs and turn on the television, go directly for their favorite cartoons.

Raheem makes it back to his bedroom to wake Glenda.

She's already awake, throwing on her robe. "No school or work today."

"I got the same thoughts going through my head. Already told the kids no school."

Glenda ties the belt on her robe. "We have no milk or eggs. Are you going to the store, or am I?"

"Let me stay with the kids."

"I'm not getting bacon."

"No swine and eggs?"

"No swine. Eggs and cereal. If I go get it, you're cooking."

"You go get it, I'm watching TV with the kids," he says. "Hurry up. I'm starving, and these kids will start complaining."

"'Heem. 'Heem. Are we okay?"

"I know what I said about pain. I'd never hurt you or the kids. And Arthur and Sandra are Arthur and Sandra, not us."

She nods, smiles, and takes off to the store.

Raheem and the kids go from room to room, double-checking that every window has been tightly shut. They put a towel underneath the back door and side door to keep air from getting underneath. It might not help significantly but it won't hurt. Raheem instructs them to not go outside. If they want to play videogames they can. They can do whatever they want to do from the confines of their home.

***

They're spitting.

That's what Glenda notices about the people in the parking lot of the small market a few blocks from her house—they do a lot of coughing and spitting. They have gone about their day, hocking up phlegm and wiping their mouths. They drink water and chew gum. To her, it seems as if everyone has been getting ready for a long smelly day when they should have been preparing to stay home.

In the grocery store, the checkout lines have recorded news on monitors. The newscaster says the smell is suspected to have caused hundreds to fall ill.

Glenda feels helpless like everyone else must feel, like she has no choice but to go about her business, hope tomorrow is better than today.

Rather than purchase only milk and eggs, she finds a shopping cart, drops a flashlight in it just in case. You never know when you're going to need a flashlight. She tosses in a few sleeves of bottled water, a bunch of first aid stuff, because, you know, what if? Did they have bandages at the house? A box of batteries is on sale, so she tosses a bunch of those in the cart. Next thing she knows, she has a stack of items she never buys—canned beans and canned chili and canned fruit. She stuffs the cart with yet even more canned goods.

After searching the entire store, she asks an employee where she can find those lame Styrofoam coolers and some ice to go in it.

By the time she gets home, the kids are complaining about being plenty hungry. Raheem stares at her and the purchases as if to say, so the world is ending now?

She says, "I saw you all messed up this morning. All scared. You wouldn't be the only one. People are scared and sick. They seem sick."

"You freaked out."

"I freaked the hell out. Why not? I feel much better with extra supplies, don't you?"

They put the groceries away. Raheem makes breakfast, and then the family eats in peace.

***

While Glenda and Raheem stay home from work, at Arthur's school there are plenty more students than usual in the nurse's office.

The nurse gives the students small paper cups of water, calls their homes to see if anyone can come pick them up to make them more comfortable. For a placebo, she places ice packs on their foreheads.

In an announcement on the loudspeaker, the principal tells the teachers to not send anyone else to the nurse, on account of there being no space for them.

Arthur is sweeping directly outside the nurse's office. The nurse shoots her mouth off like a weapon to the secretary who is passing through the nurse's office. The nurse fails to whisper her complaints about the nature of the situation. According to her, the school should be doing more. She doesn't know how, but they should be doing more.

In and out of the halls, Arthur hears kids in classrooms coughing and complaining, forever needing to go into the hallways and drink water. He watches the kids make a mess of several drinking fountains, a mess he'd wait till after school to clean up. Not yet on his shift, he tells a few teachers their kids are making the halls dangerous. He patiently waits for the bell to ring before getting to work. There are nearly a thousand kids and one of him. Best to wait them out.

The end-of-school bell makes him picture himself in Ms. Kimbrel's classroom conversing with her. When he gets the chance, he cleans up the messes on his route, and then starts for her classroom.

He barges into room 39 without knocking.

Sitting behind her desk, she taps the eraser end of a pencil on it. "Get the chair from the kidney table."

He doesn't hesitate to grab a chair, navigate through the aisles of children's desks with the chair above his head. He drops the chair in front of her desk, flips it and sits. "How are you?"

"Kids are great. They're horrible. Horrible, I tell you."

"I watched them in the nurse's office when I came in. Looked rough going."

"Oh, my Lord, all day," she says throwing her hands up. "It's not as smelly now. Way worse to begin the day. All day they were like, it stinks, it stinks. I'm telling them to read what's in front of them so we can move the day along."

"You don't think the smell is hurting people?"

"You know, I think it might be. I don't see how it's not. Did you hear about the cuts in the throat?"

"I did. Enters the body through cuts in the throat. Think. There is something that smells so bad that it cuts your throat."

"They'd tell us if it was really bad, don't you think?" she said.

"They should have already decided it was really bad, don't *you* think? Make everybody stay inside. Cancel life for a while."

She straightens herself. "If one of these kids got sick for any reason and died... If it happened at the school, would you help them?"

"By using my ability? I don't think so."

"You don't think so? Why not?"

"Not my job."

She turns her head to the side, and then slowly nods. "If you can help a child, it's your job to help a child. It's everyone's job to help a child."

"I used to think that. The people I've brought back, they haven't been too overly appreciative."

"I figured if one of these kids collapsed, you could come right on in and take care of it. You're saying you wouldn't. You can't really mean that."

"The people I've animated have always gone through something it seems. Something happens to them between them dying and me animating them. Not a good thing, either."

She frowns. "You'd be too scared to help, is what you're saying."

"I'm saying it's not my responsibility. Because of my maturity, I no longer want to pull a content or docile soul through whatever misery just so they can come back to this silly world and suffer for a lifetime. They don't smile at me when they come back. It's the opposite."

"We're better off dead."

"No one person I've brought back has ever thanked me. Except for Raheem, they're not grateful. Why is that? It could have been because they had an opportunity to get out of this place. I stole that from them. If a child collapsed right in front of me, no, I wouldn't save him or her. They're already saved from this place without my help. They're helped by being gone."

"Not helping when you can, is a macabre concept."

"You have to really lean into the idea," he laughs. "So many people want to be with their maker. When they get there, we want to rip them from their happiness so they can suffer with the rest of us. We think it's sad when they leave us. Point is, if you're ten years old, every day you live is another day of suffering."

"I should let my husband die? He's dying now, but when he does get that sick, I should let him die?"

"Don't have a celebration. It would make sense. A big-assed party—a symbol he finished his time here. Listen. Hear me out, hear me out. I remember going to see a movie about a guy who had AIDS who was trying get to know as much about his young daughter as he could before he died. He had to try to live with full blown AIDS. His daughter thought he was disgusting. By the end, there were so many tears in the aisles, I almost slipped. People were on their feet, wiping their cheeks raw, applauding the character's suffering coming to an end. If he wouldn't have died, he'd still be going through stuff, still suffering. It felt great to know he wasn't suffering any longer. The point is this: because the character died, the story took on a better shape in our minds. Not that a child's life is like a tragic movie. I'm saying their lives are a story where the suffering has ended. After it's all said and done, we'd be better off applauding how amazing they were rather than picking them up and telling them their suffering has to continue."

She stops tapping her pencil. "We're not suffering. That's a horrible thought. The people were applauding because such a horrible film had finally ended. *Their* suffering had stopped."

He stands and turns his seat around so he can sit in it properly. "I don't have to tell you it's a matter of how you think of it. I'm thinking, if you do move on to a better place, then you must be suffering in *this* place."

"It should be your job, Arthur, to see they get to make the choice to live or suffer. Because you can animate."

"For me to help them, they're already dead, is how I see it. Let them be."

"You know what you're missing?"

"What?"

"Responsibility. You're not being responsible."

With what he knows now, by helping them he might be causing more pain than he can imagine. Ms. Kimbrel's suggestion of helping those who have already died would be very irresponsible. He wouldn't save the kids, or anybody else for that matter. Nobody needs as much pain as he can offer.

Quincy's Revealing

After leaving Ms. Kimbrel's classroom, Arthur heads across campus to work through the east building. He takes out the trash in the odd-numbered classrooms, and cleans the restroom. By the time he finishes his evening break, the sun is down. He's behind schedule.

He enters Ms. Takashi's class, plugs in the vacuum he placed in there earlier, and runs it over the carpet. The stench that caused all sorts of havoc during the day has completely left. Still, something feels wrong. A familiar feeling rides him. He flips the switch on the vacuum to off.

Unlike Ms. Kimbrel, Ms. Takashi keeps her classroom clean. She has students' special assignments and awards spaced nicely on the walls. Every day it seems like Ms. Takashi has prepared for an open house event. She has tile floor, except for a large blue carpet in front of the classroom. It's where kids sit while she reads to them.

He ponders the story Ms. Kimbrel told him about his biological father. The roses. Making them fresh again. Could he find his dad? They were, apparently, in the same area at some point.

His father's abilities were like Quincy's, weren't they? What if all three of them were related? It's only now that he truly considered such a thing.

He'd love to bounce these ideas off Sandra, but until things were back to normal, he'd have to settle for telling her digitally, in his journal.

***

Dear Love of My Life,

I think you remember when Mr. Bell had his heart attack. We've talked about it enough. It's what happened after his attack that I want to tell you about. I'm almost ashamed to have not already told you. I'm only starting to understand it.

I was walking through the halls playing hooky. Mr. Bell stepped out of his class to get some air. Right there in the hallway—right in front of me, lucky him—he had a full-blown heart attack.

I hurried over to the classroom across the hall, ripped the door open and yelled into it that Mr. Bell was having a heart attack. The teacher in there rushed out, stared at Mr. Bell from a safe distance, and then urged me to go get help. My thought was that yelling into the classroom *was* how I was getting help.

Having heard my shouting, students flooded out of multiple classrooms. They stared at Mr. Bell who was sprawled out with his mouth open, his huge lump of a belly angled towards the ceiling.

The teacher I thought should be getting help stood in his doorway yelling at *me* to get help.

Ignoring the teacher, I found my way back to Mr. Bell, knelt beside him and blew air into him. An onlooker would have seen me as some kid giving Mr. Bell weird looking CPR. CPR wouldn't have done him any good. The dude was properly dead. After a moment or so, Mr. Bell rolled over, pushed himself up, brushed dust and dirt from the tile floor off his face and well-worn suit.

"I'm fine," Mr. Bell said. "I'm perfectly fine. Everyone back to class."

Mr. Bell took a long look at me, as if I did something disgusting to him. Everybody saw him eye me like he wanted to kick my ass. Truth is that he was right to look at me with suspicion. I *had* done something to him.

I've saved other people's lives, too. Not just Mr. Bell's. Up to that point, not one person I brought to life was happy I did it.

After that I dragged my feet down the hall, through the exit doors, and finally, I arrived out on the track field charged with enough negative energy that I could have jump started a car.

In the corner of the field, near the street, no one would immediately come looking for me, both because of where I was and all the commotion surrounding Mr. Bell.

Just like in elementary school, I stood next to a tree, however it had nothing to say.

The lunch bell rang. Not wanting to be found by friends, I fled to the top of the bleachers. It felt like I did something wrong. Every time I used my ability with somebody it felt like I did something wrong.

In the bleachers, nerds played board games. In the bleachers is where nerds went to commit social suicide. Nerds came in every nationality and gender. Male nerds. Girl nerds. Mexican and Black nerds were all up there in the bleachers. Asian Nerds. Nerds did not have any real sexuality. That's why they got along so well.

When the bell rang to go to class, I packed up with all the nerds. The next thing I knew, I was walking across the outdoor basketball courts.

I first heard, then saw Quincy hundreds of feet in front of the restrooms, waving his arms, trying to get my attention.

He waved to me, gestured for me to come over. "What's the deal? Where'd you go! Hiding?"

I arrived at the restrooms. "'Sup."

"Hold up, I got to take a piss."

As usual, Quincy did not carry a backpack or books. How he got through his classes escapes me.

Q's came back out of the restroom and said, "Come on in here."

I did.

The restroom had graffiti everywhere, mostly in black permanent marker. The doors had been removed from four of the six stalls. The perpetually wet, tiled floor had been carved with graffiti, as well as the mirrors above the white, porcelain sinks.

"Hey, man," Quincy said. "My dude, what happened?"

"You mean with Mr. Bell? I don't want to get into that. Weird stuff."

"My dude. Tell me what happened."

"I don't know. He fell, I helped him up. I think he's mad about it."

"You must not know who you're talking to." Quincy's face scrunched up. "Nigga, tell me what happened. Don't mess with me."

"What the hell do you want me to say?"

"Look. Look," Quincy said bringing his voice down. "I can see I'm scaring you."

"What are you talking about?"

"They said Mr. Bell collapsed, fell the fuck down right there in the hall. Everybody saw it. You didn't help him up. You did something to get him up though."

"Something like that. I guess he had a heart attack."

"They say he looked pissed as hell. Plenty of people think you did something to him."

"Can't do anything about what people think."

"You don't want to know what they say you did?"

They definitely weren't saying I brought him from the dead. "No."

"Don't care?"

"I don't."

"I forget you're in friggin high school. A kid."

"You forget you're in high school. A *kid too*."

"Mad at me?" Q's said. "I didn't mean to be so in your face like that. Sorry 'bout that."

"We should get to class."

"Hold on. Let me show you something."

He extracted a green apple with bites taken out of it from the trashcan. He held it out in front of me so I could see it clearly. The apple was deeply browned from the air.

"Keep looking," he said, slightly shaking it as if it was a snow globe.

"Look at what?"

Each time he shook it, it changed color, changed its condition. Where the bite was, it changed from brown and yellow to that beige-white of a fresh apple. The soft, browned spot under its skin stiffened and diminished and was—just like that—gone. A firm and juicy apple again.

"Your eyes aren't messing with you," Quincy said. "Understand? When you're ready to stop playing with me, I'm around." Quincy dropped the apple back in the trash, and then rinsed his hands. "Sorry for my lip a few minutes ago. Be truthful to me and I got your back like you don't know."

"What is it you did? What'd you do?"

"For right now, you can say I can make old things new. I can do that shit."

"I'm not alone, I guess." I didn't care. Surprised, sure. Didn't care. The idea of someone else having an ability made sense. Why would I be the only one? I didn't have a response to what he had done.

"I told you we need to stick together," he said.

"Who else can do stuff like us?"

"Son, it's just me and you. Pretty damned sure."

We had something in common. The real reason why Quincy singled me out from everyone else. He knew about me from the start. To recap, we had other things in common as well. We looked similar, not only because of our blackness; we were also around the same height, had a similar nose, similar complexion. Not the same but similar. Justin and Charles said we walked the same. Me and Quincy were both smart for our age. Quincy probably a little smarter. And we both had gifts. He could turn things back in time, in a way.

He turned his back on me, checked out of there.

I followed Q's outside the restroom. "How do you have my back?"

"You mean why do I have it?"

"I mean, how? I know why."

"*Why?*"

"Because you can do weird stuff like I can do weird stuff."

Quincy said, "You have to realize I've known, right?"

"How did you know?"

"I just did, man. I just did. Not too hard to understand is it?"

"I guess not."

Although I said it, I still wanted to know how he knew of my ability, obviously long before that day. For just a moment, I thought there was a bunch of kids like us with special abilities in the foster home system, separated from our parents on purpose. The idea didn't seem right, for some reason.

The late bell rang. From a distance, we could see stragglers entering classrooms.

Quincy said, "It's me and you who know about us. Nobody else."

"And Sandra."

"That's right," he chuckled. "Your rock star."

"She's my girlfriend."

"She is? Be careful with that. You're dealing with dangerous stuff. Didn't know you took it this far with her."

"I'm not letting her go for anything. Probably going to marry her."

"Does she know this?" Quincy leaned on the wall, chuckling. "You know, she has to marry you too. It goes both ways."

Despite his jovial antagonism, I felt confident. Love is something he didn't know that much about.

"Yeah, she wants to marry me. She'll say so if you ask her, no matter how many people are around."

"Okay," Quincy said, pushing off the wall. "What does she know about you, exactly?"

"She kind of knows what I know."

"Fine, then. What do you know?"

"That if you die, like Mr. Bell, I can bring you back. I can take things, objects, and make them real."

"I'm going to say this shit right here and then I'm going to leave. You don't know everything about you. You only know what you've done. She can't love you. She doesn't know who you are, or what you are. She doesn't know because you don't know."

I didn't have a response, not because he was right but because he was so upset. He'd never been upset with me before.

"The point is you don't know," he said.

Without saying goodbye, he turned and walked away.

The Future is History

Arthur cracks three eggs in a bowl, whips them to scramble. After adding pepper and salt, he takes out a non-stick pan and turns on the stovetop too high. He throws a piece of butter in the pan, swirls it briskly with a wood spoon before and dumps the eggs into it. Making the eggs lends his imagination to how Sandra must have felt when she cooked for him, when she did the little things—washed his clothes, cleaned the house. The sacrifices one makes for their significant other.

The eggs are almost done, so he extinguishes the heat.

I never did shit for her. He rarely, if ever, poured her a glass of orange juice. He never asked for her to do the small things for him, but he never did those small things for her. To his dismay, she made the big and little sacrifices that he hadn't. The culture they had made.

The eggs are perfect, except he didn't add milk and sugar. To welcome her back into his life, he'd serve her these eggs.

With the eggs on a saucer plate, he knocks on their bedroom door. Sandra doesn't respond. He knocks again, calls her name. She still doesn't respond.

"I made you eggs," he says through the door. "Haven't seen you eat anything."

The doorknob turns. She pulls it open, looks at the plate, and then at him.

"Surprised?" he says.

"Where's a fork?"

"Oh. Whoops. I'll get it."

"Don't bother." She politely grabs the plate from him, closes the door in his face.

The door clicks locked from the inside.

Figuring he's made progress with her, he makes himself some eggs as well. His eggs are more perfect than hers because the addition of milk and sugar. Sugar makes everything better. Milk makes everything fluffier.

He takes the eggs back to his computer in his office area, fires up his social media feed. There should be a lot of chatter about the horrible air quality. Not trending yet. It would. He searches the feed of his most frequent news sources. Instead of deaths, they're talking about politics. The economy is slipping, always slipping or about to be slipping. Fear. Fear. Fear. Another disease out of control somewhere, but whatever. He finds a link to a story about a mother who has strangled her son.

The world is a ghetto with trinkets for everyone to strive for.

He turns off the power to the computer, heads outside. First, he lingers on his steps, then wanders to the curb feeling heavy and bloated. A pile of useless flesh, especially without Sandra. She doesn't want him. Eggs won't win her over. *I've taken her for granted.* And he had done so for a long time.

A lanky Black man strolls in his direction on the opposite side of the street. The man looks about his age but thinner and muscular. The man has his head shaved like Raheem. Something about him seems familiar.

The man stops, drops the full black, leather duffel bag he's been carrying. "Yo, man."

The man's flared blue jeans slightly cover his sandals, his exposed feet. His buttons are open on his beige shirt. From this distance, not a cotton shirt. Hemp, maybe?

"Yo, man, it's me," the man says.

Arthur peers across the street. He knows this familiar face, knows it better accompanied by the voice.

"Quincy?"

"Arthur friggin Lowe." Quincy vibrantly nods his head, lifts his bag, and starts towards Arthur.

***

Side by side Quincy and Arthur walk up Arthur's front steps. Arthur looks Quincy up and down, impressed at the great shape Quincy is in. Quincy hasn't lost one bit of his confidence.

"Where were you going?" Arthur asks.

"Believe it or not, here. To this very doorstep."

"Well, I guess you found me."

"Not that hard to find."

Quincy saunters to the couch, sets his bag near the end table.

"You want some water?" Arthur starts for the kitchen.

"Nothing a hell of a lot stronger?"

"I don't drink."

"In the future, know that a man has to have alcohol in the house. It's not for him; it's for his guests. Kind of like giving a woman a rose. It doesn't matter if you think they like roses or not. *They do.* It's not for your benefit; it's for theirs."

"I don't necessarily want my guests drunk."

"Don't you trust the people you open your house to?"

Arthur couldn't figure out what to do with the question. "It's great seeing you. Somebody else in the area you're visiting?"

"Maybe." Quincy stands. "Can I... Can I get a hug?"

"Oh, um, sure. Sure."

They meet on Arthur's side of the coffee table, briefly embrace.

"It's good to see you and how good you've done," Quincy says. "Look at your home."

After looking around the room, Quincy makes eye contact. "You're not too happy, are you."

"Haven't cleaned since Sandra got ill."

"The same Sandra?"

"The same one."

"You married her?"

"I told you I was going to."

"You have a house, your high school damned sweetheart, any illegitimate kids?"

"Not a one."

"Pssshhh. How about that. What do you mean she's ill?"

"She committed suicide. She's getting better."

Quincy lifts his chin. "I won't ask you how married life is then."

"You know what?" Arthur says. "Maybe I don't trust everyone I invite into my home. Come back later and we can catch up."

"Nah, fool, I'm already here." With his index and middle finger Quincy jabs at the floor. "*Here*. I saw your picture at the school. I was like what the hell? Found out you worked there. Looked you up to *this* address."

"Why were you at the school?"

"I, uh, whadyacallit, know people there. Where's Sandra, anyway?"

"In the room."

"I'm going to ask. It's harder when they're injured, right?"

"Apparently. I pulled it off, nonetheless."

Quincy puts his hand to his mouth. "She killed herself?"

"She's back with us now."

"I'm sorry to hear about your situation. Believe that, believe that."

"Yeah."

"You did your thing with her."

"That's what I did."

"Although she killed herself, you guys were perfectly fine. *Are* perfectly fine."

"She's here. Alive and well."

"Alive, my dude. Maybe not well. She's not cured up here." Quincy points to his temple. "There's no reason to think when someone kills themselves, they're okay. You don't easily move on from something like that. How'd she do it?"

"Gun to the head."

"She's not going to be better from that. You've got work to do." Quincy cracks a smile. "I've got some bourbon in my bag. You're going to have some. It'll help you open your ears to the shit I'm about to tell you. You're going to hear it whether you like it or not."

***

Arthur agrees to a coffee mug of bourbon mixed with some of Sandra's breakfast tea. Sometimes she drank enough tea to keep her awake at night. She drank it in the morning, for the same reason others drink coffee. Instead of eggs, he should have offered her tea.

Mixing Sandra's tea with the alcohol should slow Quincy's drinking a bit. Why trust someone you haven't seen in over twenty years to be drunk in your house?

Quincy takes a few gulps of the tea and bourbon. "From talking to you I see you've ignored your talent, except for in certain situations. You use it as needed, which would be basically never."

"I don't have the drive. I really don't." Arthur sips from his mug. "I don't care about my ability or yours. It's been all this time. They don't matter."

"They don't matter? That would make sense if you weren't using it to help your girl. Oh, I'm sure of that, *son*."

Arthur takes another gulp from his mug. "I'm not worried or concerned about it."

"You know what they say: denial is not only a river in Egypt, ma dude. We need to talk about me and you." Quincy points to himself and then to Arthur. "Me and you."

Quincy reaches forward with his empty mug, and then sets it on the counter. "Need a refill. Never had this drink before."

Quincy snatches his bottle of bourbon from the counter, fills his mug half-way with bourbon. He plucks a tea bag from the small box near Arthur on the stove top. After extending the string connected to the tea bag, he dips the bag in his mug. "Thanks, ma dude. What I'm talkin 'bout."

"You had something you wanted to tell me? Because there's something I want to ask *you*."

Quincy gulps down half the content in the cup. "Go ahead. Shoot."

"Are we related?"

"Hell yes. Not how you think. That's going to take some explaining.

99

Better if I could show you. Going to change everything for me and you. Me…and you." Quincy finishes his drink, sets it down. "Breakfast tea and bourbon. Word."

"Your drunk ass."

"Not drunk. Yet. Nothing wrong with feeling good, ma dude."

"Are you my brother?"

"Brother? Hell, no. *Hell*, no. We're not related how you think."

"How?"

"Both ways we're related you're going to have a hard time believing." Quincy lifts his mug. "One more of these."

Quincy pours more bourbon into the mug with his tea bag. "To begin explaining, I'm going to start with how I don't think you always know when you're using your ability. I don't think you know. A lot of it must be on accident."

"If we're not related, say so. I don't have time for all this."

"You have to have time for this, fool, because it's the most important thing anyone's told you. There's a difference when you know you're doing it and when you don't. I thought you were going to mature and learn this on your own. You didn't. This is what we're going to do. You're going to show me what you can do. I want to see what you're doing that you might not know you're doing. I'll point it out."

"And then you tell me how we're related?"

"I'm just gathering the balls to say it, ma man." Quincy smiles, and then chuckles. The first sign the alcohol might be getting to him.

Arthur pictures the time back in high school, in the restroom. "Why don't you show me what you can do, first?"

"If it's true you don't know what you're doing, there are some nice sized consequences, most likely."

Arthur sets his mug down, folds his arms. "I'll wait."

"Alright. Fine." Quincy takes off his shirt and tosses it to the floor. "I look good, right?" His pectorals sag and his round belly, seemingly like a smaller version of Arthur's, slightly jiggles. "I work out. You could look this good."

Quincy cocks his shoulders back like a soldier waiting for inspection. His arms are far darker than his belly and chest. Curly hairs circle his nipples.

Quincy says, "See this tan line? Keep watching." Quincy's dark tan on his arms slowly fades to match the lighter tone on his chest. His belly slowly shrinks. "See how I'm doing everything. It's all on purpose. I don't think you can say the same. I have to stop."

"I remember you saying you could set things back. You're getting

100

younger?"

Quincy becomes stoic, especially in his face. "Your turn."

"You can make yourself younger?"

"That's the point. I can if I want to. If I were younger, I'd do a few things differently. Wouldn't you? Regret sucks. There are other approaches to some things I've done."

"What is it you regret?" Arthur says.

"I didn't have regrets until after I met, well, *her.*"

***

Arthur, you've got to understand that when I knew her, I was this guy, this thing. That's how I saw myself. When she found out what type of thing she had been having sex with, she wanted nothing to do with the thing she would give birth to. She bounced. I had the child but gave it up to travel and look for her. Originally, giving it up was supposed to be temporary. Then I kind of figured I wasn't supposed to have a kid in the first place.

She had ties to Boston and New York and all that. She was originally from Maryland. Came out here for warmer air and beaches. A fine, fine, *damned* fine woman. Everything on her was tight and firm. Trust me on that. I'm the truth.

I discovered her living in a small east coast apartment. I hid from her. She made something of herself in damned near a year without me.

She seemed happy working in a grocery store, bagging people's food, gathering shopping carts in a reflector vest. She had made some friends. I thought they'd be my way back into her life. They could give me the intel I needed to say the right things to her. I didn't do that part of the plan very good.

***

"She didn't want to be found?" Arthur says.

"Not by me. She was like, fuck that guy. Your turn to show me your ability. What's up? Let's see what you can do."

"I can't picture you with girl problems."

"Just do what you do."

"I'll animate something," Arthur says.

"Okay, anything."

Arthur gives Quincy his own version of a stoic, quiet gaze. He steps away from the counter, starts for his living room.

Quincy follows.

In the living room, Arthur focuses on the couch. "It's been a very long time since I've animated anything."

***

You say you haven't used your ability in a while, but in this world, you do things, sometimes, without knowing it. For all you know, you did it yesterday. That's how it is. You learn things without knowing you learned it. You forget things without knowledge of it. It happens, plenty. You affect people without knowing it. Perfect example. I was stalking her and didn't know it. At the time, I told myself I wanted my family back, minus the kid because, in hindsight, she didn't want the kid. If I was supposed to be with her and she didn't want a child, then maybe I wasn't supposed to have a kid in the first place.

I stalked her but didn't know I was, so I did it badly. Very not on the downlow. One day after she left her work, I asked a few of her coworkers if they knew Katerina. That was her name, Katerina. I told them I was her husband. We were never married. I told them I was concerned with her mind.

I thought she'd be okay to see me. She seemed generally happy, from what I saw from a distance.

***

"I guess you're saying you were chasing down a woman who was perfectly happy without you in her life," Arthur says. "You should have seen that coming."

He starts to animate.

Distinct indents in the shape of fingers form into the edge of the couch seat cushions, as if an invisible person grips them for dear life. That same invisible person presses against the backrests, makes obvious impressions. The indented material tears away from the couch, and then floats in their direction. The fragments hang in mid-air less than a foot from their respective faces. Arthur gazes on at the couch pieces that combine to form a skeleton of sorts.

The parts that were once a backrest resemble broad shoulders. They also resemble the back of an individual. Armrests dislodge from the couch and become floating forearms. Springs pry themselves away from the couch, spin into a torso for the animated sofa hovering in front of them. Yellow foam cushioning peels from the couch. The foam gathers on the animated sofa parts that stretch and pull into legs, merely inches above the carpet. Wood pegs dislodge from the couch and meet the figure. The pegs settle at the bottom of the figure's legs and act as feet.

Arthur steps past the animated figure to his partially dismantled couch where he violently smacks the remaining seat cushion, causing dust to rise. He blows the dust in the direction of the floating, animated thing. The blown dust circles the animated thing in a haze, promptly fills in the gaps where limbs are missing, making those areas solid—most noticeably the biceps and hands.

The thing weeps, bobs its dust-head, shuffles its pegs on the carpeted floor.

"Why are you doing this to me?" the thing whines in a little boy's voice. "I didn't do anything to you."

"What's going on?" Quincy says, in disbelief.

"This is what I can do."

"I didn't do anything," the thing pleads. "I didn't do anything."

"It thinks it's being punished, for some reason."

"I'm not punishing it," Arthur responds.

"I can help the both of you," Quincy says.

"You can help me?" the thing says, in a soft curious tone.

"Think of me as being in a white coat down to my knees with a damned stethoscope," Quincy says. "You'll be okay."

The thing becomes still. "You—you care about me?"

"Do you really know about this thing you've made?" Quincy says to Arthur. "I mean, really?"

Maybe Arthur knew less than he thought.

***

Arthur, I can see that, on a level, you know as much as you need to know about what you do. On another level, you might not know jack shit. It happened to me too. I'm looking at what you, I guess, created with your ability, which is pretty crazy, by the way, and then, staying with what I've been telling you, I didn't actually know shit about her. I thought she didn't like me or accept me anymore. I had no clue how scared she was of me. It's why I didn't know I was stalking her.

I found out I was stalking when I came to her apartment unannounced. Like I said, I thought she was generally and genuinely happy. But she screamed about how she couldn't believe she let a man run so much of her life, and how she moved to escape me. My opinion is that she ruined herself, but that's only what I think. All because she didn't want our weird kid. How she put it, she couldn't get her life back because of me. All this stuff about not being able to let people meet the real her. Man, real strong hate in my direction.

She sent me away, pissed off like you wouldn't even think someone could be. I did her a favor and left.

Days later, when her coworkers saw me again at her job, it was all drama and shit. She had told them I had abused her and that I had no business in her life. I didn't abuse her as much as she felt abused.

Still, why would I leave her alone? I wasn't doing anything wrong. I wanted her back in my life, to accept me. Not too crazy a thing. I thought my kid and her might be able to be a family if she came back.

Point is, you don't always know what you're doing to someone. People see what they want to see. Hear what they want to hear. You can animate things. You still don't have the ability to see things for what they are.

***

To admire what he's animated, Arthur lifts his gaze. "I can see some things clearly."

"You don't recognize your own voice coming from that thing?" Quincy says.

Arthur thinks back to when his old bear first opened its mouth and scared him and his mother. It did sound like his child voice.

Quincy says, "If you haven't figured this out, then you're probably leaving energy from yourself around in places, like rat droppings."

Arthur paces. "The wind—"

"—Don't try to explain it. Even when I try to explain shit like this, it doesn't make sense." Quincy holds his index finger up to the thing hovering in front of them.

Quincy says to it, "It's okay. Give me a minute."

"Okay," the little boy voice of the old bear replies.

Quincy says, "When I was younger, weird shit happened, got me? As I became a man, things happened only after I told them to happen, not on accident like when I was younger. I picked up how to do it. It's a maturity thing. You didn't know enough about your talent to see how you might hurt people with it. And don't get it twisted. You are hurting people—people you don't know."

Quincy wags his finger at the thing in front of them. "Give us one more second, little guy."

"Okay," a hole of dust in the shape of a mouth responds.

Jutting a finger at Arthur, Quincy says, "There are consequences. What do you think happened to your old bear?"

Figuring this a rhetorical question, Arthur waits for the answer.

"See, you have no idea. What can happen is something my dad had to tell me and show me. Learning is always done the damned hard way. I still learn things the hard way. Even now I learned a lesson: I shouldn't have left you back then. I was so different back in the day. I would have treated Katerina differently, if I could go back."

***

Nowadays I would have let her be. Back then I couldn't let her go.

She couldn't do anything about me being around, either. She was stuck. I thought we had a chance.

When I had a chance—one last chance—I threatened her. I told her I'd use my ability on her to screw up her whole life. She couldn't tell anybody about my threat because nobody, and I mean not a damned person would believe her if she told them that her ex was going to make her young again so he could ruin her life a second time. The point is she believed me. She believed me because she'd seen me do it to some dickhead, I don't even remember his name. Made the dude a kid. You don't touch my girl and talk shit. Agreed? Cool.

My threat scared the hell out of her.

Moments before Katerina's death, I pounded on her apartment door, all tired, and drunk, and homeless, and hungry, and in love with her ass.

I kicked the door down. Inside I see her pissed off and scared of me, pressed against the far wall, in her panties. I gave her that look. I shouldn't have given her the look. The look said, you knew it was me, and you're in panties.

I told her straight up, "We can do this again. We can start from the beginning."

She responded by jumping out the window. Right out of it.

Katerina lived on the eighth floor. She broke herself. Broke her face, her neck. Her legs.

I might have been able to save her, could have got to her before she was gone and made her younger, which would have healed all her injuries. I might have been able to. I didn't try because—now listen to me on this one—the moment had sobered me up, made me see things clearly. I had to move on. She already had. That's the lesson. Just like I did for you, I showed her my secret. It didn't sit well with her. That was that. If love doesn't want you, don't chase it. Don't bring it from the dead, is what I'm saying.

You don't know the effects of your abilities. I don't know if anybody knows the extent of their abilities.

Choking

I spent a few more weeks in that town, my mind full of her. Arthur, it turned into months, believe it or not. I was broke, not only in the wallet, but in my head. Broke, broken and busted in a place where I saw most things as bad, badder and worse.

I traveled from there but stayed right around that area. I made life in shelters, ma dude, made friends I only met once because the next time I saw them they were crazy or laid out on a stretcher or they were suddenly a different person because the streets had got them. Yes, I was, in many ways, stalking her ghost for a while, man. I still thought she made me feel good. Now that I think of it, the things that make you feel good, are, most of the time, the cause of you doing the worst things to yourself and to others.

When I finally had the guts to get back to my son, that's when I met her. Yet another woman, by chance. Love at first motherfuckin sight. Trinna. Her real name is Trinity. You know her. You know Trinna Kimbrel.

***

Arthur vehemently shakes his head. "You're saying you met Ms. Kimbrel. *When?*"

Quincy folds his arms. "Yeah, this story's really about you. Always been about you. Now, listen up. When I first saw her, I felt like I knew her. The feeling makes no sense. It makes sense that it makes no sense because it's that wow, you know what I mean? She just fit into my eyes in a certain way. That wow. Everything about her was meant for me to look at. I saw her on the playground. Your playground—".

"—My playground?"

"I knew it was your playground because Dana had told me so. I knew where you lived because to find you, I had to get a hold of Dana. See that. I found you. People from the shelter place I left you with told me about your whereabouts. They told me personal shit. Secretly. Discreet is the word I'm looking for."

Arthur lurches forward. "That makes you my dad?"

"I had no damn business with you in my life. I let you go. Sorry, son."

"You made yourself young again?" Arthur lets out a series of scoffs.

His hands on his hips.

"Once I saw Trinna, I had no future without her in it. I mean, before even talking to her I could hear her voice; I knew what she sounded like. I knew who she was. I just knew, know what I mean?"

"I'm not hearing this." He glances at the thing hovering in the middle of the room. It whispers a series of sounds, maybe words but Arthur ignores it.

"You're my dad," Arthur says. Not a question; a realization.

"I should have come back for you a very long time ago. I'm sorry."

"Shit!"

It made sense, how Quincy could make things newer, younger. How he met Ms. Kimbrel. How he knew Dana and Bixby.

Quincy says, "Trinna is the one who convinced me that if I wanted to get a chance to know my son—to really actually know my son—then I had to find a way to walk in his shoes. It was her. I dropped myself in age just like I showed you I can."

"Are you shittin me?"

"No shittin."

Arthur covers his mouth with both hands, shocked.

"I became a dude your age who kind of guided you, no more than I normally would. The thing about being a dad is you can't be with your kids at school. I could. Other dads couldn't. Dads can't really talk to their son's about girls. I could. Point is I did, but Trinna moved on. So, it was a sacrifice. She got married. Come to find out, she has a new name. The thing is, dudes like me are sick of giving up. I gave up on you. That won't happen again."

"Okay, okay, okay. You were always looking for me."

"Years later, while searching for Trinna, I found you again. Saw your picture on the wall at the school. From there, looked you up, got an address. There you were, right in front of your house—if I were to guess—waiting for me."

"She's the one Quincy told me about? You told me about."

"Yes, Trinna. I remember those times in the parking lot, skateboarding around. I couldn't explain it then. Still can't."

"Shit."

Arthur pictures himself in his childhood bedroom with his old bear and thinking his mother didn't want to be near him. "Women are eventually repulsed by us."

"Do you understand what I'm telling you?"

"I mean Katerina, Dana, Sandra. We destroy the women around us. Did I get that right? Is that what you're telling me?" Arthur slaps the cushion of the animated thing near him.

"That's what you're going to think?"

"What am I supposed to think? And, now, I don't have a friend from back in the day. Quincy. I guess he's gone or never been there."

"If I can't be your dad, why can't I be your friend?"

"Off the top of my head, you don't seem to care about all these people you've hurt, like Katerina. Do you care since you managed to just get over her? Don't seem to have a problem with how she died. You just up and moved on, just like that?"

"I moved on," Quincy says. "Not just like that. I did move on. I'd rather your mother be Trinna. She's never been afraid of you."

"My mom jumped out of a window. Sandra shot herself in the head. Dana, she fled out of my life. There's something to that, women close to me learning to basically hate themselves."

"Not with Trinna. She's accepted you. She's accepted me."

"How do you know?"

"Well, son, how I see it—you have to believe in something at some point." Quincy looks around the room. "Listen, if you never see me as your father, in the end it won't matter. What's important is you learn to not do things on accident. What's important is recognizing things for what they are. Me being your dad," Quincy nods, "is how we're related. You can be more friggin grounded, now, with a piece of your past in front of you."

"You're never going to be my dad."

"Why is this happening?" The thing's whisper turns into a solid complaint. "I didn't do anything, I swear."

Quincy rotates his head to the side to hear the thing better, and then focuses on Arthur.

"You don't hear your kid voice coming from it?" Quincy says. "I hear my son, scared of himself. You don't hear that?"

The thing softly says, "It hurts."

"Why does it hurt?" Quincy asks it. "What the hell hurts?"

The thing responds, "He keeps stabbing me."

"I didn't stab anything," Arthur says.

Quincy guides his hand over the hovering couch cushions. "Tell me about him hurting you."

"He. Keeps. Stabbing me."

"Where does he stab you?"

"All over. All over all the time." The thing shakes in mid-air.

"You know what, little guy?" Quincy says. "Whatever he does, he does it on accident."

The thing breathes heavy and raspy, as if it recently completed a run. Dust from it flutters to the floor.

"Why doesn't he know?" it yells.

"He'll stop, I promise." Quincy taps his own chest. "I'm the truth. I won't give you anything other than that."

"You'll make him stop?"

"I'm going to make him stop. He's not bad. He's ignorant."

Dust sprays from the things head. "He won't stop."

"Yes, he will," Quincy says.

"I'll let it go," Arthur says.

"You can't only put it out of your sight," Quincy says. "Your ignorant ass has to actually let it go."

Quincy puts his hand to his mouth. The stench is suddenly horrible.

Arthur does the same, squints without realizing it. With the familiar reek banging on his throat and lungs, Arthur wills the thing away, wills a part of himself he's been torturing, away.

The dust limbs of the whining, conjured child-thing fall like snowflakes, then raise in every direction before disappearing into the growing stink of the room. The parts of the couch drop to the carpet in a collaborative thud.

Arthur opens his eyes, puts parts of the once floating couch back where it came from. He coughs a bronchitis cough. He snatches the spring-torso from the floor, quite certain it won't fit back with the sofa properly. "I'll have to stop by the Goodwill and find another couch. This one's done."

"Did you let him go, or is it we don't see him?"

"I don't know."

Quincy carefully steps towards Arthur and the disassembled couch. "You have any of that bourbon left?"

"Show me that thing where you get younger."

"Not a good idea. If I turn myself younger or too young, I have to stay that young. If I turned you young right now, you'd be stuck that way until you grew out of it."

Arthur coughs. "That's crazy. You made yourself young again. I haven't seen you since high school. You've been doing what since then?"

Contemplating how his old friend is also his dad, Arthur coughs and chuckles simultaneously. The absurdity of it all deserves at least a chuckle.

"Yeah, this shit is messed up, right?" Quincy says. "I've been living, man. I've been living, doing this life thing. I, what, worked in a bookstore, the same one for a lot of time. You know I love the books. I traveled like all get out. If you're me, have to go off and do your thing another way. I have a lot of regrets. A lot of people from a lot of places don't give a damn about me."

"Why would you come back now rather than ten years ago?"

Quincy scoffs. "I couldn't risk it. I have to look pretty much exactly like I did on the day I left. She has to believe me. Already waited long enough for her. She has to believe me. That's how I feel. She has to believe me."

"You're going to be young with her, so you can live a life with her."

"I couldn't risk there being any doubt of it being me. Why would I risk that? If I have faith in her, I have to give her a damned, damned good reason to have faith in me."

"You could have been around."

"You never wanted me around. Did you search for your real dad growing up, or make an attempt to find him? The answer is hell no, because you didn't want me around. I could see that. You don't have issues from me not being around. You had a father. By getting Bixby for you, I did my part. To be real, me being a normal dad isn't and wasn't going to happen. Not how my DNA is set up. So, whatever judgment you have is fine by me."

Movement from the threshold of the hallway makes them turn their heads.

Sandra stares at them, her sweats cuffed at her ankles, her hair down her back.

"Holy smokes, Quincy. You guys still know each other?" She shakes her head. "No, nobody knows Arthur. Nobody knows you, right, Arthur?"

She and Quincy step towards each other until they embrace in the spot where Arthur's couch-thing had stood moments ago. The two let go and move away. Quincy kicks the couch spring to the side.

A grin brightens her face, something missed since even before her death.

"I'm glad to see you out here," Arthur says to her.

She frowns.

Quincy draws back as if to say, hey, girl, look at you. "After all that I heard happened."

She closes her eyes, takes a few steps backward.

Arthur stares out his living room window, tries to ignore what smells like mustard produced in pipes polluted with feces.

Quincy says Arthur's name in a soft monotone.

Arthur's tongue won't stop scratching the back of his sore throat. A dizziness seizes him. He wheezes, has a hard time keeping air in his lungs.

"I can't breathe," Arthur pants. "I'll be fine."

"It's real bad in here," Quincy says. "You cool?"

"Not cool."

"You not okay?"

"No…I'm okay. I'm…good. I'm…good." Still panting, Arthur gazes again out of his living room window.

"Who were you guys talking to?" she says to Arthur. "It sounded just like you. But younger."

There's something in her eyes and body language that Arthur imagines is compassion. "I can't breathe," he gasps. "Fuckin, damn it."

Quincy says, "Lay down."

"I'm going to die right now."

A heavy pounding on the front door. Everybody in the room stops moving and stares at it.

"Arthur!" It's Glenda yelling from the other side of the front door. "Arthur!" The knob turns, the door flings open. "What the hell?"

Arthur bends to one knee, pressed down by the weight of the smell coming from outside.

Glenda has never met Quincy, but ignores his presence, the shock of seeing Sandra up and dressed. "Tracy and Shelly passed out. They need your help, Arthur."

"Oh shit. Okay. Where's Raheem?"

"Work."

"I'm sorry." Arthur coughs.

Sandra gasps. "Where are they?"

"They're in their room where they should be. Can't we just go, already?"

"I can't breathe." Arthur grips his neck with both hands. It's like concrete solidifying in his throat. He uses his final breath to call out: "Daddy." Then he drops to his knees and falls on his face.

Crisis

With Arthur face-down on the floor, Glenda jitters from anxiousness. *Why didn't I already call 911?*

"Sandra," Glenda says, her voice wavering, "call somebody. Get 911."

Glenda can barely hold back tears. Without Arthur her kids will die.

Despite Arthur's condition, her children need to be the focus right now. Glenda swallows reality whole. Worry for her children goes down with it. She flees to her house where she rushes up the stairs to check on her kids. Maybe they weren't already dead earlier like she thought. Panic might have caused her to misjudge everything.

Tracy lies in the middle of the bedroom floor on his back, palms up with his eyes open and mouth agape. His shoes untied. They are always untied.

Glenda turns her attention to the lump under the blankets on Shelly's bed. The lump is her incredibly bright daughter who loves to play, loves to ask questions, and learns very quickly. Glenda steps over her son—whose tongue is backed up in his throat—to get to Shelly's bed.

It's here that she knows for sure that she doesn't have kids anymore. She only has what's left of them. In front of her, only remnants of something deeply loved and cherished, but not her kids. The remains of them.

Knowing Shelly and how headstrong her daughter had become, Glenda imagines Shelly had gone underneath the blankets while she choked, not realizing she was dying. That's the thing with the insidiousness of the stench. People didn't realize they were dying. Raheem, her daughter, her son. Maybe Arthur.

Considering the circumstances, Tracy might not have heard his sister choking. Shelly had probably died first, leaving her brother calling his sister's name, alone, as he choked to death. The stench had gobbled Tracy up so fast he didn't make it downstairs. The stupid mother she is, she slept through the whole damned thing. Although they were still alive when she went to Arthur's, she couldn't wake them, which was suspicious, but...

She'd need to call Raheem at his work and tell him that, Shelly, their own December baby, and, Tracy, their son born a year and two months before her, had both died.

The fireman said they should have a mask, yet nobody in her family had a mask. She didn't try to get masks, either. She and Raheem had talked about moving out of the area, but she never pressured Raheem into doing so. They never searched for another home, not even online.

What to do with the bodies? Take them downstairs? Leave them where they are? How is this supposed to happen? What is this?

She runs downstairs to phone Raheem.

His phone rings and rings, rings, and rings.

Their living room never seemed so empty. Usually, the kids caused so much movement in the house that at times it upset her. The current calm means her children are dead, called home to the Lord.

Glenda drops the phone on the couch, starts up the stairs to retrieve her children. One hesitant step after another, presses her up the staircase.

In their room, she shuts the windows on the far side to keep anything or anyone from looking in. Only family is allowed. She lifts Tracy from underneath his neck and knees. His dead weight sits in the cradle of her arms so perfectly, the moment must be preordained. She's meant to carry him down these steps in this very manner.

Step by careful step she finds her way down to the living room with her son in her arms—his limbs swinging. In her mind, she hears him ask if he's going to wake.

"No, sugar," she answers. "I'm sorry, you're not going to wake up."

"Where's Daddy?"

"Daddy is at work. He doesn't know yet, sugar. I'm going to set you down right there on the couch so when the paramedics come, they can, let's see, get to you easier. And you'll be comfortable."

"What about Shelly?"

Glenda sets him down on the couch. She pets his head, rubs his cold cheeks, takes a few steps back, and stares at him. His death certainly caused by her. She convulses in tears. She's been more mindful of the petty stuff than of her children. Giving her children life and taking it from them are somehow cut from the same process.

Dejected, she starts up the stairs to retrieve Shelly.

The ringing of the phone stops her. It must be Raheem. It's like her feet are buried in carpet while she tries to reach the phone, it takes such an effort to get to it.

"Hello," she says into the phone.

"Glenda, are you okay?"

"No, I'm not," she stutters. "Our babies…"

"*What.*"

114

"I have Tracy downstairs and Shelly is upstairs under her blankets."

"I only wanted to see if you all were okay."

"They're not, 'Heem. They're not. I am; they're not." She sniffs, and then pauses like a statue with her mouth open.

"What the hell happened?"

"They're not okay they're not okay. I'm sorry I'm sorry."

"Coming home right now. Be cool, it's going to be okay."

"No, it won't."

"Coming home right now."

"Come home."

"Glenda."

She sniffs and coughs, has snot run down to her upper lip.

"Glenda," he whispers. "You need to lock the doors. Lock you guys in. It's some bullshit going on out here. Lock everything and get the bat. I love you. Be there soon."

"What's going on?" she asks, but he's already hung up.

***

Sandra and Quincy watch Glenda quietly stroll out of Arthur's house. They watch her burst across the driveway to her place. With their eyes on her, neither of them budge.

Quincy hunches over speechless, next to Arthur's body. His fingers on Arthur's neck, and then wrists, to get a pulse.

"Can you help me?" Quincy pleads to Sandra.

As angry as Sandra's been at him, his sudden demise befuddles her. Is he truly gone? Alive and dead are blurred.

She whips her head ninety degrees so she can see out the kitchen window, imagines what Glenda must have been going through next door at her place.

Quincy flips Arthur over with both hands. "I can't make him younger. Never done it to someone who is dead."

"I don't know what you're talking about."

"Can you help me?"

She stares at him.

"Come on, help me put him somewhere better," Quincy says.

She folds her arms.

"Step aside, then. Step *aside*."

He kneels, grabs Arthur's ankles, and pulls him into the room behind them that has Arthur's computer and futon. Again, kneeling, he slides to the middle of Arthur's body, places one arm underneath his

115

legs. Another arm under the middle of his back. Quincy lifts Arthur onto the futon, leaves Arthur's arm and leg to lazily hang off.

Quincy exits Arthur's office, finds Sandra in the living room staring at the front door.

"The last thing I'm going to say before I go," he says. "After I leave, don't call anybody."

"It's too polluted out there to go anywhere."

"Don't call anybody."

"You're going to leave him here?"

"Aren't *you*? You don't give a shit. That's what you're saying, right? Okay, then don't give a shit. I'll be back for him."

"I'd do it again. If it was up to me, I'd put the gun right back to my head and pull the trigger again."

"Don't let me stop you."

"You don't know what happened between us."

"He did nothing to you, not on purpose. I can vouch for that."

"He abused me."

Her words are a jolt. For a moment, to him, she ceases being a person and becomes a subject, a thing that speaks in tongues, spells out detailed lies.

"Bitch, you don't know what type of ghetto you're spitting from your stupid face."

"I know you think I'm lying."

"You're drooling that false shit."

"I'm like a puppet with no strings."

Quincy thinks of the thing Arthur conjured not too long ago.

"Shit," Quincy says. "Don't completely blame him. He's not the only one with abilities."

She takes a moment to think about his words. Her face twists into something that disagrees with the rest of her. "You're talking about you?"

"I'm going to leave. Come back for his body."

"Did you hear me? You're talking about you?"

"It's all me."

She looks him up and down. "If you hid something that well, it's lying."

"Not that it matters." He finds the couch and collapses into it. "Shit doesn't matter."

"What are you talking about?"

"Give me a second. I'm drunk."

**

Several of Raheem's staff no-called no-showed.

Unless they're in the hospital and not able to use a phone, he's going to fire them the first chance he gets. Employees who don't care for their jobs are one of the challenges of managing The Cheap Dream chain of dollar stores.

Being short-staffed doesn't matter for the time being. Customers aren't present this morning. While the store is slow, Raheem checks emails in his dusty office. The stench that killed him not too long ago has crept in, but he can ignore it for a bit. No one has pinpointed where it comes from. Most likely from a far-off factory or from the beach, somehow. He feels safe from its effects. He knows Arthur will be there for him. Regardless, he feels fine and everybody else seems fine. The day goes on without delay.

Raheem sits in front of a two-sided window. He watches employees work and not give a damn he's watching. Or they don't believe he's doing it. The employees are the biggest threat to steal merchandise.

Scott stands at his register waiting for customers who aren't in the store yet. It takes everything in Raheem's power to not judge the twenty-something-year-old kid negatively. Scott stands there, leans on the register. He should sweep the floor or wipe something down or face an aisle. Anything.

Raheem exits his office in a huff, meaning to nudge Scott to do some actual work. When he gets to him, Scott has his hand over his nose, his palms covering his neatly trimmed mustache. Scott breathes hard, eyes Raheem as if to say something.

"Are you okay, man?" Raheem says. "What's up?"

"Can't breathe, Raheem. Can't breathe."

"You can't breathe?"

Scott might be going through what Raheem himself had gone through not too long ago. If so, then this young man's life might be in danger.

"I think you'll be okay," Raheem says. "You want to have a seat? What's up?"

"People are dying from it, Raheem."

Scott breathes more intentionally. Deep breaths, while he struggles to savor every inhalation.

"I don't want to die here," Scott says.

"You're not dying."

"Are you a doctor, or a store manager? You look more like a store manager."

Raheem gathers himself, wants to slap the kid, fire him on the spot for being a lazy bonehead. But Scott has a point.

Raheem says, "Why don't you get away from the register? Just don't talk shit to me right now. Go get some air."

Scott covers his mouth, heads straight for the exit doors.

In search of someone else to man the register, Raheem starts for the loading dock. Patricia and Ronal should be out there working as a team. Patricia can work with the customers if they happen to come in, so he'll move her to Scott's spot at register.

Out back in the docking area, neither Patricia nor Ronal are doing their job. Instead, they're sitting on the edge of the loading bay next to each other, Patricia's arm around Ronal's neck.

Employees just don't care about their jobs nowadays.

"Guys let's get to it," Raheem starts. "I'm sending Scott out for a minute so, Patty, can you grab a register? I'll help with the shipment if need be."

Patricia faces Raheem. "Ronal's not feeling it, I don't think. Look at him."

Raheem's initial reaction to the moment couldn't have been correct. Now he's convinced two of his employees are sick from the air. Raheem again recalls his symptoms before he himself had died.

"What's going on?"

"He can't breathe," Patricia says. "He can't talk."

Ronal, a middle-aged Mexican man with a huge pot belly, and a thick black mustache going down the side of his face, sits with his head down, gasping.

Ronal never lies, never comes in late, so whatever has been happening to him, it would be better to hear it from him than from Patricia, a dumpy gossip queen who always finds reasons to not work.

"Let him talk," Raheem says.

"I'm telling you he can't."

"Ronal, what's the deal?"

Ronal grabs his throat.

Raheem grabs Ronal by his shoulders. "Hang on." Raheem looks at Patricia. "Leave now to get him to the hospital."

"You want me to go where?"

Thinking better of making Ronal go anywhere, Raheem calls 911. Raheem positions himself slightly at the back of Ronal, but mostly to the side and ushers him through the store. He calls 911 from his office. The operator says paramedics will be there as soon as possible.

He pulls the phone from his ear. "As possible?"

"As soon as possible."

'As soon as possible' implied nobody would be on their way anytime soon or not fast enough.

He tosses Ronal in the back seat of his car and starts for the hospital.

The lobby of the emergency room has a population of people gradually choking. Maybe because he had died before, but he notices these people are having different symptoms of the same issue. He sees an older woman reading a magazine, struggling to swallow. Kids playing near the books and magazines, sneezing and coughing. Most of these people are on their way to their deaths. They just don't know it.

Present hospital workers wear masks. A visitor might not think hospital staff wore the masks to protect themselves against the stench, but he figures that is exactly what they are doing.

Prior to his death he didn't wear a mask, had always felt fine, just like everybody in here must have. After his death he felt fine, still didn't wear a mask or do anything differently, simply because he lacked symptoms. Simply because he thought he was safe even if he died.

He closes his eyes, finally, deeply contemplating the vulnerability of himself and his family.

Sitting Ronal in the chair, for the first time, he imagines a disease killing people seemingly randomly because its symptoms are hidden and ignored. This epiphany is so distracting he doesn't acknowledge his phone ringing until it's already gone to voice mail. Soon, when people start collapsing dead in the streets from the sickness, it'll be craziness.

He checks his phone, sees Glenda has called. Instinctively, he calls her back, hopes things are okay, though he assumes they aren't.

"Hello," she answers.

"Glenda, are you okay?"

"No, I'm not," she stutters. "Our babies…"

"*What.*"

"I have Tracy downstairs and Shelly is upstairs under her blankets."

"I only wanted to see if you all were okay."

She says, "They're not, 'Heem. They're not. I am; they're not."

"What the hell happened?"

She says something that doesn't register.

"Coming home right now. Be cool, it's going to be okay."

"No, it won't."

Although he had said things would be okay, he can't be sure. "I'm coming home right now."

119

"Come home."

"Glenda."

She sniffs and coughs.

"Glenda," he whispers so the emergency room won't hear. "You need to lock the doors. Lock you guys in. It's some bullshit going on out here. Lock everything and get the bat. I love you. Be there soon." And then he hangs up, anxious to get home.

***

Raheem resists the urge to weave in and out of traffic. Being pulled over and ticketed will only slow him down. He thinks this as he pulls over for yet another paramedic vehicle racing through traffic.

The radio reports of an elevated number of people being admitted to hospitals for unclear, yet possibly related reasons: sporadic, irregular breathing, headaches, flu-like symptoms. People are urged to stay indoors and get checked out if they have symptoms.

Raheem's shoulders stiffen, almost certain the public will not find a cure for the symptoms of the stink. There are too many people ignorant like him in dire need of a medical help.

He arrives in his driveway, quickly shuts off the engine. What lay in front of him might change things as much as his fleeting moment in the afterlife. He catches himself grinding his back teeth.

He pushes open the front door.

Glenda sits on the living room couch between Tracy and Shelly who are lying down.

"Are they okay?" he says.

Glenda's hands go directly to her face. He can tell she's been crying, as she avoids his gaze. He gets on his knees and gently touches each of his children on their respective foreheads. He places his index finger on Tracy's lips. His children are cold, lifeless bodies. He stands, and then drags himself to the living room, on his way to Arthur's house. With a dead family, he needs another miracle from Arthur.

Down the steps and into his driveway, Raheem kicks rocks to the side. He guides himself across Arthur's driveway, up the steps. The stench in the air, the distant sirens. The hollow wood of Arthur's small porch beneath his feet. Moths resting in corners of the porch, draped in cobwebs. Chipped wood on the handrail. The thought of his children having left him, leaves him with a feeling of individuality he has never known.

He turns the knob to see Sandra in Arthur's living room with a sloppy individual he's never met. The sloppy man lurches forward, sandals barely on his feet, spittle at the side of his mouth.

"Where's Arthur?" Raheem says.

Quincy and Sandra first gaze at each other, as if the other is supposed to say something.

"He's dead," Sandra says. "How are you? Oh my *gosh*, how are you?"

Raheem gasps, "Where is he?"

"He's in there," Sandra says, nodding towards Arthur's office.

Raheem tiptoes past Sandra and Quincy. He touches the wood door, slides it open to see Arthur lying half on the futon, half off, his face turned to the side, tongue hanging. Imaginary flies circle.

Not fully accepting Arthur's death, Raheem moves in reverse back into the living room, brows furrowed.

Before Raheem can say anything, Sandra firmly grabs his hand. "We're going to get through this."

"We already didn't." Raheem yanks his hand from her, cocks his head to the side, begins his descent back to his place, solemnly dragging his feet.

Inside his home, he finds a spot on the living room carpet in front of the couch and Glenda's feet. She glares at him, implies with her eyes that it's not his fault, that she has already taken the blame herself. He reaches out, places his hand on her knee to console her. He shouldn't have gone to work and let his family die. He should have stayed home and helped them.

"I'm so sorry, baby," he says, tears at his cheeks.

She replies with a blank stare.

He closes his eyes, and gently places his hand on Tracy's forehead. "We can't leave them here."

While touching his son, Raheem's body goes limp.

Sirens streak down the block. One vehicle, then another. Then another vehicle, and then another. The world outside choking on itself.

A light illuminates Glenda's face. She sits straight up.

"What," he asks.

"We wait."

"We what?"

"It took some time for Arthur to bring Sandra back, didn't it? She had been dead for over a week."

"But—"

"—We wait for Arthur. Somehow, he's still with us. We buckle down. And we wait."

Conspiracy

Glenda knocks on Arthur's faded, blue wood door.

Raheem stands behind Glenda. He stares back at their home, second-guesses not bringing their kids over, regardless of their condition.

Sandra swings Arthur's door open, then holds it in place.

Glenda says, "Can you help us?"

"I can let you in."

"A start." Raheem nudges Glenda forward.

Glenda steps across the threshold. "This whole thing is insane."

"The craziness has been my life," Sandra adds.

Raheem maneuvers past them. "I'm Raheem," he says to Quincy.

Quincy stumbles from his seat on the couch, tilts his cup of coffee and bourbon until it spills. "I won't let this be the end of him."

Glenda solemnly says to Sandra, "My kids aren't with us anymore."

Sandra bites her bottom lip.

Glenda slings her head to the side, stunned by the question she must ask: "Arthur can still *fix* them?"

Quincy steps over the coffee table, and let's himself fall back on the couch. "And you guys don't even give a damn he's dead."

"Excuse me. Who is he?" Glenda points at Quincy.

"I'm not sure anymore," Sandra says.

Raheem says, "Arthur needs to finish what he's here for. It doesn't make sense for him to save me and not them."

"He wasn't here for you guys," Quincy slurs.

"Sandra," Glenda says. "How do we do this? How does he get back to help us?"

In a plea to Sandra, Raheem juts his palms out. "*Please*, think about Tracy and Shelly. What needs to happen to get Arthur back so he can make them better?"

Sandra turns to face Raheem, who is a solid foot taller than her. "I'm not helping him, even if I could. Not thinking about it. If anything, I need to make sure he's dead for good."

"You had a gunshot wound to your head," Raheem says. "You should think of how lucky you are rather than what you think he's done wrong to you."

Sandra turns her attention to Glenda, although speaking to Raheem. "I can't do anything for him anyway."

Glenda says, "We're only thinking of Tracy and Shelly."

Quincy yells. "Unknowing and trite, is what you all are."

"Don't start." Sandra stabs a finger at Quincy. She shifts her attention to Glenda. "Quincy's an old friend from junior high and high school. He's drunk."

Glenda lashes out, grips Sandra's shoulder. "I don't care what you think about him. I flat-out don't care." She whispers, "Does he come back to us, somehow?"

Sandra straightens herself. "I've suffered more, much more than you could ever know. I love your kids, but I'm telling you, we have to hope Arthur stays dead."

Glenda takes a step back. "You're saying he *can* come back?"

Quincy manages to lift himself from the couch, stumbles around the coffee table, and gently places his coffee mug on top of it as he does so. He goes stiff for a second, and then punches the coffee table with his fist—a tight jab that cracks the glass from end to end.

"I came all the way back here just to watch my son die?" Quincy gives a piercing gaze to everyone in the room. "I guess he's moved the hell on, hasn't he? I damned well guess that is what the hell it is." He slowly slides his feet into his sandals. "I thought I could help but I can't help shit, never helped shit. Did this all wrong." He lifts his voice. "Family is a myth. It's just people and blood, and fuck this." He shakes his head a few times. "*Fuck* this."

They stare at him as he drags his feet out the front door. "Fuckin damn it!" he says from the back of his throat, punches the door on the way out.

Sandra waves them along towards the kitchen. "Let all that go for a minute. He says weird things. Hear him say Arthur is his son? Don't mind what he says. I don't know him anymore."

Glenda closes her eyes tightly, clenches her hands into trembling fists.

Raheem grips Glenda's shoulder, still trying to console her.

"You're going to have to be patient." Sandra walks away from them, towards the kitchen. "Come and sit with me in the kitchen. You need to know something about Arthur."

"We know about him," Raheem says.

Sandra continues away from them.

Raheem and Glenda follow her through the kitchen, on their way to a built-in table area at the far end of it.

Raheem stops at the sink, gets a few strips of paper towels, folds them over and hands them to the women.

They all sit at the table, hold the paper towels over their noses and mouths to filter out the smell in the air.

"I'm going to tell you guys in a different way," Sandra starts, "because I want you to hear me. Them dying is not the worst thing that can happen to them."

Glenda crosses her arms. "You need to say something that makes sense. Whatever you just said is some bullshit."

"Raheem knows what happens when Arthur brings you back," Sandra says in an even tone. "Did he swallow you?"

"What are you saying?" Glenda says, swinging her body to face Raheem.

"I was trying to tell you," Raheem says. "There might be a lot of pain. To me it felt good, in way. You come back through a lot of pain, so you're changed by being back here. It's the biggest way you know you were there." He rubs his head. "You learn from it. It doesn't feel good, but it feels, uh, justified. You're alive because of it."

Sandra gazes at Raheem with disgust. "Justified? By pain? No."

Raheem says, "Pain brings us life."

"I'm not going to focus on stuff we don't really know about," Glenda says, raising her voice. "If learning about it isn't going to help, then I'm not going to focus on it. Jesus, you don't think we're wasting time?"

Sandra slaps the table with both hands. "I think there's a chance Arthur makes it back, merely because it's him; I can't say he definitely won't. What I want to tell you is that if he makes them alive again, like you want him to, then he can control them from that moment on. They're really his slave at that point. When he comes back, Raheem will know. Your husband will start doing things that are out of character. I knew other people it happened to. It happened to me. You feel part of him. Arthur is a depressed, lonely, heartsick, selfish, immature person when it comes down to it. That's what he leaves his people with. The thing is they like being that way. You won't know the difference between his will and yours. That's what you want for Tracy and Shelly, is what you're saying, by wanting him alive. Even if you kill yourself, he can keep controlling you. This is what you want for your children."

"Why didn't you?" Raheem says.

"Why didn't I what?" Sandra responds.

"You make it sound like you could have killed him if you wanted to."

"To be honest, I sat in that room, looking at the area where I killed myself, half thinking of doing it again. There's still part of me that, I suppose, loves him." She chokes up when she says love, like a long-time guilty prisoner finally confessing. "Like I said, he has that over me. *Us.* In more than one way, it was easier to take my own life than his."

They sit there for a moment, letting the smell of the world swarm over them.

"Will you help me?" Sandra pleads. "Will you help me kill Arthur, if doesn't stay dead? Help me kill him."

***

With her arms folded at the table, Glenda stares at Sandra.

Then she gives the same gaze to her husband. "What do you think?"

"I'm not killing anybody," Raheem says.

"You believe her about what Arthur is, and what he can do? You say you won't kill people, but you'll let Tracy and Shelly go through the pain you apparently went through, as if it's a good thing. I say 'as if' because, here's Sandra, someone who would never hurt anybody or anything, saying she wants to kill this man. Raheem, he's already dead."

Glenda switches her focus back to Sandra. "You're saying Tracy and Shelly will have more of an attachment to Arthur than to us, than to me, and Arthur won't even know what he's doing."

Glenda shifts her attention back to Raheem. "You think Arthur is more important than our kids?"

Sandra taps her feet on the floor so fast and hard that everybody can hear the thumping. "He can cause more harm than you know."

Glenda says, "Can't we move away from him and take our chances? You don't think so?"

Sandra intertwines her fingers together, rests her elbows on the table. "Raheem, are you willing to move away from Arthur, to be with your kids away from him, assuming Arthur does find his way back to this shit-hole world? You won't be willing to move away, I bet."

Shaking his head, Raheem grabs Glenda's wrist. "I'm seeing a life where we don't need to worry about dying early, where we have control over things, where we can gain a life perspective for us and our kids."

Glenda frowns, and then her jaw drops.

"Put it this way, Glenda," Sandra says. "If he comes back, I would want him dead, but a piece of me won't let myself hurt him. I'm asking for your help."

Raheem vehemently shakes his head. "I'm not killing anybody."

Glenda pushes Raheem. "Get away from me."

He braces himself, keeps himself on the bench.

She shoves him with both hands, leveraging her weight behind the push. "I want you to get away from me." She shoves him again, "and to stay away from my kids." She shoves him yet again. "Keep your pain."

Raheem stands. "Go ahead and plot. Keep in mind you're thinking about killing somebody. You're talking about murdering this man after he helps you in a way that you could have never done by yourself. You're going to kill him for performing miracles. You want to turn your back on me, because I see him as special, because I want to live with miracles. You're choosing Sandra's fear of Arthur over miracles? You're choosing straight fear and hate over love and understanding, over giving someone a chance. *That's* what's happening." The wrinkles in his forehead scrunch together. With a grunt, he stomps off through the kitchen. He slaps the wall on the way out, continues through the living room and out the front door before finally slamming the door behind him.

"I get it," Sandra says. "I get it."

"Do you? I'm at a loss."

"Raheem gave me an idea I wouldn't think of unless someone like you was involved. If Arthur does return, let him bring your kids back."

"—And *then* kill him."

"That's where we get our head-start. You take the kids away. I get far from here. Raheem can stay to see if Arthur is able to return, again, after that. He can be with his miracle."

Glenda nods.

Sandra says, "I bet you're looking at me, thinking how did we get here, really? How did I get to the point to where I am now?"

"If you're good to talk about it—"

"—We need to talk about being abused if that's the case. If we get the chance."

"Is that what happened?"

"Definitely. You're saying Raheem never abused you? *Never* has?"

"He has not."

"Uh huh. Don't judge me."

Glenda stomps towards the living room.

"No, stay here," Sandra says. "Don't leave. No need for that. I'm sorry."

"I can't do this. I don't know what I'm supposed to be doing right now. I don't get it."

"I'm sorry. I don't know what I'm supposed to be doing either." Sandra's face scrunches up. "I do know Raheem can't possibly help right now."

Sandra gently touches Glenda's arm, as if Glenda has been recently burned. "Arthur's online feed is more up-to-date than network news. Let's see how bad it is out there. Check his feed, see if it's safe to travel. It might not be."

Glenda tugs on a single braid. "I'm just not thinking straight."

They enter Arthur's room. Inside, they peer down at Arthur's lifeless body, it reaching out in a frozen gesture to nothing in particular. His stiff jaw squared and locked shut.

Sandra steps past him to the front of the computer monitor. "Come here."

Sandra nudges the mouse so the screen turns on. "Just get around his hand. It's a small area, but I can make do like this." Sandra adjusts the screen so Glenda doesn't need to come all the way next to her where there will not be enough space between them and Arthur's body. "I'm going to look through his feed. Do you want me to click on any of his stuff?"

"I have an account."

"Want me to log him out?"

"I'm just saying I know about this." Glenda cannot manage to take her eyes off his body.

"Well, do you want me to click on anything or...?"

Sandra clicks on a link claiming to have information on a health epidemic in their county. To their surprise the link is to a blog site with a focus on hypertension.

"Nope." Sandra goes back and clicks on something related to "Mysterious Deaths" in their county.

"I can't do this." Glenda waves her hands, backing out of the room. "Can't be in here."

"I'm so sorry."

Sandra follows Glenda out of the office, watches as Glenda paces in the living room.

She's completely desensitized to death, Glenda thinks of Sandra.

"Let me turn the TV on." Sandra presses the button on the television. It's already tuned to a news station. The current news story is about trying to identify gunmen in the downtown area. The next story is about how hundreds have been hospitalized due to throat lacerations that have led to sudden choking, for some, and death for others. People are advised to stay indoors, if possible.

"They're trying to kill us off," Sandra mumbles.

The news report went on to show video feed of busy hospitals with some people recovering, talking about their issues—dire stories about people who didn't survive, families devastated.

Glenda huffs through her nose. "How does this help anybody?"

Sandra dips her head between her shoulders. "I'm on the side who is glad he's dead."

Glenda breaks down into tears. "My kids are dead, Sandra. Like *fuck*, you know?"

Sandra exits the living room, reenters Arthur's office, leaving Glenda to her tears. "Don't just leave. Tell me before you go."

Sandra continues searching online for updates on the current situation. She sees an icon to the left of the internet window she's not seen. A word processing document icon labeled, *Sandra*.

She double clicks the document to open it.

My dear, Sandra. When I go back to that moment when you shot yourself, I get stuck...

Sandra hears Glenda in the other room, apparently coming close to choking on her own tears. All the while, Sandra reads. As the stench invades her nostrils, she reads. A short amount of time later, Sandra calls out to Glenda, to make sure Glenda is alive.

"I think I'm fine," Glenda responds.

Sandra looks directly down at Arthur's body on the futon behind her seat. She stares at him, modestly triumphant. It's not that she's angry at him as much as she's sure she's gotten over the hump of a long, desperate moment. She flips off Arthur's body. "*Fuck* you."

Arthur's jaw, as if trying to respond to her remark, slowly begins to shut. His teeth clench together.

Her back stiffens, in anticipation of what might happen next.

Slower than his jaw had closed, it opens, and then he is motionless again.

"Glenda!" she yells. "Glenda!"

Glenda rushes into the doorway of the office.

"I saw him move." Sandra flips her hair behind her ears. "I *thought* he might find a way back."

"How do you know? How can you tell?"

"His jaw did this thing."

Glenda stares down at Arthur. "I can't be in here," and then she stomps out of the office saying, "I can't do this." In the living room, she stands near the window, gazes out at the street.

Sandra creeps close to Glenda. "Your situation will be easier after we've killed him."

"No way is any of this ever normal again."

"You know how I've told you about me and Arthur in high school.

You can see why I wouldn't tell you everything." Sandra finds herself holding her breath, waiting for Glenda's response. "Why don't I do that now?"

"Anything to convince me to help you kill him."

"I have to. I don't think we have a lot of time."

"And."

"Let me tell you about a situation with him in high school. Changed everything. You'll understand a little better. After that we can find bullets to my gun. I'll load it. You can pull the trigger if you want. You're going to want to kill him after I tell you this."

Sandrahood

Glenda, I'd like to tell you what it was really like being with Arthur. It wasn't like how I told you.

We had been together since junior high.

Imagine you meet this boy, super young. You meet him again when you're a bit older, and again when you're a still little older. Forever you keep meeting him, it seems. He was always there.

It's why it made so much sense for us to be together.

Believe it or not he was attractive back then. Almost nobody else thought so, but I did. Arthur held himself so that he walked straight up and down, but soft. Nothing imposing about him. Nothing to be scared of. You'd think he'd listen to you, no matter what. He did too, or so it seemed. He always had his eyes on me.

Imagine finding out the person you're supposed to be with is not only perfect for you, but he does real magic.

He used his abilities with elegance. He made abrasive things, like rocks, move how they should move if they were alive. He made the world seem like how it should be.

Imagine this. You're a sophomore in high school, listening to people your age and older complain about how they're not in control of their life. Arthur was *actually* in control. If anything will make a person stand out, controlling the physical world around him would be it. For a small amount of time, in the beginning, I could visit heaven by standing next to him. You probably can't understand it. I bet Raheem can.

His control turns out to be the problem. There are times when his control is downright miserable.

Let me tell you a story.

One day a good friend of his, Charles, was hitting on me. Charles was always hitting on me. Arthur didn't know because he didn't need to know, if you know what I mean. Charles thought of himself as the reason why any girl had a vagina. You know, at first, he flirted like anybody else might. By high school he started getting aggressive, in his own way.

There were times when he'd try to hold my hand, and I was like, you're Arthur's friend. Didn't say anything to Arthur. He'd pinch my butt with Arthur right next to him. I knew Arthur didn't know because Arthur was soft. He'd get upset if he thought Charles was doing something like that. With his powers, I didn't know what would happen if he really got upset.

It turned into, Charles, long hair and all, one day grabbing my ass. Really grabbing it. He was playing. I told him to quit it. He took it well. He was like, hey, I took it too far. No hard feelings. I'm sorry. I was like, cool. Moving on.

I swear, the next day he did the same thing near my locker. I always saw him near my locker after second period. I remember slamming it and yelling at him. He didn't stop walking. Him and Justin just kept going. I figured I had to report it to somebody. I didn't. Instead, I decided to tell Arthur.

Same day, after school, at my place—Arthur's dad couldn't stand me so we couldn't ever go to his place—we're in my room talking. I'm like, look, Charles is a piece of work.

He puts down the pen. He liked to lay on my bed and draw. He sucked at it, but he did it anyway.

Arthur said, "Well."

"Well, what?"

"Girls like him. He's got all that hair. He's all buffed out."

"What're you saying?"

"Well. Were you flirting with him?"

I said, "After all this time why would I flirt with him now?"

"Not flirting, but you know when you're doing something he likes, or might like? If that happens, does he notice?"

"You're asking me if I'm doing something to allure him without trying?"

"I mean, if you know he likes what you're doing, and you keep doing it—"

"—Huh. Today he comes up to me and grabs my ass, and just like, grabbed it. Justin was right there. *Right* there. Does it, you know, *matter* what led to it? Think about it, if I'm the one trying to get a rise out of him why wouldn't he tell you? Why wouldn't he tell you I'm hitting on him? Why doesn't he tell you he's not cool with me hitting on him? Why not say something to you?"

"What makes you think he hasn't?"

"Did he say something?"

"I'm not saying you would try to lead him on. I'm saying he's been my friend for a long time. I don't remember him lying to me."

"Ask Justin what happened. Call him up."

"Why?"

"You'll see he's not going to snitch on Charles. He'll lie. They lie. Charles is his hero or something. They'll make me look like a liar."

Right when I said it, Arthur's face twisted.

"Don't be mad," I said.

"Would you rather be with him or me for your first time?"

I sat next to him and put my hand on his knee.

I looked him directly in the eye. "My first time is going to be with you. Don't talk about it to Charles. I seriously think he's trying to have sex with me. The whole wanting a virgin thing."

"You're not flirting with him? At all?"

"See that's weird to me. No, I'm not."

"Right now," he whispered. Not one of those sensual whispers. This was a dare. He looked over at the door. "Your dad won't come in."

"Um, are you kidding?"

"Not at all. Not. At. All."

"It feels weird."

"Right now, come on."

"No," I said.

I could tell by his look and his body language he wasn't taking me seriously.

Then I could feel something on me, all over my body, under my clothing and on my skin, like the thinnest ever layer of warm pudding.

"Are you doing that?" I asked him.

"Doing what?"

The next thing I know I'm lying on the floor with my legs open. I went to the floor on my own with the help of an onslaught of thoughts that weren't mine. What do I mean by thoughts? The thoughts I had, the ones that made me unzip my jeans, had a physical emotion attached. What I mean by physical emotion is, along with the layer, I could feel a wave of him rush through me, just kept pushing through, like a flood of him under my skin. A, um, wave of thoughts in my blood, like the first time nicotine gets to you. I could physically feel it while I wiggled out of my pants. Not my thoughts I was working under. I was only in control of my actions to the extent that the layer of him and imaginary film let me be. That layer of film, that pudding feeling is Arthur.

I said to him, "I don't know what I'm doing."

"Are you sure?"

He asked because I was crying. That's how bad I felt, how dark and disgusting. At the time, I thought he fucked me despite me crying because he felt I was trying to prove something to him; he thought I felt guilty for leading Charles on. I think he thought I decided to give it up to appease him.

That was my first time with Arthur or anybody.

That's the kind of control he has.

I'm telling you about the layer first coming to me. I'm telling you, up to this point, it hasn't completely left. You've never met me. You've known a version of me. A place holder.

Like I said, if it comes to it, if I can't, you need to pull the trigger.

***

Sandra slides the closet door open, hoping Arthur has placed the gun she killed herself with back where he always kept it. She taps around on the shelf in the closet, not tall enough to see up there. Thick dust gathers on the tips of her fingers.

She relaxes, lets her hands drop to her sides. "I don't think it's up here."

Glenda has all the dresser drawers open. "Not in the drawers." She's tossed the clothing on the floor and into piles.

Sandra steps away from the closet. "And not under the bed. What the hell did he do with it?" She says it more to herself than Glenda.

"Personally, I'd get that thing out of here so fast..."

Sandra slides her feet forward, inches towards Glenda.

"What's wrong?" Glenda says.

Sandra throws her hands out in front of her, lets them slap her thighs. "I died in here."

They both take note of dark, crusty, dried blood around the base of the larger dresser. Similar blood marks near the head of the bed.

Sandra cups her mouth. "Everything is wrong."

"It *is* wrong." Glenda starts stuffing the drawers with clothing. "Should we tie him down?"

"He shouldn't know our intentions. We need to have vanished."

The women march to Arthur's office where his body has curled itself up on the futon in the fetal position.

Sandra twiddles her thumbs. "Did I look like this?"

"He had a blanket over you. He didn't even want to see you. He slept next to you. This is how Tracy and Shelly will be?"

"I can't do anything about that." Sandra sits in the seat in front of the computer monitor. She looks at the icon on the screen, the one with her name on it. She moves the mouse in a circle. After double-clicking on her icon, she sees words aimed at her, talking to her. "What is this?"

Glenda pulls Sandra's attention away from the words on the screen. "I keep imagining my kids next door by themselves."

"Raheem is there."

"Doesn't matter. I can't explain to you how far apart we are right now."

"When Arthur comes back, he'll help them. Remember that. You can have faith in that. I told you, he has that kind of control. I didn't exaggerate, at all."

"I had the most normal life."

"No life is normal," Sandra says. "Some of us have a lot more junk to think about than others."

Sandra scrolls down to the bottom of the document to see what his last thoughts were that he put to screen.

"It's so hard to believe this is all going on," Glenda says.

Arthur's fingers suddenly extend.

"Goodness," Glenda mumbles at the sight of it.

Sandra's back is to Arthur, as she stares at the screen. "You want to know what I was thinking when I killed myself? I was so depressed that I honestly thought a part of me must have been killed by the film I was telling you about. Imagine that. I was emotionally synced up with him, in a way, somehow. You know what my last words were. My last words were, hmpph, I said, 'fuck you, Arthur,' then I…" With her hand she imitates having a gun to her head.

Glenda presses back tears. "I can't imagine."

"I was dead. There wasn't any shiny light. I didn't see my family. My life didn't flash before my eyes. You want to know what happened when I died?"

"You remember?"

"I can recall, I think, every minute."

***

Out in front of me, a beam of bluish-white moonlight shined in through a wide hole in the ceiling. The area where I sat was too small to let me fully extend my arms. Imagine a truly over-sized coffin, with splintery wood walls. I had my legs straight out in front of me. My lower legs and feet covered in a shadow so dense, it gave the illusion of peering in at a deep cave.

I yelled a quick hello to see if anyone might respond. There was no response, not even an echo. My instinct said I was in a box outside somewhere, which explained the moonlight shining in through the large hole above me; however, I couldn't sense space outside of the box. It's hard to explain, but I quickly understood that nothing existed outside that box, despite the light. Inside the box was the entire universe.

I remembered putting the gun to my head, cursing at Arthur, and yanking on the trigger. I *had* to have killed myself. Put it this way: I have a hard time believing in ghosts because, come to find out, you can easily tell when you're dead.

You might say, hey, I could have been unconscious.

No.

You might say, well, you could have dreamed it.

I'm saying, no, I didn't dream it.

I shouldn't have to argue I was dead either. You saw me.

On the edge of the huge shadow in front of me, I focused on someone or something lurking. It waited, maybe not sure I saw it. It was breathing quiet and slow.

I didn't have a lot of room behind me. Couldn't move backwards much. As the figure leaned out of the shadow, into the beam of moonlight, I recognized it as Arthur. He was gripping a sharp knife, reflecting the moonlight. I can't think of a time when I had been more terrified. My body recoiled as far back as it could go. Arthur lurched forward and jabbed a knife into my thigh, and then my other thigh, and then my torso, repeatedly. I curled into a tight ball, absorbing the knife being punched into my thighs, into my back, into my shoulder, the back of my neck. I heard myself screaming from the type of pain that eventually strips the breath out of you.

I didn't look up because I didn't want to get stabbed in my face.

I'm certain I had somehow died in there. I know I was already dead, but I died in there, too, regardless, from the stabbing. He did it again. In that moment, I knew I had gone to hell. I was going to be stabbed to death for the rest of everything. After each stabbing I came back to life, I kept getting stabbed to death by him.

You're thinking I must have made it up. I'm telling you what happened. Don't try to take it from me.

I finally fought back. It couldn't make it any worse. Arthur would not stop killing me.

Then something changed in him. He paused and stared at me. Too dark to see his eyes. He dropped the knife, opened his jaw, and started putting pieces of me in his mouth. First loose skin and muscle, I was so mangled. Then he was eating me, biting huge chunks from out of me. I can't describe how it is to be chewed. Each bite hurt in a different kind of way.

After he swallowed me, that's when I found myself back here, with my dried blood at the bottom of the dresser, on the rug, on parts of the mattress.

Now he can do all that to me again.

Personal Hell

"What are you doing?" Glenda shouts from her cross-legged position on the living room floor.

Sandra, in Arthur's office, stares out the window, knowing any minute he would lift himself from the futon.

"*Sandra*," Glenda yells again, this time more desperate.

Sandra strolls into the living room. "Don't be like this."

"You're saying my kids will be like puppets. They'll need to be murdered by him, somehow, to get back to me?"

Sandra shifts her weight to her hip. "Puppets?"

"That's what you're saying isn't it?"

"All that hurt for them, yes, I guess, but he never tried to hurt me." Sandra says it in a small voice, with a question in her tone.

"Does that matter, suddenly?"

"After reading what he wrote to me a bunch, he never tried to hurt me."

Glenda rises. "Isn't he why you killed yourself?"

The confidence Sandra had possessed in the short time since her return, faded. Sandra, out of nowhere, reverted to her gentler person, back to the simple, photogenic person with the bright smile. Sandra's current condition might be proof of Arthur's control over her. Until recently, Glenda had not met the real Sandra. Now, the real Sandra had faded into this puppet.

Sandra's eyes glaze over. "Remember I told you about the film?"

"The pudding."

She wipes tears from her cheeks.

"Uh-huh."

"I can feel it all over me. It's here. Completely here, again. He's back."

Glenda eyes the doorway to Arthur's office, waits for him to emerge.

"You have to help me do it," Sandra pleads.

Glenda reaches out, grabs Sandra's hand, and then squeezes. "We're going to find that gun."

"His words… He really didn't mean to hurt me at all."

Glenda straightens herself out. "Do you feel you still love him?"

"I guess so."

"Just because you love him, it doesn't mean he gets another chance; it doesn't mean you need to be with him or think of him in some high regard. You can love bullshit, but it doesn't make it not bullshit."

"I can feel it."

A loud smacking sound, like a muted clap, gets their attention. They turn around to find Arthur barely holding himself up, slapping the wall while trying to keep his balance in the doorway. Finally, he grips the frame. His knees shake. Spittle drips from his lips.

Sandra rushes to him, lowers him to the floor.

"The kids," he says. "Are the kids okay?"

Glenda and Sandra look at each other.

"Get him some water, Glenda."

Glenda flees to the kitchen, finds a tall plastic cup, fills it with tap water. She takes her time on the way back, places the cup in his hand, holds it in his grip until she senses him pull it away from her.

Arthur sips the water, takes a deep breath, and then sips. "Are they at your place?"

Glenda nods.

"Are they okay?" he asks.

"No, they're not," Sandra answers.

He presses himself to his feet. "I don't know if I can do it to them. It's too much."

"You're not going to help them?" Glenda says, in a gasp.

"It's too much pain to come back. I won't put them through it. I won't."

"And you know this because of the pain you went through to come back to us?" Glenda says.

"I know, for sure, because…" Straining to point at Sandra, he says, "Because she swallowed me."

***

I opened my eyes to a darkness. Made me anxious.

At first, I thought I passed out and you guys had dragged me into a dark room somewhere for some reason. There weren't any doors or windows or a closet. Light, as if from the moon, beamed in impossibly from the low ceiling about ten or so feet up ahead.

I couldn't fully extend my arms. With my hands above my head, my fingers barely grazed the ceiling. I frisked myself, hoping to find something to dig at the ceiling or the soft wood walls. Had to get out of there. I felt something smooth and sharp near my leg along the edge of the wall. A knife. If I didn't know better, I'd think it came from my kitchen, which made zero sense.

The knife was no help in breaking through the ceiling. I knew I'd never get through it.

I yelled at the top of my lungs.

I leaned forward and saw on the other side of the light. The area wound up being a type of tunnel. A tunnel didn't make sense but there it was in front of me. I gathered the knife in my better hand, and slithered forward like a snake through grass, across the wood flooring.

Nearly across the moonlight, the sight of your feet and ankles and legs stopped me. The rest of your body hid in darkness.

Once you got wind I was there, you quickly sat upright, crab-walked a few feet backward. You gathered yourself, scooted towards me into the light.

I sat up as well, figuring I must have unconsciously conjured you. I'm sure you remember me animating things into you for fun every now and then. Out of sand, sometimes out of mud, from leaves or whatever. Never on accident. Animating is a reflex. It's me moving my energy around. That's how I understand it.

"Arthur," you said.

This version of you was foreboding. "You have to save those kids."

You were you in form only; it was actually me I was looking at. Like with my old bear, like with anything I had ever animated. It was always me. You were me telling myself to come back to the real world and save the kids.

I had died.

"You know you're not stuck here," you told me.

The key to getting out of there, I thought, was to get rid of that version of you, to get out of my own way. I had to take you out, no matter what, and it wouldn't matter how long it took. It wasn't you, because, like I said—it was me. *My* energy, *my* words. *My* hell.

You weren't a person but rather a thing conspiring against me. More me conspiring against me, like I've always been. I've always been in the way of myself.

"Baby," you said, "you have to let me stab you." Your arms and hands had collapsed at your sides. "How do you not know this? You have to be weakened."

I needed to get out of there. I, uh, I, uh, stabbed you with my knife, right into your thigh. With the moonlight above me I could see how easily and quickly you could be mutilated. You died right in front of me. It didn't stop you from opening your eyes and screaming. I had to keep doing it. I had no choice. I kept killing you, I had to get out of there.

Even right now, it feels like I murdered you.

***

I'm sorry, Sandra.

I kept thinking if I wasn't murdering you then whose blood was it?

I'll have to confess, a part of me—it's not that I would hurt you, but it's not like I had been in love with you every moment of every day.

I did not earn my depression. You did it to me or helped it along.

I saw you were, basically, always in the mood I was in. I don't know, I think part of you is fake, is all I'm saying, so maybe I had some anger while stabbing you. You smile when I smile, cried when I was depressed. Then you killed yourself, making all those smiles not matter. It made those smiles years of lies.

With the moonlight on you, your bloodied eyes fluttered open. Hunched over you, I flung the knife away.

Do you remember twisting into a ball, shocked at not being stabbed anymore? I saw you heal, as if I was supposed to do it again. You got to your knees, doubled over, like you were in pain.

"You're going to save those kids," you told me.

I'm sitting there, finally sure that I was you. Am you.

"It's only a little less painful than you might think," you told me.

When the first knife blow came it was a relief that it came from you. You stabbed me to weaken me, then you put your lips over my feet, kind of like a snake gobbling an animal larger than itself. You chewed your way up my leg. A soothing, continuous pain I can't explain. But sharp blasts of energy brought me back.

I won't put those kids through it, not if they're going to be swallowed and stabbed, just to choke to death again. I won't.

Submitting

Arthur's suddenly living husk holds itself up in the doorway. Sandra next to him, dismayed at his recounting of events during his death.

Glenda shuffles her feet, straightens herself. "Don't say anything. If the real Sandra isn't speaking, then don't say anything. Not about this. The real Sandra, not the puppet."

"The same thing that happened to me happened to him," Sandra says, "only from a different point of view." She touches Arthur's face. "Tell me you know what that place is."

She says it with his own emotion coming out of her, he thinks. It's a bit clearer that she acts how *he* feels, sometimes. She doesn't do it because of how right they are for one another, like he's thought.

"You want to know if it's real or not?" he asks.

Glenda says through a frown and a stiff lip: "Raheem talked about that place. She talked about it. Now you."

"It's a place you made." Sandra grips his arm. "It's a place you make for people you bring back."

"Not on purpose," he says.

"I know."

Arthur says under his breath. "Mr. Bell, Raheem—"

"—Me," Sandra adds, "yourself."

"That would mean I brought myself back. Through you?" He latches on to her forearm. "Help me here."

She helps brace him, inches him off the wall.

He pictures her with a knife. He licks his dry lips.

"You shouldn't do anything for Tracy and Shelly," Glenda says, a knot forming in her stomach. When she exhales, it's the last breath of the person who birthed two kids. The new person is childless and helpless.

Sandra, with her blank face, reaches around Arthur's body to grab Glenda's wrist. "You have to help me. I can't do this."

Arthur centers himself, stretches his limbs.

"Arthur, you have to let her go," Glenda says.

Arthur pries loose Sandra's hands from Glenda and holds them in his palms, as if they're the thinnest of glass. "I'm supposed to let go of the one person who makes me happy? I guess you're going to say what I did is unnatural. It being natural or not isn't something I care about." Looking at Sandra for affirmation, he says to Glenda, "We've been through a lot. Too much to throw it away when we don't need to."

"But…" Glenda turns her head away. "You brought her back for love, knowing you're hurting her? Isn't that why you said you wouldn't help my kids? You have no idea what you're doing to her."

"Do you want another chance at us?" he says to Sandra. "Did I hurt you too much to make this work? Did I do that?"

He closes his eyes in wait for a reply, and then lends his attention to Glenda. "They're kids, Glenda. It's different."

Sandra drops Arthur's hand, keeping eye contact with Glenda.

"You know what she told me when you were dead?" Glenda starts. "She told me you control her, like you pull her strings. She's not her. I think it's true you do pull her strings, accidentally. She told me if you bring my kids back, you'll have control over them in the same way you do her. I'm scared of that, don't want that. I'd rather they were dead than live a life controlled by you."

"I don't know what control you're talking about."

"I'm telling you, Arthur, that's not necessarily true, and the fact that you don't always know makes it worse. It makes you more dangerous than anything. My children are who they are, not who you make them. It's supposed to stay that way. Everything you're part of is not yours, you piece of *shit*. You know what I'm talking about."

Glenda reaches out and grabs Sandra's hand again. "I think you know what I'm talking about. Now you have to let her go."

Glenda pulls Sandra towards her.

"I love you," Sandra says to him.

"Because of my control," he says, intertwining his fingers, "you mean like—"

"—A slave," Sandra says. Her shoulders stiff, her head down, her brows furrowed, but her voice soft and cordial. "You're ugly on the inside. You're abandoned, you're bitter, and lost. I want out. *I want out.*"

Arthur walks away from them, towards the coffee table. He covers his mouth in awe, thinks back to her shooting herself in the head.

His shoulders sag as his life with her flashes across his mind's eye. There were times when Sandra said she felt like he controlled her. They argued over it. He never saw himself as a controlling person. Sometimes she appeared sickly, struggled to speak, claimed she needed to find a way to get away from him, but they always made up. Or did they? There were so many moments when she felt despondent, at the same time he felt the despondent. It's not that they had so much in common as much as they were shared the same emotion. His. They both understand this.

Sandra says, "I hate that I love you."

She collapses to the floor, exhausted, and then gathers herself, her legs straight out in front of her, her hair in her face.

Arthur says, "I don't know how to let you go."

Glenda firms her face. "I was going to let you bring my kids back. After that I was going to stab you to death. From there me and my family, along with Sandra, we were going to leave town."

"To get away from me when I came back again."

"What do you think about that idea?" Glenda adds.

"I understand. Maybe they don't have to go to that place I somehow created, now that I know I'm doing it."

"I'm not living in your world of maybe," Glenda says.

"Where are they?" Arthur says.

Glenda waves her arm in the direction of her home. "Raheem is with them at our place."

Arthur bites his bottom lip. "I don't want to be stabbed though. Shoot me properly in the head with the gun Sandra shot herself with."

Glenda shakes her head. "We can't find it."

"It's under the futon in my office." Arthur smacks his hands together. "It's there."

Glenda retrieves the weapon from under the futon. She returns to them with a sense of relief.

"Have you shot someone before?" he says, overly aware of the gun in Glenda's hand.

"Arthur. Shooting you won't be hard."

"Of *course* not."

***

Arthur agreed to bring Glenda's children back to life, and then let Glenda shoot him to death. This way he'll avoid accidentally controlling her kids, and they can escape. Hopefully, Sandra will stay with him on her own.

Arthur leads Sandra and Glenda out of his house, down his porch steps.

Glenda has the gun in her hand, as she steps outside. "What. The. *Fuck.*"

From across the way, Glenda watches Raheem squatting on their lawn, staring across the street at their neighbor, Mrs. Ferguson.

Mrs. Ferguson—a fragile old woman stumbles around on her front porch—grabs her throat with both hands. Her dress looks like a yellow tablecloth trimmed to ankle length. Mrs. Ferguson's husband, Ronnie—

his body is mostly in the house but he's lying in the doorway, his head blocking the die-cast iron screen door from shutting.

"'Heem," Glenda yells to her husband. She sets the gun down on her lawn before she jets across the street and grabs Mrs. Ferguson from under her arms. Mrs. Ferguson's hands keep going to her neck as she wheezes, unsuccessfully attempts to speak.

Arthur rushes across the street. "What are we doing?"

"We're going to help her."

Glenda says to the old woman, "You're going to be perfectly fine. Arthur here might be able to help you. Let's go, okay?" Glenda and Arthur start back across the street to Glenda's place, carrying Mrs. Ferguson by her elbows.

Mrs. Ferguson tears from both eyes, stutters, trips on her own words.

"Hang on, ma'am," Arthur says.

They finally make it across the street.

"'Heem," Glenda shouts to Raheem and Sandra who pace towards them. "Go get Mr. Ferguson. Sandra, help him get Mr. Ferguson."

Raheem and Sandra grab Mr. Ferguson, drag him across the street and into the house, drop him near his wife in the corner against the wall next to Shelly whose mouth is agape. Tracy's body lies on the living room floor near the sofa.

Glenda lies to Mrs. Ferguson, says everything will be fine.

Arthur watches and listens to Mrs. Ferguson die, because to be helped she *needs to* die.

"Where did Quincy go?" Arthur asks.

"Quincy?" Sandra says. "I don't think he said. I think you're the only one who can do anything."

"That's not true. That's not true at all."

Lay Them to Rest

Not even two blocks from the school, Quincy smells what he figures could be the physical nature of detriment.

Children will be in the nurse's office, no doubt. Everyone will have their mouths and noses covered. Why did parents bother sending their kids to school today in the first place? The general public is stupid as hell. No way around it.

About a block from the school, his imagination locks on Trinity. What will she sound like? Will she believe it's him? Maybe she won't care. There's a good chance she won't remember him, or even worse, shun him. But he knows he looks the same. He's done what he meant to do.

The street in front of the school is quiet, mostly uninteresting.

Parents think it's better to raise children in boring areas. They can build from boredom easier than accept moments of diversity and conflict that might add to their child's character.

The concrete staircase leading to the large front doors of the school sparkle with glitter. A white stripe leads from the top of the steps all the way down to the sidewalk. He could be a child here, soon. A child for the third time.

A secretary, a heavy-set woman with layers of flowing brown hair and deep brown eyes greets him at the front counter.

"I'm here to visit Mrs. Logan."

The secretary, with a blank face and then a blank smile, peels a sticker away from a booklet. She hands the sticker and a marker to him.

"Fill in your name," she says. "You'll need to keep it on. Sign in on the clipboard. Let me call down there, make sure she's expecting you. Go ahead, sign in."

As he signs the clipboard, the secretary picks up the phone, pushes a bunch of buttons on it. "Mrs. Logan? Uh huh. A, uh," she reads Quincy's name tag, "Langston is here to see you." Her eyes focus on the ceiling. "Okay." The secretary hangs up, beaming. "Who are you, again?"

"You got it right, what you told her."

"I mean how are you related? She sounded happy. I've never actually seen her happy. I'm just like, wow, who's this guy?"

"Can I go or..."

"Um, would you like a piece of gum?"

Alcohol on his breath. "Shit, I need gum?"

"Yes, definitely, gum."

"If you got some then bring it."

She digs around in her desk drawer, pulls out a stick of gum, and hands it to him, like she's holding out a message that might save his life. "A teacher smells alcohol on your breath and the cops'll come."

"Thank you. *Shit*. How good do you know her?"

"She's amazing. Bitter but amazing. Don't tell her I said that. You'd have to be drunk to want to hang with her. I'm kidding. You seem safe to me, as happy as you seem to make her. You're not a problem, right? I'm not going to lose my job?"

"I'm not even a problem."

"How 'bout I walk you down there. Keep us both out of trouble. Chew hard and fast."

Quincy nods, follows her into the hall.

She walks close to him, awkwardly so.

"It's down the hall, through the double doors. After that you veer right to the bungalows, room 39."

Quincy finds his stride slowing.

"Something wrong?" the secretary asks.

"I'll know in a minute."

"How do you know her?"

"I hope we were almost lovers, way back in the day. Going to make this happen."

The secretary stops. "I'll leave you to it."

He leaves her behind, strolls down the hallway. Lime green walls nicely decorated with book reports, and child art made with cereal and glue. Lame propaganda in black and pink bubble lettering prompting good citizens to use their 'nice words for nice results'. Room numbers next to doors indicate where learning is supposed happen.

It's baffling at how similar the setting is to when he was younger, several lifetimes ago, despite the changes in the world. Peeking into one room, he notices Lincoln Logs. The teacher still uses a chalkboard. The kids still sit on a rug, labor to stay in their skin while the teacher politely chastises and placates them. After nearly two and a half lifetimes, school refuses to wholeheartedly change. Always a new twist on the same shit. If school is about freeing yourself, then to be free you must first be subordinate, drop any ideas that might free a motherfucker.

He follows the secretary's instructions to get to Trinna's classroom.

The sun meets him outside the hallway. He trickles down the steps, follows the sun to the bungalow area where he finds himself, again, preparing to be a child, to be subordinate again, to fight himself and the world again.

Room 39 pops up on the left. The door is open. He follows the zig-zagging handrail up the ramp until he reaches the door. A rare sense of fear creeps into his bones, slows his pace.

The bell rings. The pitter patter of kids lining up at the door jars him. So many small people so close to him. Trinity calls kids' names, excuses them individually. Her voice, a muddied distortion of yesteryear. Not lacking beauty; however, diluted by symptoms of time, is all.

"Okay, walk," he hears her say. "*Walk.*"

With their hands behind their backs, the students march single file past him, towards a marker up ahead. The last one out of the classroom is Trinity. She pauses when she sees him, purses her lips, waves the kids on, and begins to weep. The kids don't move forward, despite her signal. Some of them point, and one girl gets out of line to get her teacher's attention.

"No," Trinity says. "My line leader, single file line to the cafeteria. Straight line in 3,2,1…" She claps her hands twice. As the kids file around the corner and out of sight, she cries. One hand on Quincy's shoulder, the other grips the door handle.

"Trinity," he says.

"Langston." She gathers herself, stands straight up and makes eye contact.

"Ya damned right." His chuckle is nervous. He inhales, deeply, acknowledges his absolute terror at standing before her.

"Oh, that would have been embarrassing. If it wasn't you. You're so, young." Again, she purses her lips.

"I'm very old, right here." He rests his hand on his chest, as if preparing for the pledge of allegiance. "You still smell like your same perfume, like roses."

"I look so different now, I thought you wouldn't recognize my face. You would recognize my scent. If you returned, and you did."

"What I recognize is that we need to get inside the classroom."

She admitted to having been waiting for him.

"Yes, yes, yes." She strolls to her worktable in the classroom, leans on it.

"Why are you surprised to see me, if you've been ready for me?"

Statuesque, she stares at him. "What happens next?"

He smiles. "A new life. You'll be introduced to the world as an orphan, like me, never admitting you ever had parents. At our age, deep down, we're really orphans, anyway. You can change your name, probably have to, really. You know me as Langston. This entire lifetime calls me Quincy."

The smile on her face stretches every wrinkle near her mouth and cheeks. "You're absolutely going to make me young again."

"How young?"

"I have a husband. I don't know what he's going to do. He's incredibly ill. Could you do the same for him?"

He chomps harder and faster on his gum. "Why you messing with other niggas if you knew I was coming? I could see a little bit, but you have a husband?"

"Is that a problem?" She straightens herself, meanders away from him, towards her desk.

"You want something from me. You have nothing for me though."

She clasps her hands together. "Things have changed since last time I saw you."

"Look at me. Look at me. Very little has changed for me. Know what I mean?"

"You said yourself, you're young, physically, not in here." She taps her chest. "If I do this, do I owe you something?"

"You want something from me, but you're not offering anything. Do you owe me something? Just know your husband stays."

"*You* found *me*. All I'd be is grateful." Her nose flares. "I'm not offering you any more than that."

He wipes his mouth, makes clicking sounds with his tongue. He takes a step towards her, and then another. He lifts his head, so he's staring at the small holes in the particle board, tile ceiling.

He says, "I'm going to come out and say it. I've carried the weight of you in my heart for this whole life, picturing a *mother* for my son. A *family* for my son. A family I've never had. I stayed away, thinking I had to come back at only the right time so that you recognized me, because you had to remember that, Trinity, girl, it's me. *It's me.* I knew you were my queen right when I saw you on that playground with my son. I *knew* it. And all you can be is grateful?"

"You're not going to own me."

"The only thing is your husband isn't your husband anymore. Go ahead and remember him as your husband. Go ahead and think about him. I don't care. But he can't *be* your husband."

"I'm not going to be your *wife?*"

He grinds on the gum, like a cow chews cud. "I only want to be with the beautiful rose I met back then. If you're saying I'm delusional and need to step out of here, then I'll go. My bad, my mistake." He shrugs.

"Don't tell me that's what's happening."

"I can't accept what you're offering. Like you said, I can only be grateful. That's not enough, apparently. I'll be lying if I do anything else."

"I don't think you'll be lying. You'll be lying more by staying with this dude you call a husband."

A smell, like molded chicken, circles them.

Trinity Kimbrel covers her nose with her hand. "It's so bad. Off and on, you never know when."

"You can't let it be true? In a matter of time?"

"I'd do anything to have my youth back. All I could be is grateful for that. I can't leave my husband."

"I can give you an out."

"An out?" she says.

"You have to know people are dying out there, getting sick."

"And."

"I bet hubby is dead before we make it to him."

"Tell me that was not a threat."

"Not a threat. We can go see about him. If he's alive, him too. A deal for you. Compromise for me."

"Are you implying you know something about the stench?"

"Nothing you don't know. You see it happening all around. If kids are having a hard time, then your so-called husband is. I guess, yeah, I might know something."

"What else?"

"To be real, I might know something extra. It's too late for that."

"How's that?"

"It's not a where or what it's coming from. It's *who* it's come from."

***

Trinna, listen to me.

At first this might be hard to understand: the stench comes from Arthur.

I could have helped him stop it. He died, so everything is all mucked the hell up. My son is dead, so it's all screwed up. Nothing to do now.

Let me explain it better.

My dad—from lifetimes ago—would always say a person has to ask for what they take from the world. Or, as I see it now, you need to ask for what you accomplish, or you wind up doing something else with your gift. That's anybody, not just me or him. Arthur could add life to things. Accidentally, he unleashed it on motherfuckers.

When you have what me and Arthur have, you're a big filter. The world enters you in some way. Me and Arthur can send it back out there, filtered through us, so we need to be aware of what we're putting back out there. When I make us young again, I'll feel the world moving through me, then it can come into you. From there it will do what my abilities say it can, which is make things young. That's what I can do. I can do that for you. Can't make things older. Only younger, so once we're there, we're there.

Arthur, because his dumb ass didn't know what he was doing, the world moved through him and spit out his nasty shit. He accidentally poisons things when he uses his ability. He might as well be the lead dumped in your drinking water for years at a time.

The reek we smell, it's what Arthur's depression smells like. It's what anger and frustration smell like, what people treating you like shit since being a kid smells like, like what watching the person you love commit suicide smells like. That's Arthur we smell in the air.

Arthur is a statistic, thanks to me. Thanks to me leaving him, he's that poor, Black, inner city kid who got raised by a single parent. He's the kid who never had a real relationship with an adult, who never had someone consistent who he could identify with. I don't think he had anyone to love. This kid made it through school, through the bullshit of growing up alone and by himself. How do I know that? I know because I wasn't there. His mom wasn't there. No adult was there, and when I got the chance, how can I say that I chose you over him? I'll say it like that. I chose somebody else over him, convinced I had all kinds of time. I mean, I can create time. I wanted that family, but what family? There wasn't one. I sacrificed him for that idea.

Nobody ever taught Arthur to be Arthur. A bunch of motherfuckers only taught Arthur to be nobody specific. They thought he could be anybody. People can't be anybody or anything they put their mind to, all that bullshit. People are themselves first, let's say it like it is. He's sure not like me. I guess he's dead now, so this stench is on me. In a roundabout way, I did it. I'll own it. I'll take that. Nothing I can do, but I'll own it.

I first saw signs of his condition in high school. I told his ass even then. 'You have to know what you're doing,' I told him. The last time I saw him since not too many hours ago was at a little house party back in high school. What I saw scared the hell out of me. I had no idea he had been doing what he had been doing, till then. I thought it was too late. So, like an idiot, I got out of there.

***

Arthur and Sandra were already at the party when I arrived.

A crowded, small apartment, smelling like spilled beer and liquor. A thin haze of cigarette smoke. A hint of vomit and urine. This was and is the youth, standing around either doing nothing or doing dumb shit. Youth is a term given to the youth, not by the youth. The youth have never had a representative of their own stand up for them. The only heroes in high school are fiction characters, not real people.

All these hero-less wastes of time crammed themselves into such a small place that they spilled out the front and back doors, down the walkway. Kids were loitering on street corners.

I walk in and people are pointing at me with their eyes. Some girls reach out and touch me. I used to get that from girls. They wanted to have their hands on me in some way. I'll admit it, I left a lot of them wanting more. Left a few of them pissed off as all get out. None of them my ex. I only wanted you.

Sandra greeted me with a kiss on the cheek like she always did. She said something to me. I don't remember what. Arthur greeted me with an embrace and a smile. We had become good friends, although I excused myself from his clique. Too old for that, from the beginning.

The music was so damned loud we yelled back and forth, smiling. Arthur with his beer. Sandra with a water. Might have been vodka. I still don't care.

"We're going to graduate," he said. "That's crazy. After everything that's happened."

He went on and on, from subject to subject. He talked about how his mom left him, talked about how he discovered his abilities, how he landed Sandra, and now got laid all the time. He talked about how me and him were both orphans and special.

"You're like a brother to me, you have to know that," he said.

"We're good. Nothing to talk about."

He took a huge chug from his can of beer. "It's not good. I'm not good."

I looked at Sandra. "What the hell is he talking about?"

She shook her head. She had a horribly sad friggin look on her face. It was worse because of how pretty she was. She had tight cheeks. Muscular shoulders showing through her sleeveless blouse.

When I first met Sandra, she was that chick dudes wanted to bone. Girls were jealous of her because she became popular so fast. By the time of that party, she basically had no friends. Her time would always, always be with Arthur. Like plenty of close couples, she became an extension of his laugh, of his moods. She didn't see her people anymore. It didn't stop the envy and jealousy of others. You put her next to me and people stared, curious at the arrangement between the three of us.

Charles came into the living room via the hallway, his hands wrapped around Tania's waist from the back. He kissed the back of her neck. A huge spectacle. Coming from that hallway could only mean one thing. They were banging in the apartment's only bedroom. They would have to have been in there before the party started, hours ago, for no one to know they were in there. Anybody in the know was like 'ooooohhhhh'. I, myself, was like, holy shit, what's this?

Arthur turned to see what got so much of everyone's attention and yelled "fuck".

Charles saw him, flipped his hair behind his ears, smiled, and came at us. He didn't dare bring the broad with him.

"What are you doing?" Arthur said, a kind of gloom sitting on him. "Get the fuck out of here."

Charles said, "Chill. He's not around."

"Justin's right outside dumb-ass," Sandra said.

Charles rotated his head back and forth, looked around like a bird. "Where?"

On cue Justin walked through the front door, exhaled the last puff of his cigarette. The dude had changed a bunch since earlier days. He had on a hoodie sweater. Converse. He kept his hair short and neat, only wanted to fit in.

We watched the whole thing unfold from the far end of the living room. Justin saw Tania, his girlfriend, who he had no idea was at the party till that moment. Instead of welcoming him, she had a wall up. He was like what the hell, and they argued for a while. Numerous people cleared away from them. Justin took her ass by the elbow and ripped her from the damned place.

Charles, who at most times was all smiles, stood in front of us, speechless.

"I don't know what you're still doing here," Arthur said, pounding the rest of his beer. "You screwed up."

"We're in love, bro," is the silly shit Charles said.

I'm like, "She's not the only one you're screwing."

"I know," he said. "There's nothing I can do. I love her. She's hot."

"What if Justin loves her?" I said.

"You're one to talk," he said.

"What keeps you from screwing *my* girlfriend?" Arthur said to him.

"She's not in love with me," Charles responded.

Arthur stepped into Charles's personal space. "But if you thought she did you would. Maybe we break up for a day. She gives you a look you like."

"You guys aren't breaking up," Charles answered.

Arthur looked Sandra dead in the eye and asked, "Would you screw him?"

A snarl formed around her lips. "Yeah, I'd bone Charles."

Charles' face morphed into complete confusion. I should have seen right then that whatever emotional junk Arthur had going on with him, Sandra had going on with her too, only on another level. No more than a moment before that she was as stupefied as any of us at Charles' decision to bang Justin's girl. A moment later, although upset, she said she'd bone Charles. She said it because Arthur thought it.

Then, basically on cue, here comes Justin, like an emotional knife, slicing through people to get to us, to get to Charles. When he gets to us, he doesn't say what's up or hello or anything like that. He punches Charles in the side of the head. Charles made a girl-like sound before pushing himself away, tossing himself into me. I shoved him off me and cursed at him.

Arthur grabbed Justin by the shirt. "Whoaaa, whoaaa, hang back, hang back."

Justin wasn't listening to that mess. He jumped at Charles and shoved him hard enough to send Charles flying against the wall. The whole crowd was aware of the situation, now. Some people got out of there but most gathered and yelled, did some distinctly unhero-like shit, chanting, egging the fight on.

Justin dived on top of Charles. I stepped back and let it happen. I couldn't be a hypocrite. If I were in Justin's boots, I would have kicked Charles in the mouth.

Someone dived on top of Justin to get him off Charles. Someone else jumped in, some other dude, I don't know who. All these girls were screaming. The whole thing was a mess. Someone decided to dump beer on everyone. The entire living room of people was moving, shoving, and pulling. There were some good intentions, but none of them stopped Justin from pounding on Charles's face.

Did Justin's girl come back inside to stop him? Hell no. Did she know this would happen? Hell, yes.

That's the moment I noticed it. I saw Arthur with one hand trying to rip people off Charles. His other hand was aimed at Sandra, who stood by herself on the wall. He had one hand in the pile of kids, the other grabbing for something. I'm looking at his hand, and then at Sandra, his hand, and then at Sandra. You know what I saw. She was off the ground. He was pinning her against the wall, holding her there, at least five feet away. She looked uncomfortable. Not shocked, merely uncomfortable. It's when it occurred to me that he didn't know he was doing it, but maybe it happened all the time. He was using his ability accidentally; he was controlling Sandra, while not controlling himself. To have her in the air like that, off that ground, it's thorough control.

How long had he been doing that?

I panicked. Not because of his abilities, but because I didn't want to be around when the consequences happened.

Here is the unwritten rule, what my dad said. You can do whatever you want, but if you do, it had better be intentional, and on a special occasion. It's not something you do all the time. If you do, you wind up poisoning the well.

Arthur was enabled by me to poison the well. I was being a friend of his instead of a father. He's still poisoning the well, so much so that you can friggin smell it. It's all him.

The next day was the first in grad week. That day at school was the first time I smelled the shit we all smell now. It's been building up since even before that, for who knows how long.

Should I have left him? Hell no. I thought it was tough love, leaving him alone like that. Never thought these many lives would be at risk. Not this many.

***

"I don't believe I'm hearing you say such a thing," Ms. Kimbrel says.

"Life is full of shit that's straight unbelievable and absolutely completely true."

"A person doesn't smell emotions."

"I do. I can guarantee you that."

"Because you failed him?"

"I'm pretty damned sure when parents fear their kids, and it doesn't matter the reason, at that point, they stop being parents."

"And that's you."

Quincy lifts his chin. "That's me. That's a way to look at it. Listen, I've got nothing against your husband. Let him finish his life out. Let him be most people. You and me be special. Say, yes, so we can leave all this. Start new with our own thing."

"I'll be lonely," she says.

"You'll have me. You can have your looks back. You can have what everybody, including myself wants—time. You can be more than grateful. You can be happy."

She gives one nod, like a genie. "I want to have a kid. That's what I want."

Quincy smiles. "Our child can be as special as Arthur. You know what my dad could do? He could change elements. The dude could turn water into wine. I'm not even kidding. Plastic into glass."

Ms. Kimbrel gazes up at the ceiling, closes her eyes, and nods, again, like a genie. "Okay, then."

"You don't even have to love me," he says. "As long as I can be with you, we'll figure it out, won't we."

The bell rings to end lunch.

Quincy heads to the door. "Finish your day. I'll come back for you after I go get Arthur. Figure out what to do with his body." He stops and looks around the room. "I thought he could take care of himself. The little bastard couldn't. We'll see about your so-called husband."

"Come back."

He opens the door, takes a step outside onto the ramp. "*Shit.*"

"What is it?"

He waves her in his direction, suggests for her to step forward and see what he sees.

She hurries to the door to see what's grabbed his attention so suddenly.

Over a dozen kids lie around the bungalow gasping for air, gripping their throats. A few of them look dead.

"Shit." Quincy rushes and kneels beside a little girl near the wall. He grabs her small hands, pulls them away from her throat. He looks her in the eyes which are circling in her face. She wheezes, and then stops breathing.

Ms. Kimbrel rushes past Quincy to a male child only a few feet away. "Derrick."

She doesn't bother to get any closer to him, instead desperately searches around, and then runs to the main hallway.

Giving up on the young girl, Quincy runs towards the large, concrete field, leaps over and around dead kids on his way there. On the field, kids are strewn about like litter, some motionless, some writhing like worms. He finds himself shaking his head in shock at how fast it all happened. A generation of kids, not anymore. He briefly sifts his thoughts for a solution.

He runs back to Ms. Kimbrel's class. She's not there so he yells for her.

In the main building, Ms. Kimbrel checks inside several classrooms. Nobody is in there.

In the staff lounge several teachers hunch over on the long table. Others lie on the floor, their throats swollen. She's never seen swollen throats. She coughs involuntarily, to expel something from her throat. Can't stop coughing.

Grabbing her throat, she makes her way to the Principals office, staggers against doorways. The Principal lies partly under a desk, in the administration office. The dead secretary is in a doorway on the way out the back door. She must have tried to escape. Ms. Kimbrel steps over the secretary, whispers for the will of something higher to intervene.

She's outside again, in the quad.

She sees through open classroom doors, and windows, fellow teachers consoling children, children crying. Staff bewildered, lost and lame.

She jogs back to her classroom, looks for Quincy. He stands with his hands in his pockets. He's been waiting for her.

It feels as if her throat is closing, like her chest might explode.

Quincy rushes to her, hands flailing.

She falls to her knees.

He catches her before she hits the ground, then lays her flat. He puts his mouth to hers, and then blows.

My Dear Sandra

Compelled to follow Arthur, Sandra heads outside with him, picks up the same gun she killed herself with from Glenda's lawn, and enters his car.

Arthur backs his car out of the driveway, as if he's going to work on a normal day.

"Where to?" Sandra says, staring forward. "The school?"

"Believe it or not. Find Quincy. Please don't ask questions. Not trying to convince anybody of anything. We're past that point."

Pulling up to a red light, they see people across the street pound on the glass doors of the convenience store. For the first time ever, it seems, the store is closed. Would-be patrons line up along the ground-to-ceiling window, slap it, yell into it, most likely at the workers inside.

The light turns green. Arthur drives the speed limit, makes sure he doesn't run over bodies lying in the road. He weaves around them without slowing. Cars behind him do the same.

Sandra points at the once live objects in the road, nearly speechless. "What the *fuck*?"

Arthur keeps his hands steady on the wheel, checks his mirrors, as he normally would. The real issue is the people who had not been through the types of trials he had been through—they hadn't died or brought anyone back to life, or had not seen their wife commit suicide—would panic at the state of things.

"I don't smell anything." He takes one hand off the wheel. "I guess whatever the smell is, it's worse now even though it doesn't smell as bad."

They stop at another red light, at a four-way intersection. Sirens scream, approach from in front of them. Meanwhile, on the cross street, a police cruiser speeds passed. The ambulance passes them and is now in the past.

Distracted, Arthur fails to advance on the green light. The car behind them finally screeches around them, and then another does the same.

Arthur locks his sight on a homeless man sitting on a bus bench in front of the gas station to the left. The man is still, his eyes open, as he gazes off into forever.

"What are you doing?" Sandra asks.

Arthur places his hand on Sandra's thigh. "I'm sorry about

everything, baby."

"I know." She taps his hand. "I'm not mad at you. I can forgive you."

For a second, he imagines her as a child. What if she really has forgiven him? Something turns on in him, at the thought of being forgiven. A light-weight energy swirls in his joints, in his feet. It's like being a child.

Sandra lifts the gun from off the floor, places it in her lap.

He gets out of the car, heads for the man on the bench—a Black man with living-sky blue eyes. A heaviness presses on Arthur's chest—a sudden sadness for the bum in front of him, something he didn't feel even five minutes ago for all those people in the road. The difference between now and five minutes ago is that five minutes ago Sandra had not forgiven him.

At the far end of the gas station, an officer sits in his patrol car, weakly protecting the gas or the gas station attendant. Drivers honk at Arthur as he strolls diagonally across the street. Once across, he sits next to the bum, taps him on the shoulder.

Traffic erratically presses on, stops, and goes, and honks. Machines screaming in a mechanical language.

The homeless man is undoubtedly dead. His head sits crooked on his neck. His dirty, gray, cotton shirt too big, filled with holes around the neckline. His face so dirty Arthur can't easily see his skin. His hair stiff from the amount of dirt it holds. The man's corduroy pants, too big to be originally his, probably something found along the way.

The life in this man, Arthur understands it as something floating about in the wind, something that, at one point, Arthur carried in his feet to find Sandra. Life is in the wind.

Arthur gathers energy from within himself, leans over and kisses the man's forehead, just as he did when he placed Sandra in their bed to bring her back to the land of the living. Arthur smiles, feels that same wind from his childhood, and lends it to the homeless man, as he squeezes the bum's hand. Arthur squeezes, until the man's body shakes in one solid convulsion. The man spits and shouts.

"Oh, my lawd," the man says in a tinny, much smaller voice than anticipated. "Oh, my *lawd*."

"You okay?"

"You have a quarter or a dollar? If you have a cigarette?"

"I don't."

The bum deeply focuses on him.

Arthur gets to his feet, moves to the edge of the curb. He waits for traffic to die down so he can safely make it back to his car.

Arthur looks back at the officer in the patrol car. The officer is in the same position as moments ago. Arthur saunters to the patrol car, looks inside the cracked window, sees the swelling of the officer's neck. He lays his hands on the officer's forehead through the open window and invites the wind from his childhood to move through the officer.

The first thing the officer does upon waking is grab his own throat, look up at Arthur, and reach for his weapon.

"Whoa, whoa, sir," Arthur says.

"Step away from the vehicle," the officer says, firmly.

"No problem." Arthur backs away a few steps, his hands up.

The officer quickly exits the squad car, breathing heavily. He slams the door behind him, cranes his head at Arthur. Slowly the officer steps back against his car door. A man easily over six feet tall, husky, middle-aged and clean cut, leans back, his bottom lip slightly trembling. The cop closes his eyes, and a single tear forms in the corner one of his eyelids.

"Why don't you get back in your car," Arthur says.

Respectfully, the cop follows the instruction.

Arthur jogs through the gas station, to the middle of the street where his car is parked.

"Were they dead?" Sandra asks.

"It wasn't like before. Felt different." He gets in the car with Sandra, which is still running.

"How so?"

He grips the steering wheel, smacks it twice, and grins. "Because of you everything is different."

"What."

"I absolutely feel different."

As the light turns green, Arthur presses on the accelerator. They progress a few blocks. He can't stop himself from scanning the area for dead people.

He says, "I should have been helping all along, instead of protecting myself. I can make this all better."

To the right is a small playground with a tetherball court and a few picnic benches. He pulls over, eyes what he thinks is a situation. An EMT vehicle flies passed them, sirens blaring up the street.

Kids in the park gathered around a motionless pit bull. The dog lay in the lap of a boy with no socks. The boy's shoes are untied, his hair not combed. Two younger boys surround him.

Arthur and Sandra approach the scene with speechless caution.

"Do you mind?" Arthur says to the boy who holds the dog's head in his lap.

"Mind what?" the boy says, first looking at Arthur, then Sandra, and then Arthur again.

"Let me help your dog."

A strong kid, muscles more formed than Arthur's. Ashy knees, and braces on his teeth.

Arthur easily moves one of the children to the side, leans down and presses on the dog's belly.

"Get off my dog, bitch," the boy yells.

Arthur's first thought is, no, this is *my* dog. He doesn't want the dog, and he doesn't want control of it either. "You can have your pet."

With that the dog lifts its head and snaps at Arthur.

"Lassie!" the boy says, smacks the pit bull and hugs it.

"Friggin Lassie?" Arthur says.

Sandra smiles from ear to ear, then heads back to the car ahead of Arthur.

At the car, the bum with the living-sky blue eyes waits for them.

Across the street, the officer Arthur saved is in his patrol car gazes at them through sunglasses.

"That's them, right?" she says.

"Guess so."

"Following you?"

"'Scuse me," Arthurs says to the bum at his driver side door.

The bum says through his own stink, "Can't I get a dollar? I'm playin, I'm playin."

Ignoring the bum, Arthur sees the little boy and his friends approaching, barely trailing Lassie.

"What'd you do to my dog, Mister?" the boy yells.

"I'm not sure. Get in, Sandra."

Arthur and Sandra load into the car. He shoves his key back in the ignition. He'd happily save anyone he saw, anything he saw on the way to the school. His positivity should reflect in Sandra's body language, maybe in what she says.

He yanks the wheel into light traffic.

"They're following you," she says.

"*Us.*"

"No. *You.* People you brought back to life are following *you.*"

"How do you feel?"

"I'm fine. I think I'm fine."

"Are you sure?"

"Let me go."

"I'll let you go. Go ahead and go."

"Can you leave me be?"

"For good?"

She says, "I love you, but can you let me go, please." The confusion in her. "I don't want to kill myself again."

"Things will be better," he says. "Let me make it right. Make it how it was."

Up ahead, it's obvious they need to stop. Two cars have collided in the intersection. The side of one car looks like something clawed metal from the side of it. The second vehicle's front end is crumpled like abused tinfoil.

Instinctively, Arthur pulls to the side, gets out and searches for victims. Chances are, at least the driver of one of the cars choked while driving. The stench being the cause of the accident. Somebody around here is dead.

Sandra jumps out of the car but stays where she is.

The officer Arthur saved stops next to Arthur's car and watches.

Arthur approaches two body bags on the sidewalk. Fire trucks and firemen with gas masks surround one of the smashed vehicles. Police officers block one direction with flares, the other direction with a patrol car, lights flash in the early evening.

As Arthur arrives closer to the bodies, firemen approach him.

"I can help," he says.

They politely grab Arthur, tell him to go away. He thrusts one off him. An officer grabs his arm.

The policeman Arthur saved runs up to them, yelling, "Let him go! Let him go!" He steps between Arthur and the other officers.

The scene is a shoving match between police and firemen.

"Everybody calm down," a fireman yells.

Passersby have their camera phones out, take pictures and video.

The officers step back while Arthur advances on the body bags. He kneels, grabs what he thinks is an ankle of someone in the bag. He doesn't need or want to see the body. He didn't need to see Sandra. He sure doesn't need to see these people. It's only a second before the wind from his childhood is moving through the body in the bag.

The firemen lift Arthur up from under his shoulders, desperately trying to control the moment. They pull him, as he fights to see if the body starts to move. It does.

The officer he saved points, "Look! Look! Look!"

The small crowd watching panics at what they see. Some flee under cars, while others sprint down the street, turn back for a glimpse of the miraculous. Others keep their cameras pointed at the body bag.

The body struggles to get out of the bag.

Arthur strolls to the second bag, lays his hand on what he thinks is someone's chest. He knows he's releasing his energy into this person. He knows he's filling this person up with a joy of being curious, of discovering; it's how the wind made him feel when he was a kid. He's somehow, for some reason, repressed it all this time. He was wrong about his ability: what he's doing is more than a reflex. He didn't put joy into Sandra when she died. He put hurt and disgust and longing into her. This same wind had filtered through some fairly, nasty gunk.

He looks back at Sandra. The wind, more like a gust, kicks up. Arthur giggles like a little boy, feels his wind leave him. He exhales, as if he's just taken his first breath.

Sandra smiles, laughs, and involuntarily claps her hands.

He thinks, *I did that.*

"Go if you want," he yells to Sandra. "Go if you want."

She doesn't move, still part of the moment, involuntarily clapping.

He stands up straight, scans the crowd for anybody so freaked out by what he's done with the bodies that they might want to harm him.

The officers stand before him, in awe. The firemen, gawking. One of them takes off his jacket, tosses it to the ground, lets his jaw hang open—a type of salute, is how Arthur sees it.

"Thank you, Jesus!" someone yells. And then multiple voices saying, *yes.*

Hearing such a thing, stops Arthur. He does a complete three-sixty, takes a good look at the entire crowd, the whole situation. To the audience, the raised dead are part of a cataclysmic event. People are dying for no apparent reason, and here he is lifting people from the dead. They're drawing conclusions.

He grabs his nuts, to hint at them they've got the wrong guy.

People snap pictures on their phones. Some are on their knees for him, because of him. His dad, Quincy, warned him about showing people his ability. It's one of the main reasons Arthur never put himself in a position to publicly showcase himself. Everything would get out of hand, just like Quincy implied. But it feels good.

"I'm not your Jesus!" Arthur shouts, turns in a circle, let's people get a good look at his face.

Onlookers peek from behind cars, from under cars, from inside cars, around corners. All traffic has stopped. People squat in the doorway of the liquor store, and peek their heads out, struggle to get a look at the situation. Not everybody knows what's just happened, but word of mouth is undoubtedly at work.

"I'm not your Jesus," Arthur repeats, throws his hands in the air.

The bodies in the bags frantically struggle, scream. A few officers come to their aid.

Lowering his head, Arthur starts for his vehicle.

Sandra waits for him in the car, but there's something else.

"You're ready to let all these people suffer, aren't you," she says. "Everyone you didn't leave dead has suffered like they never have in their life."

"No." He shakes his head. "I'm telling you, it's different. I thought you forgave me."

She holds the gun. The expression on her face makes her intentions clear; she's ready to murder him.

***

Helicopters thump across the sky.

Sandra stares out the passenger window, then through the windshield, and then back at Arthur. Again, out the passenger window.

Stress plastered on the faces of those walking about, sitting about, lying about. Some emotionally in pain, some physically in pain.

Arthur can't help the living, regardless of their hurt. To be helped, they need to choke, they need to vomit, they need to mourn and question why anything is as it is.

"You don't care do you," Sandra says.

Knowing there is no right answer he doesn't respond.

"You look perfectly fine with everything," she says. "How many do you think are following us?"

"This isn't going to end very good."

"Or at all."

"Oh yeah, it is."

He stomps on the gas, weaves in and out of a few vehicles. He makes an abrupt left. He zig-zags through a residential neighborhood, accelerates down a wide side street, keeps glancing in the rearview mirror. He stares straight ahead, drives a few minutes, turns onto the main road.

Up a few blocks, after the left, is the park. At the end of that street is where they need to go, where they'll see a cathedral for learning—a huge, square, green building with large windows. Classrooms without air-conditioning.

Coming up on the left is a park with an after-school day-care. Kids

163

have swim classes there, play tag on the park's sprawling grass area. They play board games inside, have snacks. He'd seen the program in action from across the street at the school while he did his cleaning route.

He makes the left, pulls over.

"What're you doing here?" she says, gripping the door handle.

"There are kids inside, at a program. *Kids.*"

"You don't care how much you hurt them?"

He pays no attention to her last comment. He springs out of the vehicle, sprints across the street, leaves his door open.

Not certain if she wants to follow, she waits—one one-thousand, two one-thousand, three one-thousand, four one-thousand, five one-thousand, six one-thousand—he's disappeared behind the building— seven one-thousand, eight one-thousand, nine one-thousand, and then she races across the street, bolts through the recreation center doors looking for him.

The center is empty, except for long tables with several bottles of glue, stacks of colored construction paper, bottles of glitter, and scissors. She backtracks out of there, and then to the far side of the center's facade. She meanders across the grass area towards the park pool. People lie on the ground, on the grass area on the way to the pool building. They're vomiting, suffocating, spitting. She can help none of these individuals, so she doesn't break stride, doesn't look directly at them. Instead, she dashes through the pool facility's swinging glass doors.

A commotion comes from the pool area—a distant echo filled with splashing and yelling from adults, screaming from children. The troubled sounds of people struggling to live.

To the left is the boys' dressing and shower room, to the right is the girls'. A stool props open the door to the girls' room. She cautiously enters the girls' area, kicks the stool to the side. A few kids lie unconscious on the wet, tile floor, their throats swollen. She makes short jumps to maneuver over them and through the area.

Where is Arthur?

In the showers, a little girl in a bathing suit cries, her mouth agape as she takes in shower water.

"Are you okay?" Sandra says to the girl.

The girl is no older than eight or nine, dragging her feet in Sandra's direction.

Sandra inches towards the girl, picks her up and lets the girl straddle her, as she keeps moving, searching for Arthur. "It's going to be fine. Everything's going to be okay."

Holding the girl does not keep the girl from crying.

"Where's your mom?" Sandra asks, in the most understanding and soft voice she can muster.

The girl sniffs. "At work."

"Who's in charge?"

"Coach Ron," the girl sniffs.

Arthur, where are you?

Sandra stops, sets the girl down and wanders to the indoor pool area, holding the girl's hand.

Several kids stumble and choke. Lifeguards, as well as dozens of children float face-first in the pool. Two adult males splash around, gather kids, bring them to the edge of the pool, yell profanities while trying to lift the dead and dying out of the water. The screams have faded since she heard them outside.

"You're going to be fine," Sandra says to the girl. Both of their hands tremble against one another. "What's your name?"

The girl sniffs, and coughs, simply can't control herself. "Bobby."

"Bobby?"

There he is.

Arthur waits patiently next to the bleacher.

What's he waiting for?

Then the realization he can only help after they've died.

She watches in dismay, as the last few stumble and fall to the concrete of the pool deck. Small children. The most harmless things possible, on their knees, and then on their hands, some dry heaving. She turns Bobby around so she can't see, knows she's already seen plenty, and can still hear enough.

Finally, Arthur walks towards the men who have given up gathering children in the pool. Their faces of utter disappointment and defeat. The kids died too fast to be helped.

Their cotton shirts reveal the men as staff, employees of the program.

Arthur says to them, "Pass them to me. Let me help."

"It ain't worth shit, man," the first staff member says. "Call some motherfuckin body. Call somebody," he says with his voice breaking. "What the hell?" It didn't sound like he believed in the actions of his own words.

The other man, much thinner, coughs, splashes the water in disgust, and has nothing to say.

Arthur reaches out to them. "Pass them to me. Let's get them out of the water."

The staff member, in tears, pushes a body up to Arthur.

Arthur takes the first child, drags him all the way against the wall. He comes back and struggles to lift a pudgy kid from the water, drags him all the way to the wall as well. He comes back and picks up a third child, and so on. By the time all the kids are out of the water, the thin staff member is out of the pool, staggers backward in shock. Nearly falls back in the pool. All the kids, poolside, are alive again, coughing, in a good way, expelling water from their lungs, simply clearing their throats.

"Arthur!" Sandra calls to him.

He points to the exit doors. "We go!"

"Her." She points to the little girl. "Bobby."

"Parents will pick her up. These dudes will deal with it. Let's. Go."

Sandra stares at Bobby, squats, looks her in the eye. "It's okay, sweetie. False alarm, I guess."

Bobby nods, and then hangs her head. She reaches out to Sandra.

Sandra unknowingly ignores the girl and starts for the exit to meet Arthur outside. Not willing to go around the pool, she walks back the way she came, through the dressing room and shower area. She finds herself outside where, from a distance, she sees cars fly down the street in the direction of the school. Some people on bikes. Others walk. Some jog. Either way, they're heading to the school, most likely to get their kids.

At the grass area in front of the pool building, Arthur stares at the dead people lying throughout the park. He goes to them one by one. He's not touching them when they rise to their feet. They all have a similar reaction—a peaceful, yet ecstatic bewilderment.

He starts for the school where he works as a custodian, which is at the opposite side of the park and across the street.

According to Arthur, Quincy will be there.

***

The gates to the front of the school are locked.

Looking through the gates and to the other side of the campus, numerous people trickle in from the back side of the school. A rather large crowd mulls near the bungalows. The activity catches Arthur's eye because none of it looks school related, and it's near Ms. Kimbrel's classroom. A sudden burst of yelling. It all makes him uneasy.

A campus security vehicle down the block, has its driver's side door flung open.

A few individuals approach the front steps of the school, and head up through the open double doors. A few others straggle behind down the block, clearly coming to the school as well.

At the entrance, Arthur grabs Sandra's arm. He looks at her, hopes she can see how scared he is. He can't seem to reach her with words.

She rips her arm away from him, and steps into the building.

He nudges her along.

She jerks forward. "You can't *touch* me."

His hands go up in surrender. "I'm sorry."

For a moment they stare at each other.

Mumbles and scattered footsteps softly echo through the hallway, but the people making the sounds are yet to be seen. The echoes fade into the unseen disturbance.

Arthur jumps forward a few steps, stops, gazes all the way down either direction of the hallway. Sandra joins him, swivels her head in both directions.

"We don't need to be here," she says.

"*We* don't need to be here. Go if you want."

"I'm going to get the gun from the car. Nothing is safe."

"You're scared of everything."

"Including you."

Judging by her sudden change in attitude, Sandra might be freed from him.

Somehow.

He didn't understand how this all worked, but it seems as if the nature of him gave him options. How he approached himself changed how people approached him. A free-of-his-control Sandra left to get the gun.

The commotion grows, comes from the direction of Ms. Kimbrel's classroom. Maybe not a bad idea to get that gun, seeing that towards the commotion is where they need to go.

Sandra turns back the way they came.

Arthur jogs down the hall towards Ms. Kimbrel's classroom, sweating before he gets to the end of the hall.

He's quick at getting down the steps, and then to the aisle of the bungalows where parents, as if at a swap meet, sift through dead kids and crying babies. His shock does not come from seeing kids with their lives dismissed, their bodies haphazardly lying against bungalow walls. He's shocked by the wailing naked babies crawling on hands and knees across the blacktop. Babies, who are mostly naked, slap the ground beneath them, scoot out of their over-sized clothing, scrape their knees as they struggle forward.

If they were dying, Quincy would do this to save them.

Parents and relatives flip over the dead, scour the area for familiar faces. The concrete wet with tears, and the weeping barely distinguishable from yelping dogs.

A handful of people take the babies into one of many classrooms in bungalows. There are so many babies lying around that there aren't enough hands to carry all of them or move them inside. The dead kids, a clear distraction.

Those handling the babies continuously shake their heads, frown, mope. The babies are a good thing. Quincy stopped their sickness by making children infants. Arthur is sure of it.

He nearly trips on tiny hands and wrists. Tiny protruding. He's back-to-back with grown men who have become mute, not able to deal with the moment. Hushed curse words flash across faces, as well as an awkward sense of hope—hope of finding some small person, and then the hope there's no sign their small person died in pain.

They move the babies into the bungalow on the end. There must be a lot more of those babies in there.

On the far side of the bungalows—where he has no view—kids are alive. They call for their mommies, whine in pain. Adults console over there as well. Teachers, administrators, he figures. Survivors. More parents and relatives. It sounds like double the amount of people over there as on his side. It's a wonder more people didn't find their dead kids. He rationalizes it's because so many entire families are dead. Many of the parents to the dead kids are dead too so they won't show up. How many orphans will come out of this?

At least a few children were given a ball for a pacifier, as a time killer. He hears it skip off the side of a building.

It's apparent someone has organized the babies going into the classroom, has organized where all the dead kids will go, which is in this very aisle he walks. The similarity between the dead and living is that they both need organizing.

A scream, quick shuffling of feet from somewhere. The sudden scampering makes his chest tight.

Behind him, coming from the quad, a consistent trickle of scared members of the community, more parents and uncles and aunts and older brothers. They jog through, concerned and clueless. Concerned because they're clueless. In the minutes he observes, sometimes he can hear them coming but not see them coming, because they stop inside classrooms not in his line of sight, not in the bungalows but up the way in the quad. The campus rapidly fills, adding to his nervousness.

He can now discern the reunions between dead child and the living family by the sudden screams and the irrational shuffling of feet. The disturbance is now a crowd, bolstered by exuberant depression.

I need a plan.

First, he needs to forget about getting advice from Quincy; there's no way Quincy is still wandering around. The idea of Quincy disappearing and being gone forever freezes him where he stands. He doesn't want to learn about how to get better on his own. A better way is to learn through Quincy. He toils in his current spot.

Adrenalin shakes his teeth, as he resists the urge to animate every single one of these children back from the dead. Because he can save everyone, not just the dead kids. Everyone. If he animates the kids doesn't he give life back to those grieving as well? At the same time, won't people thoroughly lose their shit if they see him raise their kids from the dead? Wouldn't that mean that those watching him use his ability would see him as something bigger than he saw himself? Where would that lead? Maybe nowhere for him but for others…

Leave the world as it is. Just leave it.

Not too long ago he told Ms. Kimbrel he wouldn't help dead kids, even on campus. Yet, here he is, devising a way to save children in a way to not attract attention.

He'd feel in the right saving all the kids in front of him, just as he felt in the right saving everyone on the way here.

If Quincy is gone, then next, look for Ms. Kimbrel. Try her classroom. She might know where he is.

"Arthur." Mr. Kato, a teacher his height, taps him on the shoulder.

Mr. Kato's glasses tilt like they were knocked off his face at some point.

"Are you okay?" Mr. Kato asks.

"No."

"It's a real mess, a real mess." Mr. Kato speaks above the growing crowd. "A real mess."

"Oh, this is *so* messed up."

"It's really bad. It's a real mess, a real mess. Look at all these people coming for their kids. So many are lost."

"Maybe."

"It happened at recess. There were so many, so many of them outside, and it happened so fast, just like that," he snaps, "just like that," he snaps again, "and it happened to so many, so suddenly that we left them where they were. We decided, don't move them. To maintain their dignity or something, is what I was thinking, at first. You don't want to treat these small people as if they're trash, so you don't want to touch them."

"How many staff? Do you know?"

"Principal Dory, Georgia, Eileen, everyone in the office. Not only a few. We're lucky."

"For now," Arthur says. "It could be us later today, tomorrow evening. Whenever. How about Debbie?"

"Nurse Debra is off today, not that she'd be any good. Not about her, nobody is good at this. This isn't something anybody is good at. Look at this." Mr. Kato wipes his nose with his arm. "On the other side Mrs. Lucas has set up an information area for parents or whomever arrives. That's where everyone is winding up. The older kids are in the auditorium and cafeteria. That's what you're seeing, people coming from the cafeteria."

"That's right." He can look for Quincy there.

"I don't know what keeps people here."

"You don't think it's your job to help?"

"I'd still leave if I didn't think this was the safest place, for right now. They're checking them off as dead or alive, and..." Mr. Kato raises his hand to Arthur's face. "The babies are unexplainable. Unexplainable, Arthur." Mr. Kato walks away, biting his lip. Instead of talking, he points to the classroom where the babies are.

Arthur recognizes himself as an outsider who observes everyone from afar. From his viewpoint, everyone works together, lifts, and drags, and consoles, undoubtedly wonders why it couldn't have been themselves instead of their kids. Guilt keeps conversation about prevention to a minimum. It's not any specific person's fault, is what Arthur figures they must be thinking. They must all be taking the blame.

Arthur starts up the ramp to Ms. Kimbrel's class for the small chance she and Quincy are in there. He doesn't think they are, but they could be. He can't get there unless he steps over a little girl lying across the ramp to the classroom. She not positioned to be dumped with the rest. Not found by anybody, although she's right here at his feet. Nobody is trying to identify her like they are many of the others. He doesn't care for her name or where she's from or where she might be in the future. He simply can't take his eyes off her. Her curled hair covers her face, her hands clenched beside her thighs.

Placing his hand on her knee, he kneels, puts his face close to hers, and whispers in a single breath, "Wake up." After a short moment her fingers twitch. He darts into Ms. Kimbrel's class.

No Quincy. No Ms. Kimbrel. She hasn't cleaned the place one bit since last time they spoke. Ms. Kimbrel's scent of roses lingers, stuck to her dress which is lying on the floor in front of him. It makes sense for her dress to be here. If Quincy was responsible for turning kids into babies, then why not turn him and Ms. Kimbrel into kids? As a child wouldn't she leave her dress in the classroom? Quincy's sandals and hemp shirt are balled up against the wall.

Arthur leaves the classroom in time to see the dark-haired girl he just animated stagger towards the quad, rub her eyes, freshly woke to a scenario she'll undoubtedly have a hard time explaining.

Arthur follows the girl across the quad.

In the quad, to the left, is a single-story building, nothing but classrooms. Through the windows he sees they're empty.

The girl drags her feet forward. Arthur does the same, trying to picture where Ms. Kimbrel and Quincy went. They left campus or settled into the cafeteria in front of him. He might as well look in the cafeteria.

Quincy must have made he and Ms. Kimbrel kids again at the height of kids getting sick and dying, otherwise the two of them scampering through the halls in underwear far too large for them would have drawn too much attention. In the main hallway is where they could have liberated spare clothes from the nurse's office.

A couple of strides after the girl enters the cafeteria. Arthur does so as well.

Students are seated at every inch of the lunch tables. Teachers stand at the back of the cafeteria, blocking the exit. A few more at the entrance.

A dangerous and dying world lay outside the school. Go there at your own peril is what the adults' body language says. Many of the kids gathered no longer have homes, but the adults in the room won't immediately tell them.

"Arthur," a child calls. "Arthur."

He ignores the beckon, chooses to clap his hands three times. Then three more times. Loud, thick claps. This is how authority figures, usually teachers at the school, get the children's attention. It must have been odd for the kids to hear Arthur doing it. Custodians don't address students in this way. He claps three more times. The kids clap back three times. He does it once more. The kids clap back, and he now has their full attention. He also has the attention of other adults in the room.

"I'm sorry," Arthur says to the cafeteria. "I'm sorry. I could have found a way. I didn't."

Nothing else comes to him.

"Arthur," again a child calls his name.

The child sits at the closest table.

Barely recognizing the young boy, Arthur's spirits lift. "Dad!"

It's a small Black kid with a lopsided afro, in a school uniform. Next to the kid with the afro, a little white girl with long, strawberry blond hair.

"I don't want to wait anymore," Quincy says. "I want to go home. She's going to have to come with us."

Arthur cautiously looks at the teachers who flank him. "My nephew and his friend. I'm going to take them."

"We're on lockdown, Arthur," a female teacher says.

"Do you know of anybody on their way to help? Anybody confirm that?"

No response.

"Then you're on lockdown. Not me. Come on, kids."

Ms. Kimbrel and Quincy get off their bench.

Arthur backs out of the cafeteria, makes sure nobody tries to stop him. At the cafeteria steps, he turns on his heel. Not looking back, he quickly walks in the route he always takes leaving campus. Into the main building, through the teachers' lounge, into the hallway. He looks back at his first-grade teacher, and then his—until recently—estranged father, as children.

"You waited for me." Arthur says.

"We're not walking all the way back to your place," Quincy replies with quite a bit of attitude. "We're friggin eleven."

Ms. Kimbrel says, "Arthur, we have to think of a way for you to help all these families."

"The best way to help them," Quincy starts, "is to make sure shit like this doesn't happen again. Know what I mean?"

"Let's get to the car," Arthur says.

"Real quick." Quincy tugs on Arthur's elbow. "You have to keep it together. Know what you're doing. You see why, now?"

He did.

Although Ms. Kimbrel is suddenly young, she manages her teacher glare that says he should know better.

"You have to do things for something, not against something," Quincy says. "If there was something to practice, practice that."

"I don't know what you mean," Arthur says.

"Real quick. You use your ability on accident and there are repercussions."

Arthur tries to picture what he considers to be the wind, and how it

172

moves through him. What if it's not wind at all? Or more than that. It's something he does. A true power.

"The wind is the stench," Arthur says.

"Thank you," Quincy replies. "Now you can be more of a man. Own this."

Arthur stops moving his feet, thinks of all the people he might have killed, assuming Quincy stands correct.

"I don't think it's possible to help everybody," Arthur says. "There're too many. There're people who need help who aren't even here. There are so many people."

He sniffs the air. No stench, for the time being. He'd do everything in his power to not let it come back, which also meant thinking the best about those he couldn't help. It meant moving on. The same wind that helped Sandra killed his neighbors.

Arthur repeats, "I don't *think* it's possible to help everyone. Appreciating them is something."

Outside the school and a block away, Sandra wields the gun at his car. As he approaches, he sees she's pointing it at him, a scowl across her face.

"Ah, shit," Quincy says. "This is happening."

"What's *this*?" a young Ms. Kimbrel asks.

Arthur doesn't break stride. He strolls up to Sandra and her weapon.

With the barrel of the gun on his chest he says, "If you have it in you to let me live, I swear I can let you live, too."

Sandra's shoulders sink as she exhales. "You'll only come back to life again won't you."

She tosses the gun into the driver's side window.

"If things can be okay, I will make them okay," Arthur says.

Sandra closes her eyes, tilts her head to the sky.

"This is Quincy," Arthur says with a grin. "And do you remember Ms. Kimbrel?"

Sandra lifts a brow. "Um, what?"

Maybe she doesn't believe him but that is a moot point.

***

Despite recent events, the ride home is quiet.

The gun lay on the floorboard between Sandra's feet, a sneer slashing her face.

Quincy and Ms. Kimbrel sit silent in the backseat. Who knows what trauma they've gone through, or what trading down to such a young age does to a person? They'd have to go through the mind games of adolescents again.

They pull into the driveway between Arthur and Glenda's homes. Sandra is the first one out, taking the gun with her into Glenda's house.

Watching Sandra go towards Glenda's rather than the home they made shakes Arthur from the inside, although it's what he expects from someone who doesn't accept him. He sits, taps the steering wheel, as Ms. Kimbrel and Quincy get out of the backseat, both sliding out through the same door. They follow Sandra into Glenda's house, holding hands.

Not wanting to think too much, Arthur exits his vehicle, steps up to the front porch to Glenda and Raheem's home. He strolls into the house, finds himself near the wall in the living room next to the dead bodies of Tracy and Shelly.

"You're going to do yo thang?" Quincy says.

"Yes, my *thang.*" Arthur lays a hand on Tracy, his other hand on Shelly. "Why don't you come back to us?" Arthur whispers close to the kids' faces. "Come back to us."

"What happens now?" Ms. Kimbrel says, in her child voice.

Glenda says from the top of the staircase. "We wait."

"Where's Raheem?" Arthur says to Glenda.

"Thank you, Arthur," Glenda says.

"Where's Raheem?" Arthur repeats.

"Praying about pain, somewhere."

Arthur looks at Quincy, as if Quincy should know better. "Go get them some water."

Quincy jets off to do just that. Interesting how he has the body language of a child. Quincy can always be in his youth.

So, this is the woman Quincy said he was in love with, way back in junior high.

Ms. Kimbrel leans forward to see the kids better, a look of disgust across her face. "Are they…?"

Tracy's eyes open.

Arthur turns his back on the kids. "Not anymore."

Glenda races down the stairs. She grabs her son and kisses him all over his face. She rubs Shelly's cheeks and kisses her forehead. "Oh, my goodness." Suddenly, Glenda is awash with concern. "Are they going to be okay?"

With more than a hint of disapproval, Sandra says, "Answer the question, Arthur. She wants to know if they're going to be like me, go through what I went through for all that time."

"Nothing bad will come from this," he says.

Glenda eyes Sandra, then shifts her attention to Arthur. Her kids sit up, and she hugs them, tightly. Again, she stares at Sandra. This time it's a long glare.

"I'm going to lie down for a bit." Arthur says. "I have a lot to think about. Don't we all have a lot to think about?"

"No," Sandra says. "There's nothing to ponder."

"Are you, you?" he asks her, knowing the wind he put in her, from either time, has departed. "I feel you're you."

"I will never be me."

Arthur sucks his bottom lip. "I guess I have to accept it."

"Either way it doesn't matter."

"Does it matter that I never stopped loving you?"

"Because of what you are, it's never mattered, now has it."

Moments later, Arthur kicks off his shoes in his living room, knowing his life with Sandra has ended. Obviously, she'd move on to whatever else or wherever else her imagination leads her.

Broken glass from his coffee table is scattered near the television. Not minding the mess, he retires to his office where he sits in his office chair and nudges his mouse to wake his computer. He first thinks to check his social media account. What is the media saying about what happened today? He goes with the second idea, to continue writing to Sandra. No matter how much she hates him, he will write to her.

He types to her in his digital journal for about an hour before hearing the front door open. Is it her? If it is, it's because he still might have a chance with her. The upcoming moment needs to be unquestioningly on her terms.

Don't force anything.

Sitting in his chair and facing the doorway, he waits for her.

Suddenly she's there, holding the barrel of the handgun. She reaches out to hand the grip of the weapon to him.

His shoulders slump. "Oh."

"We all need our own lives."

"About the kids? Don't worry about the kids."

"You know what? I'm not worried about any kids. Glenda—"

"—In time she'll see it's fine."

"When I say we need our own lives, I mean me. Do you understand what I'm saying?"

"I swear I'm sorry for everything. I'd take my own life if it'd do any good."

"We both know it won't."

"I do love you so much. If we share the same emotion, I'd love that," he says, grinning.

He takes the gun from her and drops it on the futon. "You couldn't have disliked every single moment. You have to have good memories."

"I want you to go into the most empathetic part of yourself. When you get there, do so knowing you're an abuser. That's how I want you to think about it, as an abuser. Now, as an abuser, you're here telling your victim, who you've been abusing since their adolescence, that surely, she must have enjoyed being abused, at some point."

She leans over, puts her hands on her knees, like a runner after a race.

She says, "I walked over from Glenda's going to shoot you. I was going to shoot you at the school when you arrived at the car. I didn't expect you to be with kids. I only wanted to shoot you in the face, because, no, it wasn't *all* bad. And I *hate* the fact." The word 'hate' comes from the back of her throat. "Are you going to let me stay dead?"

"You're confused."

"I'm not. I want to be dead."

"No, you don't."

She had handed him the weapon. If she wanted to be dead, she would have held onto it.

"What am I supposed to be doing?" she asks. "Going about my days? I can't just up and have a normal life."

"What I did to you was wrong." *Not abuse.*

"Maybe wrong is never wrong to the ignorant." She yanks her hair behind her ears. "If what you did was wrong like you say, then why not accept what the victim says?"

"I'm not going to say I abused you. I'm not going to say that."

"You'll admit what you did was wrong, though. What the hell was so wrong about it, if not abuse?"

"The control—"

"—Is how you abused me."

He puts his hand to his forehead. Judging by the look in her eyes, she assumes that if he doesn't say what she wants him to say then he's lying to himself and to her. But he's already admitted ignorance and wrongdoing? He can't do much else. How can he admit ignorance, and at the same time say he didn't do to her what she's charging him with? If she's going to judge him, what are the consequences of his actions?

He says, "If I did what you say I did? I can't take it back. You're absolutely free to go. Nobody is keeping you. I don't want you here if you don't want to be."

She chokes up, nervously wipes her hands on her pant legs. "I *do* want to be gone."

"Then go."

"I'll always be stuck in this long moment with you, no matter what." She holds out her palm. "I want to be gone."

"Then—"

"—I want to be gone," she repeats and nods, her hand still outstretched and shaking.

"I'm supposed to hand it to you?" He lifts the gun from the futon.

Handing the weapon to her, he figures he's giving her permission to do with it whatever she chooses. A blessing. It's a promise of the unknown.

He lifts the gun from his futon, feels its weight in his grip, and then hands the weapon back to her. "This is what you want?"

In one motion she brings the gun directly to her temple and blasts a single bullet through her head. Her body collapses in the doorway. Her blood splatters everywhere to the left of her, on the door frame, the wall. Sandra is limp and broken and useless. She looks, probably, a lot like how she must have felt for years at a time during their relationship.

Arthur gave her permission.

For hours he sits in his office chair, softly turns from left to right.

His social network feed shows a thread of news.

The gun he gave her lies next to her body.

Finally, his guilt rattles out of his quaking body in the form of vomit.

When he rises to his feet to begin the imminent duty of cleaning up, he is resolved, having been through this before.

***

A few weeks later, Arthur knocks on Glenda and Raheem's door.

Raheem answers but doesn't say anything. He walks away shirtless in his morning slippers and baggie sweats.

"What's up, 'Heem?"

Raheem stops, turns to look at Arthur. "After a while you start to forget what it feels like. You know that, right?"

"That's a good thing." A hint of disappointment ribs Arthur, knowing the most negative part of himself had latched on to Raheem, as it had with Sandra.

Raheem nods towards the staircase. "They're upstairs. Don't make them late."

"'Heem."

177

"*Ra* heem."

Arthur lets go of the urge to plead for Raheem not to kill himself. "Never mind."

Raheem continues to his room, probably to finish getting ready for work.

It makes sense that Raheem and, albeit mostly Glenda, agreed to take in Trinna and Quincy, understanding the kids' unique situation. Today, Trinna and Quincy will try to enroll in the very school where Ms. Kimbrel taught less than a month ago. They share a room with Tracy and Shelly, sleep on the floor and roll their blankets up, daily, until the spare room, which has been used for mostly storage, is cleared out. Arthur would have allowed them at his place, but Quincy didn't like the idea of his son being his dad, in any way.

Arthur makes his way upstairs and into the kids' room.

Shelly ties her shoes on the edge of her bed.

Trinna is in the corner with her things.

"Good morning Mr. Lowe." Shelly grins, like sunshine through rain clouds. "Thank you for the best friend."

"Is my niece your best friend? What's Tracy going to say?"

"He's my brother. It's better to have a girl best friend."

Shelly finishes tying her shoes, and stands, ready for school.

"Where are the boys?" Arthur asks Trinna.

Trinna has been ready for school, from the looks of it, for quite some time. Her backpack is on the bed, bulges with what Arthur figures are binders. Pens stick out from a pocket on the backpack. A sweater tied around her waist

Trinna says, "They're in the bathroom getting ready. Girls first and then boys. Raheem is kind of traditional, in many ways." Trinna says to Shelly, "Can I meet you downstairs?"

Shelly thinks about it for a second, gets the hint, and then says, "Okay." At first, she skips, and then walks out the door and down the stairs.

Trinna begins to roll up her blankets. "You're here for what purpose?"

"Saying hello."

"I'm going to see you later on at the school."

Arthur steps over and grabs a blue teddy bear off the desk near Shelly's bed.

"You're going to keep missing her a bunch aren't you," she says.

"My heart is one hundred percent broken."

"That's part of being in love, don't you think?"

"Apparently."

She places the blankets in the corner, pats them down several times. "Being a kid, you want to do more things. Impulses are a joy." She smacks the blankets several more times, saying, "Bam, bam, bam," as she does so. She gathers herself. "Do you regret cremating her? You can't bring her back."

"There might be a little regret there. At the same time, there's no risk of that evil assed smell taking us out because of me." He bites his lip. "All because of me."

"Some beautiful things happened to some of us because of you."

He contemplates all the supposed good he's done. He thinks of how much better he can make things in the future.

"Well," she says. "I'm going to school. Excuse me."

She runs across the room, and then out of sight.

He hears her stomp down the stairs.

Arthur smacks the teddy bear and his hand together, as if he's pounding a catcher's mitt. For him, being a kid again would be too dangerous. It's the bile built up in him beginning in his childhood and adolescence that killed a great deal of people. He has more control if he's positive and mature. Everything is easier if he's positive and mature.

He takes the teddy bear next door to his place, sets it on the futon in his office.

The bear sits behind Arthur, silently watches Arthur interact with the computer.

Focusing on his computer, social media still can't explain the tragic events from a few weeks ago. There were symptoms, though never a cause for the symptoms, therefore no real cause for all the deaths. Then, poof, the symptoms were gone. Poof, the mysterious smell was gone as well. Would they be back? Nobody knew. A total mystery.

The teddy bear wiggles itself off the futon, finds its way beside Arthur. It grabs the mouse, guides the cursor to the icon on the screen labeled "Sandra". The old bear double-clicks the icon to open the document.

Arthur begins to type:

Sandra,

I know this entry will never reach you, but there's still something I need to say.

It's about a memory from our beginning days of junior high.

One day, during passing period, I saw you from down the hall. I was at my locker. I just couldn't get enough broken syllables out of my mouth to say anything.

You locked your locker, and then started my direction. It was one of those rare moments when you weren't with anyone. I thought you were going to do what you usually would do and stroll right by me without a glance. Instead, you stopped about ten feet away and searched for something. No matter how many times your eyes should have met mine, they didn't.

I thought you couldn't see me because we were most likely in different realities. Different worlds. To me, you were basically only a daydream at that point.

Sandra, I'm sorry you lived so much of your life in that daydream I forced you into. I think the best I can do is learn to not hurt people. Maybe, in a way, compassion is something you enabled me to embrace. If you'd allow it, I'd like to see it that way. I won't bring you back. That's my promise.

That day in the hall, I'd like to believe you were, in some way, searching for me. I'd like to think you eventually found the real me, and me the real you.

That's the best we can do.

Maybe I'll see you in the next life.

My love.

My dear, Sandra.

U.L. Harper is a former journalist from Long Beach, California. He now resides in the evergreen state of Washington with his wife and daughter.

For more of his writing, stop by http://www.ulharper1.com/

Don't hesitate to connect:

Twitter: @ulharper

Email: ulharper1@gmail.com

CPSIA information can be obtained
at www.ICGtesting.com
Printed in the USA
LVHW090452261020
669798LV00030B/716/J

9 781087 919768